THE LIBERATION'S CHILD

THE
LIBERATION'S
CHILD

LUCY CRUICKSHANKS

First published in paperback in
Great Britain in 2022 by Polygon,
an imprint of Birlinn Ltd.

Birlinn Ltd
West Newington House
10 Newington Road
Edinburgh
EH9 1QS

www.polygonbooks.co.uk

9 8 7 6 5 4 3 2 1

ISBN 978 1 84697 577 6
EBOOK ISBN 978 1 78885 379 8

The publisher gratefully acknowledges investment from
Creative Scotland towards the publication of this book.

Typeset in Bembo by Polygon, Edinburgh
Printed and bound in Great Britain by Clays Ltd, Elcograf S.p.A.

For Tate

Do not be fooled by the date or location.
This novel is based on real and recent events.

It was election day, and the sky was turning the lilac of a bruise above Trafalgar Square. Theodora Baxter sat atop her daddy's shoulders, her skin tingling, heart thudding and body braced against the surge of the crowd. There were more people here than she'd ever seen in her life at one time. More than she knew existed. In every direction, the roads and pavements in and out of the enormous open space were blocked. Cars and buses had abandoned their journeys, and people clambered over bonnets and onto rooftops, stamping dents in the metal with their dancing feet. Men had mounted the steps of the monument too, hauling their wives and children up beside them, and their fists punched the air as they shouted and cheered. They straddled railings to reach friends and threw their arms around each other. They hung from the lampposts, waving their flags. Entire families stood shin-deep in the fountains. It was like a party, thought Thea. Like the whole world was happy. Music pounded through her, and she fizzed with the beat of it. There were five men on the stage, striding its length and back again, and waving, pausing only to hug. The one with the glasses and yellow sweatshirt had a microphone. When he spoke, the crowd roared and heaved towards his voice.

There was a shove from behind, and Thea dug her fingers harder into her daddy's hair. He called up. 'You OK?'

She yelled a reply, hoping he'd hear and not take her back. They'd been swept to the square from the Roundhouse with her mummy and their neighbours, and she didn't want to go home. A man had been shouting in the courtyard outside her tower, cupping his hands to his mouth and screaming, 'LANDSLIDE! IT'S A LANDSLIDE!' Panicked, Thea watched him from the bedroom window, far below and frantic. Her eyes leapt from his face to the sky-high blocks like her own behind him, then to the slashes of sunlight between them. She held her breath and waited for the onslaught of sticky wet mud to swallow the concrete, like she'd seen on the telly in a programme about forests, and then eat him too. She didn't know where it would come from in the centre of the city, but she felt the hot rush of terror all the same. It wasn't until her daddy had wriggled her shoes onto her feet and swung her out from the apartment that she'd wondered if maybe she was the landslide – and her mummy and daddy and everyone else. Around her, the entire Gritstone Estate was emptying. Residents spilled down the stairwells and into the lukewarm evening, to the streets beyond the courtyard, in a single, liquid movement, swamping everything that stood in their way. She'd seen Marie and Nathanial from school with their big-boobed, waddling aunty, and Mrs Shah who worked at the care home with Mummy, and the man from the nineteenth floor who walked with crutches, and the woman with red hair who left food out for the foxes and made the people on the ground floor mad. Josh Springer had grinned at her, poking his tongue through his gapped teeth and snapping her off a length of his liquorice before the torrent of people dragged them opposite ways. Even Mr DeSouza was there, and he never closed the cafe. Not even on Christmas Day. She wasn't sure if she'd ever seen him out from behind the counter. She'd snorted a laugh at his skinny white legs.

Now, a chorus of 'Free and Equal Britain!' was spreading through Trafalgar Square like flames, each rising voice sparking the one beside it until Thea was certain that every person in the city was chanting, and she was right in the centre, at its heart. Her daddy tilted his face, and she saw the corner of his mouth stretched to a smile like hers was, singing, and she knew they weren't leaving anytime soon. Thrill shot through her. Where he held her at her knee, she could see his wristwatch. It was later than her bedtime. She knew it was. The light was fading. Perhaps it was later than she'd ever stayed awake. She was meant to be scrubbed and changed and ready for her story when the little hand was on the seven, but here she was with her parents and her friends and the whole big city. At the party! The hand had already slipped past the eight.

The noise of the crowd overcame the music, and Thea pressed herself into her daddy's shoulders. On the stage, the men had lined up and were clapping. Grinning. The crowd struck their hands together in imitation, high above their heads and perfectly in time. There was a shift at the top of the square, in the farthest corner, a break in the solidness and its steady mood and movement. Thea's eyes jumped sideways, and for a second she caught sight of a horse with teeth bared, rearing, the policeman on its back thrusting downwards with his rifle and striking the blunt end into the scuffling crowd.

'Thea!'

Her gaze snapped back. Her mummy had climbed onto the plinth, squeezing herself on the narrowest ledge of stone aside the giant statue of the lion, and her skin, hair and the beast's mane glittered beneath the streetlamp in shades of gold. Reaching out, she passed Thea the sign that they'd made together from a flattened cereal box then cupped her daughter's head in her hand, smiled hard and leaned towards her.

'Hold your banner up, sweetheart. Hold it up so they can see!'

She planted a kiss onto Thea's cheek and scratched behind her ear before releasing her, and Thea's heart skipped two-time as she pushed her arm up, stretching, stretching, as tall as she could, taller even than she stretched to reach the tin of biscuits at the back corner of the kitchen counter, willing the men on the stage to look her way. THANK YOU, said the big colourful block capitals. 'THANK YOU!' she yelled.

As she tried to shout again, a lump of something hard and unexpected in her throat stopped the sound. She shivered. Was she going to cry? She wasn't even sad! She would draw a picture of this later, she thought, so she'd never forget it. The crowd and the lions, the streaked sky gleaming, the stage and the men. She would use the pencils from her birthday. All the colours. She'd draw everyone smiling and dancing and happy, just like in real life. Everything will get better now, her mummy had told her. It's the liberation! Once in a lifetime, her daddy had said. She didn't need to know the details. Whatever this was, it was beautiful, wasn't it? She felt it through every twist and turn of her insides. How could so many people mean anything else? She squeezed her eyes shut and pushed her banner higher, and let the cries of 'Free and Equal Britain!' pulse down to her core.

Yet when she opened her eyes, Thea wasn't where she thought she was. Her father wasn't holding her. Her mother wasn't smiling. She wasn't six years old. Her limbs were long, lean and fully grown again. She tried to drag her vision into focus. The light above her hummed, glowing blueish. Her head stung. When she blinked, an image of her parents' bodies flickered behind her eyelids. They hung limp from their nooses, their eyes bulging and bloodshot. There was a moment of confusion before the realisation. Her hand sprang to the curve of her belly, but instead of the ripe, firm roundedness she expected to find, her fingers sunk into rotten-soft fat. The pain was instant, complete and consuming, an explosion of scalding-hot shock through her body. They'd sliced her open, just as they'd done to her parents. They'd pared her out, like a fruit. Stoned her. She was on her own. The baby was gone.

THREE MONTHS LATER

1

Thea sat at a desk in the centre of the Archive, leaning towards the screen and frowning, ignoring the ache at the base of her spine. She had chewed her pencil to a nub, and she pulled it from her mouth, dug a soft splinter of wood from between her teeth and rolled it on her tongue before spitting it away. She squinted harder, spinning the pencil in her fingertips. The man staring back from the screen looked listless. He was older than Thea, but not by more than a few years. Late twenties, probably. Thirty at most. He had thick, dark brows that met in the middle, and his eyes, dull and distant, were set deep beneath them. His nose was long and crooked, like it had once been broken, and there were freckles across the bridge of it. Did the man she want have freckles? A snarl escaped her. His lips were two stubby grey slugs, fat and shapeless, not at all like they should have been. Disgusted, she bit her own lip and swiped him sideways. No. Not him. The next face appeared.

Outside, a cloud shifted, and Thea raised her gaze to the vast, domed ceiling. The August sun was arrowing through the high windows, laying scorching yellow ribbons across the floor and illuminating the rows of silent figures where they sat shoulder to shoulder along benches that fanned like bicycles spokes from the middle of the circular hall. Heat struck hard with the light, and she wiped her face on her fraying sleeve then tapped her watch, waking it. Her stomach twisted. Already, she'd been three hours. She rubbed her thumb over the smudged glass and dismissed the messages that had stacked up. She was damned if she was giving Springer a second of thought today.

Her eyes slipped back to the benches and the people absorbed in their miserable tasks. They were raking through the faces of the missing and the dead, the condemned and the condemners, all dumped together and decaying into one. The Archive was no different from the graves that pocked the landscape. From Newcastle to Norfolk, Cardiff to Cornwall, excavation of the communal pits was finally complete – leaving gaping cavities in the dry months and mud-brown lakes in winter – and the world's largest ever DNA identification programme was underway. Almost every UK citizen who survived the FEB era – those four catastrophic years of Free and Equal Britain that followed the election – had submitted their genetic profile in the hope of finding answers about the people they loved most, but the painstaking task of making matches was still decades from being done. Now, fifteen years after FEB's demise, those too old, sick or desperate to wait for official results came, like Thea, to the British Museum's old Reading Room to trawl the photographs, prison logs and scans of scrappy, hand-scrawled confessions. So many people had wanted to enter on the day it first opened that the riot spread through half of London. The UN was forced to use the cannons, and images of raging, water-soaked survivors facing off with black-clad soldiers were beamed around the globe. *Is Britain Relapsing?* the headlines read. The Archive still always had a line at the door. New information was added almost daily – every fresh DNA result listed, every newly surfacing FEB-era photograph or snippet of data logged. It drew back wave after wave of the grief-stricken.

Except these people weren't like Thea. Not really. Thea knew what had happened to her parents. She wanted to know *who* did it. She pressed the balls of her hands into her tired eyes, listening to the collective hiss of whispered voices and the scribble of pens on paper. Beneath the Archive's church-like canopy, she felt the weight of unsaid prayers. When she finally found his face, she would remember. She knew she would. When she looked into his eyes, there wouldn't be doubt.

'Thea?'

Jemima's hand on her shoulder made Thea start. She looked up and flashed a mechanical smile, twitching her fingers and slipping her notebook underneath a sheet of blank paper before the old woman could see. For a while, when Thea had been pregnant, she'd been able to draw all sorts of things; the sycamore by the underpass that led to the Roundhouse, or the birds darting and dipping above the towers, or the skyline from her window. They were just scraps of the whole – leaves and gliding wings and streaks of cloud behind the concrete – but they were there. They were something. Now she was back to scribbling little more than the same face that she strained to remember, unsure whether each sketch honed his details or blunted them, whether her pencil took her closer or further away.

'Hi, Mima,' she said, letting her friend kiss her cheek.

Jemima dropped into the chair at Thea's side and placed a book on the desk. *The Infinite Horizons of Space* by S.F. Leckie. She rubbed a wrinkled paw on Thea's thigh. 'Perhaps this one will be your passion, sweet pea? Perhaps you'll be the first person from the Gritstone Estate in space, eh?'

Despite herself, Thea let her smile settle in. She knew Jemima's game. *You need to find something that you love, Theodora. What makes your heart sing? Let it lead you to the future. Away from London.* Away from the past was what she meant. Thea had tried to explain that she couldn't – she wasn't ready – but Jemima persisted. *One day, sweet pea. One day, it'll be time.* Thea picked up the book and slipped it into her rucksack. Jemima had given her a pamphlet about veterinary nursing last week and a biography of famous female journalists the week before. Once, she'd brought a book on how to build racing cars. Another day, it was *The Easy Way to Learn Mandarin.* Thea knitted her fingers over Jemima's, linking into them. 'Maybe, Mima,' she said, and squeezed. 'You never know.'

A grin stretched across Jemima's face, and she pulled a bar of chocolate from her pocket, peeling back the wrapper and bending the soft brown oblong until it broke in two. 'Have you eaten today?' She passed Thea the bigger chunk.

Thea slipped the sticky sweetness into her mouth and nodded as it melted on her tongue. Jemima stared for longer than she needed to, and Thea's eyes dipped as she felt her lie exposed. There wasn't anyone in her life – perhaps not anyone anywhere – more giving of their time and kindness than Jemima Earl. When Thea had first staggered through the Archive's doors as a teenager, overawed and afraid but utterly desperate, Jemima had plucked her from her knees and helped her through. She had taught Thea to read beyond her basic, stunted schooling and gifted her book after beautiful book. Jemima always checked she'd eaten, bringing her iced buns and apples and packets of papery crumbed ham. For year after year, she made Thea cups of tea, and sat and listened. She told Thea gently when it was time to turn her screen off, and she let her sit in silent, simmering fury until she'd calmed enough to face the long walk home. There wasn't anyone else to whom Thea had been able to tell the story of what happened – she didn't know anyone who had not been at the Roundhouse that day to see it, and that was entirely, unbearably different – but Jemima had teased the thorns of it out of her. Slowly and tenderly, she'd done her best to dress the wounds. She was one of those rare, precious people with the ability to always find the positives, and to give more than she took. Thea never fully understood why Jemima had chosen her to give to, but after years of no one else caring, she felt so glad to have a friend.

Nobody knew the Archive better than Jemima, either. Before FEB, she had worked as a school librarian, and when the moment came, she'd been swift and shrewd in snapping up a safer job. She'd worked in Whitehall for the full four years, organising the incarceration records. She once told Thea that she'd known eventually the world would come for justice, and she kept those records as clean, clear and detailed as she could, so that one day there would be evidence of who had blood on their hands. Thea swallowed the melted chocolate and dragged her knuckles across her mouth. On the far side of the room, she could see the guard at the Archive's security desk skipping through the rolling news bulletins on her own screen. Every page was an image of the courthouse, the plush light-wood interiors or the grand stone facade. The guard paused on a page and took a bite of her sandwich. The video was soundless, but the pictures were unmistakable. They were the same ones that beamed from practically every screen in the city. There was a lone man in the dock with his arms folded, defiant. He looked down through the bottom of his spectacles. A lump lodged in Thea's windpipe. One man and one trial was better than nothing, apparently, but was there anyone who didn't have blood on their hands? The trial was nearing completion, the verdict due in just a few days, and the defendant and the decision of the stern, glossy-haired female judge that presided over him was all anyone could talk about.

Jemima followed the line of Thea's stare. She drew a thin breath. 'You've been here a lot this week, Thea,' she said quietly. 'Even for you.'

Thea's eyes sunk to her lap. She flicked her head.

'I don't know whether to worry more when I see you or when I don't.'

'I'm doing OK.'

'You sure?'

She nodded. She wasn't sure. She rarely felt sure. It had always soothed her to come here, or at least she could pretend that it did for a short while – for the seconds, minutes and hours when she felt that she was moving forward, working through options, making progress and inching closer. Recently she found herself having to stay longer and longer and work harder and harder to feel any relief. But what else could she do? She couldn't bear to stay at home and hear the sounds of families through the Roundhouse's walls: the laughs and disagreements of everyday supper times, the toddler upstairs with his flat-footed scampering, Nina Farrell's newborn as his squall rang down the hall. She sniffed, and her hand slid to her belly. It was still bigger than it should have been, soft like dough and with puckered skin. This morning, the wound had been weeping again.

Jemima knew Thea's thoughts. Her frown thickened. 'How's the pain?'

Thea shrugged. Another lie would not get through, she knew. 'About the same. It comes and goes.'

'Still bleeding?'

'A little.'

'You need to see a doctor. Get yourself another lasering.'

Thea picked at her chewed, stumpy pencil. They both knew she didn't have the credits for that. Loss gnawed at her. She had called the baby Laurel, even before the girl was born. There were not many memories Thea had of her parents, fewer still where they were happy, but she remembered the one holiday that the three of them took to Devon the year before the election, when things like that could still be done. They caught a coach with tokens they'd saved from the newspaper, and she'd beat her father in a running race along the beach at Dawlish when he'd pretended to trip in the warm, coarse-grained sand. She'd saved a photograph from that day to her Archive homepage. Andreas and Rose Baxter and five-year-old Thea, beaming. She could see the edge of it peeping from behind the parade of faces, a sliver of green grass and blue sky, her mother's shoulder, tanned and smooth. When they'd returned to the caravan that day, her mother made a wreath with leaves from the laurel hedges that grew around the campsite and placed it on Thea's head for victory. She'd not known the leaves were laurel then – she wasn't even sure they were now – but she'd collected up the scraps of that precious memory, pieced them together as best she could and embellished them, to give her something bigger to clutch. She missed her parents more than ever since Laurel. She wished they were here to tell her things would be OK.

Jemima placed her hand on the back of Thea's head and scratched behind her ear as you would a cat, like Thea's mother used to do. 'You're seeing her today, aren't you?'

Thea nodded, and sadness backed up inside her. 'At four,' she said. 'They've given me an hour this time.'

'Come for supper tonight, will you? I'd like to hear how she's doing.'

Thea dragged up a weak smile, and Jemima nudged closer, wrapping her arms around her. Her scent was sweet like the chocolate, and warm and musty.

'Don't worry,' she whispered into Thea's hair, holding her. 'You're doing so well. You'll get her back, sweet pea. Your parents would be proud.'

2

The aeroplane banked right and jolted, sinking inside the dense layers of cloud and beginning to bounce. Dominic Nowell stretched in his seat, the chill settling instantly over him, and stared through the scratched plexiglass window into a blindness of dazzling, whipped-up white. In his chest, the knot was yanking tighter. He didn't like not being able to see where they were. Minutes earlier, the captain had announced their descent into London Heathrow, and the passengers around him were rousing themselves, stifling yawns and buckling seatbelts in readiness to land. He shifted again, nudging his shoulder against his sleeping wife in an attempt to wake her. He needed Tess to tell him to stop worrying, and he wished – not for the first time – that he'd had the balls to come back earlier, only so he wouldn't have to do it now. There was a rumble as the aircraft's internal workings cranked, a lurch that made his hands leap to the armrests, and then the plane emerged beneath the clouds into a clean, calm glide. He looked at the land, taken aback by how close they were. The clouds had been low, catching him off guard, and here it was already, the city he'd loved but been ripped from so abruptly. When he'd taken this journey in the opposite direction, he'd been thirteen years old and rigid with terror, wrapped in a foil blanket from the US Embassy, his brother still covered in vomit by his side.

Dom swallowed down a rising swell of anxiety. He'd only seen London from the air that once, but its image was seared into his memory. Almost two decades had elapsed, but the Thames looked exactly as he remembered it, snaking grey-brown though buildings that grew bigger and thicker as the city intensified, with boats of all sizes tearing ragged cream ribbons in their wake. He recognised tower blocks and skyscrapers too, some directly and some from photographs he'd seen since, and from movies and the news. Despite the dull light, they shimmered. Parkland grass and sport fields were scattered between them, muted and patchy in their greenness. They were edged by the darker, murkier hue of trees. On a strait of water, he found the Palace of Westminster. His eyes scanned involuntarily northwards, chasing cars along narrow streets that looked all alike, though he doubted that the university campus where he'd last seen his mother and father would be distinguishable from the air. The monument was clear, however. The immense burnished-copper archway straddled the complete width of Regent's Park, its soaring, delicate coil glinting and casting a scythe-shaped shadow across the land.

The plane tilted again, and Dom took a steadying breath, bracing against the seat as though he might be tipped out. Despite careful landscaping, the criss-cross scars from where FEB had turned Regent's Park into allotments were still visible, drawn to the surface by summer's heat.

A drop in altitude made Dom's stomach roll, and the pressure mounted inside his head. He held his nose and popped his ears. Just four years of Free and Equal Britain had resulted in the deaths of 16 million people, either through execution, starvation or the spread of disease. It was a figure that the world still struggled to comprehend. Britain's social, political and economic infrastructure had been decimated, and even now, fifteen years after the fall of FEB, she was only clambering to her knees.

To think that the entire course of his country's history – and a large part of the rest of the world's history – had been altered by a single line of wayward malicious code still blew Dom's mind. He was a child of post-post-9/11, born into an era when Western politicians had abandoned the War on Terror but its legacy remained. Politics was dominated by unease, a fearfulness of any form of action or anyone different. Isolationism was rippling through nations; walls were being built and barriers erected. It was a time of impending European collapse and divisive rhetoric by bullheaded world leaders. Liberalism, the promised golden replacement to fascism and communism, was failing to deliver on the promises it had made. The gap between rich and poor was growing faster than ever. Centrist politicians were evasive and self-serving, unable or unwilling to see the discontent that brewed. When populist groups sprung up from across the political spectrum, they were treated with derision by the established elite.

It wasn't long before the Party for Free and Equal Britain emerged in the UK as the figureheads of popular dissatisfaction. With magnetic leadership and a talent for tapping into the pain and rage of those who felt ignored, the party gained support at rates previously unseen in British politics. The rattled Old Guard bandied together in a fragile alliance, deriding the party and their followers as ignorant and self-sabotaging. When they threatened to outlaw membership, there were riots on the streets of every major city. It took the military to regain order, and curfews ensued, but the groundswell of anger continued online. The first hack came shortly afterwards, eradicating the balance sheets of companies deemed to be servicing the rich. The government was quick to blame FEB, introducing sweeping legislations aimed at eliminating dissent, including near-blanket Internet blockage for everyone without a university degree or exceptional dispensation. Three prominent FEB politicians – the representatives for Central Bedfordshire, Luton and North Hertfordshire – were shot and killed at a public rally opposing online regulation, and rumours gained traction that the government had been involved. Unrest grew, and the more the government blamed FEB for the hacks and violence and regulated against them, the more support surged. In a last-gasp bid to retain power, the government repealed the Internet blackout, and the following month, the most calamitous cyber attack in the history of the world took place.

Subsequent studies showed that the Zero Virus had most likely been aimed only at the accounts of the most wealthy politicians in Britain, but an error sent it running free, linking from account to account, person to person, business to business, institution to institution, until the balance of virtually every bank account in the UK was wiped irretrievably to nil. It spread beyond Britain's borders, eradicating the balance of any account with a UK association and leaving pockets of devastation globally in its wake. An entirely new global currency – credits – was required to piece things back together. Nowhere, however, was the damage more complete and shattering than in Britain. Businesses collapsed, hospitals ceased to function, no one could buy fuel or food. The country was in chaos beyond comparison. The government said it was hallmark FEB tactics to attack the rich with disregard for consequences. FEB argued the Coalition was attempting to frame them. They had a track record of state-sponsored violence, didn't they? Some even argued it could have been a foreign government with an interest in causing chaos in Western democracies. It was never established who wrote the Zero Virus, but the emergency election – a misguided attempt to shore up power – was a total FEB landslide. How could it ever have been anything else?

Sickness rolled through Dom's gut, and he reached up and pulled the shutter down across the window. Through the gap between the seats, he could see the woman in front was watching the trial. Her headphones were on, so he couldn't hear what the journalist was saying, but the screen cut from the newsroom to the Old Bailey courthouse and Judge Mabel Lyons, and then to the infamous photograph of the young FEB Five. They were in Trafalgar Square on the day of the election, on a makeshift stage with the sun setting behind them. Their arms were around each other, and they were smiling. Laughing. The architects of Britain's demise. Billy Slade was on one end in a bright yellow sweatshirt, looking relaxed with his fist in the air. He was a fisherman's son from Grimsby, a man of the people with the jawbone of a cartoon superhero and charisma seeping through every pore. Beside him stood James Easton, a veteran of the Iraq War with a public-school background that he somehow managed to keep quiet, and a missing leg after a run-in with an IED. Edward Wade was next, the West Country boy made good, a builder who'd earned his pre-virus millions importing fuse boxes from China. Eric Simmons leaned against him, older and plumper than the rest. Before FEB, he'd worked for a series of charities and lobby groups, covering interests as diverse as animal rights and tobacco promotion, their political aims seemingly less important than the stridency with which they were pursued. Carl Hamilton was last and the only one not smiling. Slade's childhood friend, he'd been a chemistry teacher in one of Grimsby's most deprived postcodes, and though he preferred to keep away from the limelight after the election, his fingerprints were on all of FEB's most barbaric acts. Slade and Hamilton aside, the men had come together through the protests, uniting behind a thirst for power and their shared understanding of the alchemy that anger, fear and hopelessness could achieve. They knew how to spark a flint into flame. Dom squeezed his eyes closed, nausea pounding through him. They'd had none of the knowledge or skills required to rebuild the country and – even more damningly – little intent to do so.

'Sir?'

Dom opened his eyes, and the air stewardess gave him a practised smile. She indicated to the window.

'Shutters raised for landing, please.'

Dom nodded and fumbled the plastic upwards. The stewardess paused, her eyes hovering on his trembling hands. She tapped Dom's shoulder gently and smiled again, more warmly.

'Don't worry. We'll be down in a moment,' she said, before moving on.

Dom's cheeks burned, and he stuffed his hands into his pocket, feeling for the safety of his pot of pills. He hated when people assumed it was nerves. The Hamilton Shakes, they called them: a life-long side effect of exposure to Tremor Gas, the sixth-generation nerve agent created from agricultural pesticides not outlawed under the international Chemical Weapons Convention – and FEB's favourite method of crowd control. The gas was otherwise known as hamilditiophosphate, named after its creator, the chemistry teacher turned genocidal despot, Carl Hamilton.

With his hand inside his pocket, Dom flipped the cap and extracted a pill. He crammed it into his mouth, dry, and forced it down. Between the seats, the woman's screen strobed with photographers' flashbulbs. Slade was the only one of the FEB Five who'd been brought to trial. Wade slit his wrists as NATO soldiers dragged him from a coal chute in an abandoned Lake District cottage, three days after ground troops went in. Simmons surrendered a week or so later and was being prepared for prosecution when a bodged attack on his transportation convoy – whether an attempted assassination or escape was unknown – left him in a persistent vegetative state. He now spent his days in a secure unit in Berkshire, where it cost hundreds of thousands of credits to keep him alive. Easton, Hamilton and Slade had disappeared. It was a decade before Slade was located in Sudan, tracked down by an intrepid journalist, having changed his name and taken a job at a Christian aid charity, of all places. Hamilton and Easton were still on the run.

'Where are we?'

At Dom's side, Tess stirred and straightened, rubbing at the imprints of her pillow on her tawny-brown cheek. He let out a long breath, the relief that hearing her voice alone could provide, and teased a crumpled loop of her hair that was sticking upright. He flattened it for her then lifted her hand and kissed her knuckles. 'Over the city. Won't be long until we land.'

'You OK?' she asked.

'Nervous.'

She glanced through the seats and saw the woman's screen. 'There was never going to be a good time to come back, you know? It was always going to be hard.'

Dom clamped his teeth on a snag of thumbnail and tore, not answering. He knew she was right. Tess was always right about things like this. Fear had kept him away for nineteen years already. For all that time he'd pretended that he didn't need to return. She linked her arm through his and snuggled into him, squeezing, then reached across his body and tapped his watch. The photograph lit on his home screen. He smiled at the sight of it. Warmth filtered through his insides. Yes, Tess was right. He would focus on the good things. He could do that, couldn't he? Outside, the buildings grew larger and closer, and the land fled by, blurring. He took a deep breath and braced himself for landing, feeling as though his past and future both hurtled towards him, and he wasn't sure which one would reach him first – nor if the impact might break him.

The plane nudged onto the tarmac, and from somewhere in the cabin a cheer rose. There was clapping. This was it, Dom thought. I'm here. We're doing this. There's no turning back.

3

Outside the museum, Thea's watch buzzed. She stamped down the stone steps, emerging from beneath the portico and squinting through the afternoon's glare, seeing the glass light again with Springer's name. She swiped the message open, cursing. He never gave up.

I'm here. Where are you?

Thea stopped dead. Her eyes leapt across the plaza, finding Springer at the gate to Great Russell Street. He was scanning the space like she was, searching the throngs of tourists, school children and downcast Archive trawlers, and blocking her escape. She ripped her watch from her wrist and powered it down, stuffing it to the bottom of her rucksack and keeping him in her sight as she backed away. She'd bought the watch second-hand from the man who ran the Gritstone's entire tech economy from his fourth-floor flat, but she'd not had the credits for a security update, and no matter how many times she changed the GPS to private mode, it always reset, and Springer tracked her down. She slipped into the gap behind a van selling ice-cream cones and coffee to a Japanese tour group and skirted the edge of the sun-bleached lawn, heading towards the side of the museum that was covered by scaffolding. She ducked beneath its green mesh awning and hurried along the corridor, emerging at the railings on the museum's north-east edge, out of view from the heaving courtyard and Springer's gaze. She hauled herself over the wrought-iron spikes, and the wound in her stomach screamed a warning as she thumped to the ground.

Wincing, Thea dragged herself up. Colours spotted through her vision, and she pressed a hand to her belly, sucking air deep into her lungs as she moved away. She'd have to deal with Springer later, but at least that would be afterwards. She'd have had her time with Laurel. Calmed down. A familiar jab of anger fired through her. She couldn't remember the moment when she and Springer had stopped being best friends. They were both alone together in their Roundhouse homes at one point – her without her parents and him without his mother and sister – but it must have happened one day that they made their choices differently. Grief did different things to different people. Thea turned against everything FEB for her survival. Springer chose to turn towards them instead.

It was hard to argue that he'd made the wrong call. He'd had more food, more people looking out for him. They'd given him better work duties and taught him to read. Even now, his position as the Roundhouse's warden had its root in those days. Every morsel of power and influence in Britain today, however big or small or pettily exercised, could be traced back to the choices a person made during FEB. Thea would leave, one day. Sometimes when she thought of it, she could hardly breathe for wanting. She hadn't said it out loud, but it must have been obvious to Springer. As soon as she had Laurel and was done with the Archive, Thea would quit her job and get far away from the Roundhouse, London and Britain. It didn't matter where she went or what she did when she got there. All that mattered was that it wasn't here.

Her hands balled to fists in her pockets, and she quickened her pace, swinging around the corner. It had been eighty-four days since Thea had slept in a bed beside her newborn daughter, and it was all Springer's fault. In those three long months, there had only been three visits; three times that Thea was allowed to hold her baby, to breathe in the milky-sweet scent of her skin and feel those tiny fingers wrapped hard around her own. She crossed Euston Road, not waiting for the lights to change. The cars hissed to a halt, but the guilt crashed into her. It had been the start of May. The heat was settling in for the summer, and she'd been working overtime at the Oakwood Hotel. Springer had got her a job as a waitress (and not let her forget it), and she'd been trying to cram as many hours into the days before she knew she would have to leave for the baby, but her feet were swollen, and her belly was heavy, and she'd thought it was only the temperature that made her head swim. Then she'd blacked out on the kitchen floor. When she came to, the drugs had paralysed her limbs, but her mind was instantly lucid, horrified and terrified, panicking beyond panic that they had taken her daughter, until the moment she saw the girl in the cot at her side.

Thea's relief was short-lived. The Oakwood's head chef had made a call to Springer, and he was already at the hospital when she woke. He'd given the doctor permission to check Thea's credits while she was unconscious, and they'd come to the conclusion she was TTS only: Treat To Survive and nothing more. As soon as the feeling came back to her legs, the doctor asked her to leave. She might not have minded, but they'd already made arrangements for Laurel, and Springer had signed them off. It wasn't unusual for someone as incapacitated as Thea and without any blood relations to have care decisions referred to their warden. It was a system that had begun with the first post-FEB government, since so many people were left without next of kin. In the years since, warden responsibilities had expanded almost beyond recognition. Central government provided local councils with a budget to hire wardens in whichever communities they saw as having the need, yet they rarely appeared outside the estates. They were assigned as building managers, regeneration champions and community representatives, as well as emergency points-of-call, and the job attracted a certain calibre of applicant. In practice, they were often lawmakers, judges and juries. Spies.

Thea's jaw set. The fact that Springer had been operating within the expected boundaries of his job description for once did nothing to soften the blow of losing Laurel. The baby had a fever, and TTS could be extended for minors. Afterwards there were charities that would step in for her care. Thea had argued against their separation, but she was tired and confused and drugged and raging, and despite the claim he was helping, everything that Springer had done was wrong. Monthly visits were promised until Thea had saved the credits deemed reasonable to take Laurel home. The doctor made it sound easy. It was temporary. Not unusual. The hospital would get Laurel's vitals steadied and then send her to the children's home. Thea could collect her when she was feeling better. When she wasn't alone and broke and useless, he had meant.

She clenched her fists tighter, her footsteps reverberating through the split in her stomach. The sound of the trains arriving and departing from Euston Station clattered between the buildings, and she could smell their diesel and the uncollected bins. The station's long wall was layered with year upon year of graffiti that the council had been too preoccupied to deal with, but there was plenty of it fresh too, the paint dribbling from the lettering's edges as though it were still wet. *FIRSTS COME FIRST. POWER TO THE SALTERS. SPOONIES PISS OFF.* Thea focused on her feet, on keeping their rhythm. At the start of FEB, everyone was given their category. Officially, you were either a One or a Two. Ones represented the way of life that the new government was striving to achieve. Ones were model citizens. As a Two, you were indicative of all that was wrong with Britain and that needed to be eradicated. You were there to confess, repent and change.

Unofficially, the labels evolved more brutally. You were either a Salter, so named because your family was salt of the earth – hardworking, no-nonsense and under-appreciated – or you were a Spoonie, because you were born with a silver spoon in your mouth. Besides, what illness was more chronic and life-defining than privilege? At first, to be a Spoonie was just something to be embarrassed about. Later, you hid it or paid with your life. What it meant to be a Spoonie altered too, as the months and years progressed. To start, Spoonies were those whose families had old money. Then it was anyone who owned their own home. Then anyone who had been on a foreign holiday. Ate in restaurants at weekends. Owned a car. The way it worked out – though the government never articulated as much – there was never a Salter who wasn't a Cat. One. There was never a Spoonie who wasn't Cat. Two. Thea's family were Salters. Her mother worked as a kitchen hand in a care home, and her father packed spices on a factory line that yellowed his fingers and made him smell like the curry house on Worthington Avenue. In the long run – when the food ran out and FEB's hold became fragile – it didn't make a difference what category you were.

Thea shoved the memory to the back of her mind and turned the last corner, slowing at the sight of Little Doves Children's Home. Her hands uncurled, and she found her notebook in her pocket and thumbed the edge. The only calmness she'd felt these last three months was when she'd held Laurel. She could hardly believe the strength of love and pain that came with someone so new and small. The notebook's thin paper rumpled in her fingers. It wasn't only the man's face she'd drawn on the pages. In miniature, amidst the endless versions of him, she'd drawn her baby too. The sun burned onto the nape of her neck and nerves rippled through her. But had she? The child she'd scribbled was beautiful, pudgy and peaceful, but what if it wasn't Laurel? What if Thea remembered her daughter's face no better than she remembered the man? She might walk inside the children's home and see a dozen sleeping infants, and not recognise her own.

She shuddered, stiffening and forcing her feet forward. The road was set back from the main thoroughfares and quiet; cars neatly parked, no pedestrians and only the faintest breeze. From the railings, a wood pigeon puffed his chest and cooed, watching Thea with ink-drop eyes. She looked away, tasting the acid from where Jemima's chocolate had met with the emptiness in her stomach and bubbled back. Springer's mother had made them a pigeon pie to share, once. That was before the pigeons ran out too. Seeing wildlife in the city could still surprise Thea. The Ministry of Resources made a show of saying that things were improving, but rationing was as strict as Thea could remember, and the food banks ran on empty. She usually picked from the plates that she cleared at the Oakwood, but she'd been too full of anticipation about Laurel to eat anything this morning.

She climbed the steps to the children's home and thumped the heavy brass knocker against the wood. The bird startled from the rail and fled with beaten wings. Thea straightened her t-shirt, smoothed it over her stomach. Waited. She rapped again, listening for footsteps. She couldn't hear them. She couldn't hear anything. There were no cries, no shouts, no sounds from any children. Looking up, she saw that the windows were all closed. It must have been twenty-five degrees. Why weren't the windows open? Were the curtains drawn too? Her eyes flicked sideways. Every other townhouse on the street had opened its windows. They glinted in the sunlight. She moved back to the pavement, squinting at Little Doves, working her way up the building, searching each pane for movement and feeling her heart-rate spike. She realised the sign above the door was missing. The cloud with the outline of the bird in flight was gone.

'Hello!' she yelled. She could hear herself panicking. 'Are you there? Hello! I've come to see my baby.'

The reply came from behind her. Thea turned to see a scruffy, barefoot man exiting the doorway opposite, lugging a bulging black sack down the steps towards the street. At the kerb, he threw open a bin and lobbed the sack inside. His voice was faintly amused but not unfriendly.

'You're wasting your time, love. They moved out last week.'

4

The screen inside the Driverless Express said twenty minutes to West Kensington. Dom and Tess faced each other across the taxicab, their ankles touching as the car sped smoothly and silently along the motorway. Tess was absorbed in her own screen, swiping through Maya's adoption documents and seeing that everything was in order. It would be, Dom knew. She'd checked and re-checked a hundred times since leaving Washington DC, but anything would do to distract from the nerves. Dom understood. He didn't feel like talking either. He'd expected that being on the ground might have made him feel calmer – more rooted – but instead, the feeling of free fall continued. Everything about the world outside the cab was too familiar, like time had stopped and waited for his return. Grassy, litter-strewn banks lined the roadside, giving way at intervals to bland office blocks and budget hotels. The sky sat low, grey and threatening rain. Blue and white signs with names like Twickenham, Hammersmith and Kew Gardens dredged up sharp shards of memory. Sheep grazed in the occasional parched field. He pressed the button to draw down the window, and the smell of the summer city was as he remembered. The petrol stations had been replaced with charging terminals, and he could see the traffic drones overhead, but everything else was so eerily similar that he felt the past was slithering around him. Squeezing. The US had seemed so endlessly vast when he'd first arrived there. Britain was small and smothering by comparison. The other cars on the motorway felt too close to him. When they entered London properly, the roads were even narrower. Buildings loomed over them. Dom could have reached from the window of the taxi and touched the mothers on the pavements with their prams.

He rubbed his face and tapped at his watch. *Landed. Journey fine. On our way to meet Maya. How was the interview? So weird being back.*

He paused. Deleted the last four words. Pressed *Send.* Their plane had arrived later than expected, and it was already mid-morning in DC, but Tim wouldn't have been waiting for the update. He wasn't one for worrying like Dom. Tess said it showed what a first-rate job Dom had done of being a big brother, absorbing the fear for him, but Dom wasn't convinced. There hadn't been a day in life after their parents died when Dom didn't feel that he was hanging by his fingernails. He'd wanted to shield Tim from so much more.

Look after your brother. Those were the last words his father had said to him as he'd shoved the boys inside their mother's office at University College London before slamming the door and sprinting towards the screams and the gunshots, in search of her. He'd not meant forever, although that was what it turned out to be. A federal scheme for refugee FEB children saw Dom and Tim flit between four foster families in three years before finding something steady. Then, at eighteen, Dom became Tim's legal guardian. It was ridiculous how protective he still felt of his little brother, and how proud he was too. Tim worked for the FBI in forensic accounting, tracing the movement of cryptocurrency linked to criminal activity across the world. He'd run point on some of the highest-profile fraud cases in recent years and, at only twenty-seven years old, was now interviewing for sector head. His office was two blocks south from where Dom worked as a senior vulnerability manager in Tech Infrastructure for Recovering Nations, one of the newer departments at USAID. Dom spent his days devising and implementing tech strategies to shore up the computer systems of credit-strapped, struggling governments worldwide. It was a job he was happy to do and ashamed of in equal measure. There was no kidding himself that his childhood experiences hadn't led him to it, and he knew that the things he did there made a difference. Yet his office was safe, so far removed from the realities of where the Zero Virus had hit. He could turn his screen off in the evenings, go home, have a beer and a takeaway and almost, *almost*, forget.

The cab turned from the main road, arriving on a tree-lined street with terraced houses that looked a little untidy but nothing like derelict, and anxiety pushed its way from his stomach to his chest. What was it that he'd been expecting to see? The burned-out carcass of Britain? He should have known that the news streams only showed the worst and most hideously compelling snapshots. In the eyes of the UN, this was officially still a developing nation, but he reminded himself that the downfall had started with runaway code, not a hail of bullets. When the bombs did come, they were few, precise, swift and so utterly ruinous to FEB that it was disgraceful it had taken four years for the world to intervene. Ahead, the traffic lights leapt to red, and when the cab halted before a parade of shops the difference between then and now made itself known. He kissed his teeth. The shops weren't shops, he realised. There was a clothing exchange. A shabby-looking food bank. A branch of the Missing Persons Reparations Bureau. The kerb had crumbled to dust, and the weeds were overgrowing. A dog looked dead behind the bin. Embedded in the wall beside an innocuous-looking car park was a fist-sized disc, blush-pink and glinting in the sunlight, embossed with a number. His heels jittered on the floor. Dom remembered similar plaques from his childhood – royal blue ones with white writing that were set into the brickwork of buildings across the country to celebrate historical figures and note where they'd lived. There were more than a handful of them near his mother's UCL office, and she'd point them out on walks to and from the station. The Charleses were her favourites – Darwin and Dickens, pioneers of body and mind. These pink plaques commemorated history, Dom knew, but they weren't for celebration. Instead, they marked execution sites and kept count of the dead. His mouth went dry as he read the record. *Hooperwell High Street. 316.* On the shuttered-down store beside the car park, he could see the ghost of partially scrubbed graffiti. DEATH TO SPOONIES. Taunts shrieked through his memory, and he felt in his pocket for the bottle of pills. This was why they had come back to Britain. He knew this was the reason. He'd give Maya the chance for something better – like he'd had. He'd protect her as fiercely as he had his brother. Tess and Dom would be her escape.

The lights changed, and the taxi hooked left onto Beauden Crescent. Dom shuffled across the cab, pulling his wife into him and kissing her forehead. She leaned against him, not speaking. It was Tess's idea to come. If they couldn't conceive a child of their own, what better place in the world was there to adopt from? They followed the dog-leg of the road, searching the double-fronted townhouses with their big bay windows for number 89. Severe male-factor infertility. That was what the doctors called it. It was most likely another side effect of the tremor gas – studies had found patterns – although the attack hadn't prevented Tim from producing two perfect kids. Dom never begrudged Tim his easy happiness, and he loved Sasha and Finn completely, though he couldn't help feeling a pang of envy too.

It was the day of Finn's christening when he and Tess made their decision. Tess stood in Tim and Katrina's glossy white kitchen, at the countertop spread with celebration food and blue confetti, rocking their gorgeous, sleeping infant on her shoulder and picking at a cupcake topped with sugar booties. The makeup couldn't hide that she'd cried. It was four weeks after their embryo transfer, the only successful transfer they'd managed, with the only successful embryo the IVF had created with Dom's feeble sperm. In the night, Tess had stirred, and Dom had turned to see her clamber from the bed. As she padded to the bathroom the moonlight fuzzed her hair and made her silhouette ghostly, but he'd seen at once the blots of dark blood on her white nightdress. Grief powered through him. He closed his eyes and waited for her howl. The clinic wasn't open on weekends, so they'd missed Finn's church service as Dom sped to the emergency room and Tess shook with sobs beside him, and though the doctor was patient, kind and gentle, there was nothing she could do to change the scan's outcome. They were told that miscarriage was only slightly more likely in IVF pregnancies than natural ones, but that didn't make a difference. There wasn't a heartbeat. The baby was gone. Dom told Tim and Katrina that a puncture had got them coming off the junction on the 601, and the four of them laughed it off in a brisk, breezy moment. What a day to blow a tyre. Such shitty luck. In the car going home, Tess had said it was over, and Dom panicked, thinking she was leaving him. He wouldn't have blamed her. She deserved the child she longed for, the one he couldn't give her. When he realised that he was mistaken, the relief was sickening. Five years of trying and failing, of tests and procedures, hopes raised then slaughtered, five years of limbo, watching their friends have children and move from the city to houses with gardens, buying SUVs and taking vacations to Disney World while Dom and Tess scheduled appointments and calculated ovulation and doused every act of affection with pressure, and kept secrets and failed . . . *that* was over. It was the constant uncertainty that made life impossible to grasp. So much of their identity as a couple had been tied to what they'd planned for. What was left when you took that away? The only thing worse than not being pregnant was being pregnant and then not. Tess couldn't do it again, couldn't bear another miscarriage, however unlikely. They were done with treatments. They were going to adopt.

The taxi pulled up beside a smart-looking, white-painted townhouse with frosted-glass windows and bay trees flanking the door. Tess glanced at Dom – steeling herself – then paid with a tap of her watch against the screen. The door to BlueSkies Children's Sanctuary was open before they'd dropped their backpacks on the kerb.

'Mr and Mrs Nowell?' Catherine Hilton-Webb bounded down the orphanage's steps and hugged Tess and Dom in turn as if they were old friends. She smelled of mint and sweet, strong perfume. 'It's lovely to meet you. How are you? I bet coming back has been quite the experience.'

Dom took the hug awkwardly, finding Tess's hand. They had spoken to Catherine by telepresence on numerous occasions, and she knew his story. Tess had explained, hoping it would help their application, but Catherine's forwardness still surprised him. He wasn't usually one for hugging strangers any more than he was for them knowing the details of what had happened. Saying nothing was simpler and safer than saying a little and then having to explain. Yet despite himself, his tension eased. It was a relief for once that he didn't have to hide it. It was nice to feel that someone cared.

Catherine ushered them into the hallway, questioning Tess about their journey and what colours they'd picked in the end for Maya's bedroom. He zoned them out to the sound of a baby wailing and nursery rhymes playing from somewhere inside. After months of planning, being here felt unreal. They followed Catherine along the corridor, and he glanced through the crack of an open door, glimpsing a row of babies that were older than Maya, some asleep and some standing in their cots, watching a nanny change a nappy nearby. His heart thrummed as he took in the surroundings. The children's home was clean enough, but plaster was flaking from the cornices, and the posters of cartoon monkeys and lions were dog-eared and fading. The children looked calm and not unhappy, but there was still the unmistakable feeling of an institution: the tang of disinfectant, rooms with not enough furniture to stop their echo, furnishings that were sparse and nothing more than functional, scuffed paint in shades of duck egg and cream.

Catherine seemed to read his thoughts. 'I know it looks basic,' she said, waving Dom ahead of her, 'but we're purpose over comfort here. Our children have everything they need, but we don't waste money on being flash. Some agencies like to put on a show for prospective parents – everything from scrimping on food to pay for adverts to keeping the children with birthmarks and lazy eyes out the way. Making sure you only see the cute and cuddlies, you know? It's vile. We funnel every penny we can into preventing children from coming here in the first place – helping little ones like Maya stay with their birth families whenever possible. We've had our two thousandth adoption this month. It's taken us a good few years, and it's not been without headaches, but I'm proud of that number. Our work is a drop in the ocean, but you know if you get your child from us, we've done everything we can.' She paused and smiled at Dom, touching his arm gently before continuing along the corridor. 'I promise we never scrimp on love.'

Dom blushed. Cheerful though she came across, Catherine left no doubt that she'd assumed he needed to be reminded of his privilege. She was only partially right. He did feel shocked, tired from the flight and dazed from the onslaught to his senses that the trip had so far been, but he hadn't been disgusted by the orphanage's appearance. He and Tess knew that the UK adoption scene grappled with those who were out to make a quick credit from their clients. They'd done their homework, choosing BlueSkies for its impeccable reputation. Instead, Dom had been trying to organise the slew of new sights, information and feelings. As he was doing so, one had risen to the top like a bead of oil through water: shame that he hadn't been back before now.

Catherine stopped by a door at the end of the hall. 'Well,' she said, turning back and smiling. 'Shall we meet your little girl?'

Tess fired Dom a look – not panic but somewhere close. He felt it too. Through the door's glass panel, they could see a young woman with her back to them and hear the water running as she rinsed a bottle in the sink. Catherine dipped inside the room and said something quietly, and the woman nodded and placed the bottle onto a rack. She dried her hands and slunk past them with a shy smile, before disappearing along the corridor. Catherine held the door, and Dom and Tess crept forward. Maya was asleep in a crib that looked the same as what Finn had been in when they'd visited the hospital; one with clear Perspex sides and a swinging metal frame. The air had that light, powdery talcum scent that hung around Tim's house. Sunlight had torn through the clouds and spilled softly over her body. Dom stepped beside the crib. Tess clung to his hand. She was shaking. Maya looked so small and peaceful and perfect, swaddled in a lilac muslin that was covered in tiny grey elephants.

Tess tucked back her hair, leaning over the cot. 'Oh, Dom,' she whispered, pressing her hand to her mouth. 'Look at her.'

Dom couldn't speak. He wrapped his arms around his wife, clutching at her t-shirt and biting back tears, staring at the softly moving swell of Maya's breast, overcome with love for both his girls. A vision of their future bolted though his consciousness: bringing Maya home for the first time in her car seat, taking her to Tim and Katrina's at Thanksgiving, kicking leaves with a galosh-clad toddler at the riverside, listening for the school bus on their street every morning, helping with her homework, teaching her swimming, and ballet recitals and holidays and it all.

Catherine looked at Tess. 'Would you like to hold her?'

Tess's face lit up. She peeled herself away from Dom and eased the bundle into her arms, cupping Maya's dark head in her hand and pressing their bodies together. The baby stirred and yawned, eyes screwed. Tess smiled through her tears, rocking her.

'Hello, little bean. Hello, my sweet love.'

Dom blinked back the tears that had collected behind his eyes. Maya and Tess looked beautiful together, and seeing them so was better than he could ever have imagined. He had known he was excited – known how desperately he had wanted their lives to move forward – but the strength of this feeling was overwhelming. He stroked a fingertip across Maya's temple, sweeping through the tips of her downy hair. Her eyelashes fluttered, and she sighed and then looked at him. A laugh burst from his chest, and her huge brown eyes started, but then she smiled, widely and utterly luminous. He kissed Tess's lips and felt her trembling. They had been a couple on the pavement outside the orphanage. Now they were changed. At last they were *three*.

5

The telephone number for Little Doves had been disconnected. Perched on a hard chair in the corner of the police station's waiting room, Thea listened to the computerised voice deliver the same curt message that she'd heard fifty times in the last two hours – *The number you've called has not been recognised* – before cutting her off. She tapped redial on the screen of her watch, and the man at the opposite end of the row of conjoined plastic seating tutted and fired her a glare. She thumbed the button to lower the volume, and waited for the voice to dismiss her again. A strip-light stuttered from the ceiling, and the smell of bleach hung so thickly in the air that she could taste it. Her head felt as though it was being cleaved in two. On the wall behind the reception desk, the projection flicked from a newscast of Slade's trial to an advertisement for PTSD treatment clinics, to a warning that possession of firearms could mean ten years in jail. The sun radiated through the grubby glass doors, and she tugged at her t-shirt, peeling it from her skin. The room was crammed with people, and getting busier. A girl no older than sixteen, Thea guessed, was gripping the desk and speaking to the officer behind his barricade for the third time. The baby strapped to her chest was asleep, limp-limbed, soft and plump where it spilled from the carrier. Thea picked at the skin around her fingernail. They'd arrived around the same time, the girl and Thea. It must have been ninety minutes earlier. Longer. The baby had been shrieking. The girl was sent back to her seat, looking anxious. Her eye caught Thea's. The police were useless. How hard could it be to report a crime? Her own nerves smacked, her stomach cramping. Was this a crime? Little Doves wouldn't move without telling her. Would they? Something had happened. Oh, god. Was Laurel safe?

'Theodora Baxter?'

A door in the side wall opened, and a policewoman leaned out. She threw a look around, and Thea raised her hand, standing and hurrying across the room. She let herself be greeted and guided into the corridor, feeling the thick metal door clank shut at her back. She followed the officer along the long, airless walkway and into a room where the air conditioning blasted. Gooseflesh rose on her arms. The room was windowless, the size of the Oakwood Hotel's meat locker. She'd been trapped in there once, when Chef sent her in for steaks and the handle jammed. It was an hour before he realised and let her out. A pig was hanging to drain and blood overspilled the bucket; when the lights timed off, the shadow was shaped like a human. The sight had followed her for a week.

The officer pulled out a chair. 'Would you like some water?' she asked. There was a smile on her face, but it stopped before her eyes.

Thea shook her head and thudded into the seat. The

officer sat opposite. She smoothed her red-brown braid over her shoulder, and from beneath the cuff of her uniform Thea saw the sharp, slender point of what might have been a star, or perhaps a compass, peeping out. She tucked her hands beneath her thighs and sat rigid. It didn't matter what it was. There was only one reason to have a tattoo on your wrist. The *epa* had been the branding of the most ardent FEB loyalists, the two black diamonds, one for justice, one for law, overlapping at their points like handcuffs. Thea had heard that FEB stole the symbol from West Africa – like Hitler stole the swastika – repurposing its meaning to suit their needs. Most of those with the *epa* covered or removed it when FEB fell, but it always remained obvious. Her heart pumped harder. She shouldn't have come here. The police were more than useless. They were crookeder than tree roots. Everyone knew that.

The officer plucked a screen from its holder on her belt and swiped a pattern across the glass. It beeped, and the image of a microphone appeared in the centre. *Transcribing.* She spoke the date and her name, then Thea's name, and Thea saw a document open and the words appear in a hard, bold line.

'Can you confirm your address for me, please, Miss Baxter?' asked the officer.

'Apartment 82,' Thea replied. 'Eighth Floor. Roundhouse Tower. Gritstone.'

'The Gritstone Estate? This isn't your local station.'

'It was closest to where I was.'

'Who's your warden?'

'Josh Springer.'

'Do you know his reference?'

'GR-94376.'

In the corner of the screen, Thea saw Springer's photograph leap up. The officer tilted it at her for confirmation, and Thea nodded through her scowl. Even if her parents had still been alive, living somewhere like the Roundhouse meant the wardens would know everything there was to know. Springer would get pinged a summary of her police visit for certain, perhaps the full transcript before she even arrived home. She made a note not to mention his name. The government argued that being transparent helped the wardens deliver better security for their residents, as well as more thorough and appropriate care, but Thea doubted Springer was the only warden who elasticated the definition of 'appropriate'. There had been the odd protest about warden jurisdiction over the years, but those with the power to curb their influence rarely lived in a community that was subject to it, and the protests always fizzled out. *Prioritisation for reconstruction* was the post-FEB government's eternal refrain. So much to do. Manage your expectations. Aim low. The policewoman tapped Springer's face to confirm his authority and settled the screen back on the desk.

'So how can I help you today?' she asked, looking at Thea.

Thea took a deep breath. Her head was fuzzy. She felt as though she wasn't really here. 'I can't find my daughter,' she said.

The officer nodded, her faint smile giving the impression of sympathy. 'OK. I'm sorry to hear that. What's her name?'

'Laurel Laila Baxter.'

'And how old is she?'

'Three months.'

The woman's expression hardened. She stared at Thea, any trace of smile gone. 'That's a 999 job,' she said. She nudged her chair away from the table and pulled out her radio, raising it to her lips and pressing the button to speak, before pausing and releasing it. She eyed Thea sideways. 'Isn't it?'

Thea didn't move. Her stomach was liquid. She had thought about dialling, but what would she say? She didn't know that it was an emergency. If only she had gone to the Archive and found Jemima before coming here. Jemima always knew how to handle things. The officer's glare was cold and impatient, but her own shock ran deeper. She glanced down at her wrist and scraped her thumb over the thick white ridge of scar tissue that peeped out from beneath her watch strap. Springer had said she was lucky they'd only snapped her arm that day and not her neck. It was true. She knew they'd have beat her more if he wasn't there to step in. It was when they were children, back when they'd still been friends, a few months after her parents died, before his mother and sister died too. The day was midsummer-hot, no shade in the allotments, and Thea was tired and thirsty and hungrier than hungry, and she'd only stopped work for the briefest moment, only paused from digging out carrots to grab for a beetle; a fat little one that was shimmering green and purple as it clambered over the hunks of churned mud. She thought she'd been swift. Thought they'd not seen her eat it. Not heard it crunch. But of course they had. FEB saw and heard everything. The supervisor – one of the older Gritstone boys – was swift to react, leaping from his camping stool and yanking her from the vegetable patch before she'd even swallowed it. He slapped the back of her head, making her spit the gritty morsel onto the path. With the other children watching, silent and frozen, he raised his cane and thwacked it across her forearm. She heard her bone crack, saw her skin cleaved open, before she felt the pain. She whimpered, and the boy brought the cane above his head again. He was poised to strike when Springer intervened. Thea didn't know what Springer had said to him, but Springer was well liked in those days, and he'd somehow calmed the boy down. Punishments are always worse if you cry, he told her afterwards. Never show weakness. Stay quiet. Stay still. Ride it out. The lesson stuck. She hadn't cried since.

Thea sat taller in her seat, stiff-backed and lifting her chin.

The officer sniffed. In her voice, a new note of suspicion was clear. 'You got paperwork for this kid?'

She shifted, and Thea saw that the tip of the tattoo she'd mistaken for a star or a compass was letters, the stylised point of a capital A – *Alicia Jade* – beside a date from six years ago. It was a child's birthday. Thea would bet her life. Resentment broiled. She shook her head. The only people in Britain with paperwork for their children were those with credits too. Little Doves had told Thea that they'd registered Laurel in line with state requirements but that Thea would have to save and buy the papers back.

'I didn't want her to go,' Thea said, staring down the officer and grinding out the words. 'I was sick when she was born. I wanted to keep her. I'd have never done it if I didn't have to. Not if I'd had a choice. I thought she was safe.'

The officer had stopped trying to hide her distaste. 'You gave her to the Boxes?'

'No.'

'There's no shame in it, Miss Baxter.' Her tone said otherwise.

Rage sizzled through Thea. This woman didn't understand. How could she?

'I didn't give her away. They took her.'

The policewoman scowled, her radio still poised. 'Who's they?'

'I don't know who *they* are,' Thea said, spitting with frustration. *They* was Little Doves, but it was also the hospital. It was the doctor who'd said she wasn't fit to be a parent, and Springer who'd signed the most precious part of her away while she was drugged and unconscious. It was the person who'd made the rule that held her daughter hostage until she'd earned more credits than she'd had in her life. It was Chef at the Oakwood, paying her almost nothing. She stared at the policewoman's wrist with its red and black spiked writing. *They* was this woman, accusing before helping. Her hand drove into her pocket, clutching her notebook and crumpling the pages. She could feel herself unspooling, feel the threads of control that she'd bound so tightly beginning to tangle. It was the man who killed her parents, and everything he stood for, and everyone who'd left her to manage this shit alone.

'I want my daughter back!' she cried, and she rammed her chair away from the table. It toppled behind her as she stood, and she swung round and kicked out, sending it clattering into the wall. The officer backed up, speaking into her radio. The hallway door flew open, and before Thea registered what was happening, two policemen had thrown themselves onto her, and she realised she was shouting and kicking and clawing.

She flipped, boss. I don't know what happened.

Says her kid's missing.

The Boxes.

These mothers.

Don't know what she's taken.

Get hold of her elbow.

The muzzle! Where's the muzzle?

Easy now.

Just calm it down, love.

Calm down.

CALM DOWN.

She could hear herself screaming, and she was biting one of them, sinking her teeth into his hot, flabby haunch. He yelped like a dog as they prised her off, and there was blood on her chin, dripping, and the warm taste of iron on her tongue. Then they had her on the floor. It was cold and hard against her cheekbone. There were cuffs around her wrists, tight enough to burn, and she was dragged into the corridor. They carried her back, further and further, still fighting, and when the cell door slammed shut, everything went black.

6

They waited until the end of the street before they embraced.

'I miss her already,' said Tess, laughing into Dom's chest. 'We're so lucky, Dom. She was smaller than I thought she'd be, wasn't she? So tiny for four months. I hope the clothes we've brought her fit.' She hugged him tighter and looked up, her dark eyes pressing into him, gleaming in the early evening light. 'I can't believe this is happening. I thought I was going to lose it in there, you know? End up a slobbering, snot-faced wreck.'

Dom laughed too and kissed her forehead. 'You're pretty snotty now, Tess.'

She thumped him off and stuck out her tongue. 'Did you see the way she was holding my finger?'

'She loves her mama.'

Tess closed her eyes and smiled. In his heart, he felt the swell. He was so proud of her – of the both of them – and he hadn't expected to feel such relief. Never would he have believed it was possible to love anyone so completely, so instantly, until he saw Maya. He loved Tess more too, somehow, for having seen her with their child. Of course,

Maya wasn't theirs yet. Not quite. But she would be. They had paid their fees in full – their donation, Catherine called it cheerfully – and now there was only the final adoption approval left to process, and the visa application, and then they'd be able to take their daughter home. The last appointment with Catherine was set for the following morning.

He called up a map on his watch and spoke the address of the Yeandle Hotel. A blue line marked their route to Marylebone, the better part of an hour's walk away. Catherine had offered to order them a taxi, but Dom refused. Seeing Maya had buoyed him. He wanted to walk through the city. They could cut through Kensington Gardens maybe, and see if the playground that he used to visit with Tim had survived the years. Perhaps he would recognise the footpaths where they'd ridden bikes with their parents after catching the train from their home in Watford on Sunday afternoons.

He picked up their backpacks from the pavement and crossed the road, taking note of the map and then turning northeast beneath the pinking sky. The air was warm and felt cleaner than he remembered, and his steps had a lightness that he was so unused to feeling. Whatever London threw at him, he would handle it. They'd made the right decision to come. This trip was not about replacing old memories – that could never happen – but about building on them and balancing the bad ones out. That was Tess's phrase, something she'd said when Dom needed convincing. As usual, she'd picked the perfect words for feelings he wasn't aware he had. Tess was third-generation Cambodian, the great-grandchild of refugees with the money and connections to flee Phnom Penh before the Khmer Rouge seized power in 1975. Roughly a third of Cambodia's population died under the Khmer Rouge; the same proportion of UK citizens as had perished under FEB and in horrifyingly similar circumstances, while the world stood by. Tess never claimed that her family's experiences gave her authority on Dom's feelings, but she understood where he came from. Not all of it, perhaps, but more than most. Enough. She saw how his grief went beyond his parents, although that alone was crippling. He'd lost his childhood, his home, his culture, his history. It left him drifting, untethered in ways he couldn't verbalise, and she never tried to make him. She didn't ask the wrong questions, crowd him or pity him. Tess let Dom be himself, without condition. They worked well together. Never forgot their luck, even during the treatments and the failures and the misery. Sometimes he felt afraid that he might not deserve her. More than once he'd said that he wouldn't blame Tess for leaving. She had laughed in his face. *Don't be a prick.*

They crossed the road at the lights and followed its curve, and Dom checked the directions on his watch. Excitement twitched, and he looked up, trying to make out the gates of Kensington Gardens ahead. He quickened but then paused, aware that Tess had dropped from his side. Turning back, he saw her staring down a side street.

'Tess?'

'Dom, look.'

She disappeared between the buildings, and he doubled after her. She came into view again, pulling her screen from her back pocket as she walked, unrolling it, powering it up and swiping quickly. She stopped on the corner and passed it to him. He looked down at Maya's adoption record and then at the building, its large archway doors painted in vibrant red. The realisation of where they were doused his excitement. He'd been so eager to uncover something positive in his own memories of London that he'd not made the connection about where they'd pass by.

Tess crossed the road slowly but directly, stopping in front of the small, innocuous-looking metal hatch that was embedded in the wall of Kensington Fire Station.

'This was where she was found,' she whispered to Dom.

He tucked his trembling hands into his pockets. April 3rd. That was the day that Maya's birth mother – or someone who knew her – had opened the hatch and placed his child inside. Post-FEB Britain was a fraudster's dream. The regime had made no effort to establish what was owned or earned before the Zero Virus, and anyone could be who they wanted to be. Frequently, they chose to be someone they were not. In the early days of the new government, a decision was made that in order to avoid anything similar happening in the future, a drop of blood would be taken from each newborn and a Lifetime File created in their name. It would record every detail about them for the rest of their lives, from medical information to education records to bank balances, and a blood sample would be all the confirmation of identity ever needed again.

Yet even the most well-meaning solutions have unintended consequences. With state-funded healthcare long dead, women without insurance or with reasons to wish themselves anonymous – the poorest, least supported and most afraid – would give birth with the doulas in black-market clinics, and hundreds of thousands of babies remained off-file. No papers, people said. In an effort to discourage mothers from risky secret births and unrecorded children, regulations were passed about what these babies could and couldn't go on to do. Only blood-registered children were eligible for vaccinations, for rations, for school. Again, the impact was not as planned. Rather than increasing registration rates, the government found themselves with a flood of abandoned babies as mothers unable to pay for hospital births instead left their wailing infants on the steps of council offices, or with wardens or in train station toilets, knowing that the state would register them and they'd get the life they deserved. Orphanages multiplied, and motions to revoke the flawed laws were put forward, but the government was drowning in a sea of hastily made legislation in need of change. After a particularly cold winter and a wave of little lifeless blue bodies, the Boxes were introduced. Positioned in places where there would always be someone close by, mothers could leave their off-file children somewhere that guaranteed their safety, somewhere warm and away from the rats and the dogs.

Tess passed Dom her screen, took hold of the Box's handle and yanked, and it shuddered before relenting, opening with the same clang that Dom remembered from the filing cabinets in his mother's old office in the university's History Department. Inside, it was empty except for a grey woollen blanket, neatly folded, and a hand-written note that read: *You're welcome to come in and talk this through. We won't ask your name.* Dom gripped

Tess's screen more tightly. They had always known where Maya came from and planned to visit, but being here still felt like a shock. Tess reached in and stroked the blanket with her fingertip, as though it might crumble away at her touch.

'Can I help you?'

Tess's hand leapt back. There was a door beside the main archway that Dom hadn't noticed before, and a woman was standing there. She was wearing a red uniform with the gold Fire Service emblem on the pocket and eyeing them suspiciously.

'I'm sorry,' said Tess, closing the hatch. 'We just wanted to see.'

The woman's stare skipped to the backpacks. 'It's not a tourist attraction.'

'It's not like that,' said Dom. He woke the screen from where it had darkened. 'We don't want to pry. We're adopting a baby who was abandoned here a few months ago. See?'

He held Tess's screen so that the woman could check Maya's record. She hesitated, frowning, but then unfolded her arms and stepped forward to look at it.

'We usually ask for appointments,' she said. Dom glanced at her name badge. Officer M. Parks.

'We didn't know we'd be passing.'

Parks glanced back to the door and then seemed to soften. She gave a small, understanding nod. 'I've got some time. Why don't you come in?'

She led them into the station, a cool, high-ceilinged and hangar-like space where their footsteps echoed on the concrete. They slipped through the gap in front of the waiting fire engines, heading towards the far corner, where Dom could see that turquoise material had been slung like a sail. It screened the space partially, but as they approached, it revealed an oasis of warmth and colour. His breath caught. The snug beyond the hatch was another world entirely. In the centre was a Moses basket with a frill around its canopy and a stuffed-toy rabbit and dinosaur arranged at the foot. There were shelves painted white, containing a row of clean, empty bottles and cartons of formula milk, dummies, new in their brightly coloured packaging, a stack of knitted rainbow blankets, baby-grows and fleecy booties, and more soft toys. Where the rest of the station had bare brick walls, here they were painted bright buttercup, and someone had drawn flowers growing up from the skirting. There was an armchair. Cushions. It was nothing like the cold, hard hatch.

'You've made so much effort,' said Tess. He could hear the wonder in her voice and felt it too. Maya's records had her listed as *Abandoned,* a word so brutal, and yet there was something hopeful here that he hadn't foreseen.

Parks smiled. She ran a hand over the pile of blankets, taking the top one and shaking it out. 'No baby gets put in our Box because it's not wanted,' she said. 'It's the opposite. They're brought here because somebody loved them enough to do it. I know they're only young and won't remember, but we want them to feel that they're loved here too.'

'It's beautiful,' said Tess.

Parks refolded the blanket and tucked it back. 'I'm sorry if I sounded rude outside,' she said. 'You wouldn't believe how many people we get nosing around. Misery sightseers,' my husband calls them. Folks who go on holiday to rubberneck at broken Britain, to pretend they're intrepid and feel better about their lot.'

She opened a drawer in the desk beside them and pulled out a data card. She slipped it from its wallet and pressed it into the side of an idle screen.

'I make a note of every child that comes through here,' she said. 'Not just date and time and weight and all the official things you already know, but what they were wearing or if anything made them smile, whether they were sleeping when we found them, if there were any toys or letters left with them. Things like that. Would you like to see what I wrote about your girl? What was her date?'

'April 3rd,' said Tess. Her smile glowed. The report on Maya's discovery had told them the facts but was cool and impersonal, like she wasn't a real person, and Dom was suddenly desperate to learn everything about her, every detail he'd not known was missing before. Had she been crying when her birth mother left her? Was Parks the one to calm her down?

Parks pulled up a folder and scrolled through the list of documents within it. 'The 3rd of April?' she asked. 'Are you sure?'

Tess nodded. 'Positive.'

'And she came from the Kensington?'

Dom felt his gut tighten. He put Tess's screen on the desk so that Parks could see. Parks flicked down Maya's record, confirming the details with a nod and returning to her own files.

'I don't have any babies here for that date,' she said.

Tess shot an anxious look at Dom. 'Could you have missed her?'

'I can't see how. I thought perhaps the date was mistyped, but there's nothing registered at all for that week.'

'Perhaps she came when you weren't on shift?'

Parks shook her head. 'I live above the station. If I'm out and a baby arrives, they call me back.' She shifted, looking more awkward, then tapped her knuckles on the desk, as though considering if there was something more she should say.

'What is it?' asked Dom.

She pointed at Tess's screen, to the bottom of Maya's record and the signature of the person who'd documented her abandonment and passed her on to the authorities. 'See this,' she said. 'This name should be mine. It's always mine at the Kensington.'

Dom followed the line of Parks's finger, for the first time looking properly at the scribble he'd skimmed over on many occasions in the last few months. The scrawl was thin, looping and completely illegible. 'Who does it belong to?' he asked.

'I've no clue,' replied Parks. 'I don't recognise it as anyone who works here. I'm sorry.'

'So where did Maya come from?' asked Tess. She was looking at Dom, and he could hear a note of panic in her voice.

Parks could clearly hear it too, and she reached out and squeezed Tess's hand. 'I wouldn't worry,' she said. 'I'm sure there's a simple answer. Perhaps someone wrote the

– 63 –

wrong Box registration number. Why don't you ask your agency?'

'But it doesn't make sense,' said Dom, doubt creeping over him. 'We've been told from the start that she was found here. The address was always written as Kensington Fire Station. We've not seen any number. Isn't there any other way you can check for us?'

Parks smiled, but she shook her head gently. 'I'm terribly sorry, and I hope you get it sorted, but there's no doubt in my mind. She didn't come from here.'

7

It was Springer – of course – who bailed Thea out. He'd been called to the police station without anyone asking her permission. She'd have rather spent the night in the cell. Speeding home through the dark London streets, past the parades of shuttered-down bookmakers, food banks and pawn stores, she stared through the window of Springer's car and leaned away from him. The occasional off-licence glowed beacon-like between vacant shopfronts, bright lights illuminating dirty windows and lonely vendors in the gloom. Through the side of her eye, Thea watched Springer closely. He'd not said a word since signing her release form, and his hood was up so she couldn't read his features, but at least he wasn't giving her the lecture she'd expected. Perhaps he thought his disappointment was a punishment in itself. She snorted a half-laugh. As the car whipped beneath the street lamps, she saw the flash of his mother's signet ring from where it was jammed above the knuckle on his index finger. He tapped it against the buffed leather steering wheel, and the sight of it pressed at a bruise inside her. The thin band of gold sat so out of place on his rough, meaty hand.

Mullion Drive and the burned-out garages that marked the boundary of the Gritstone Estate appeared ahead. Springer yanked down his hood and rasped a palm over his buzz-cut scalp. He wound down the window and increased his speed up the ramp – as he always did on approaching. Thea's head lurched with the speed, and at the view of the thrumming night market. Barely anyone who lived in the Gritstone had what the government described as reputable income, nor the education and contacts required to compete for the coveted few positions that would provide it. They were experts at survival, however: organised, canny and industrious, and the Gritstone's self-contained economy thrived. Night came, when the police were afraid enough or paid enough to turn away, and in the concrete square that sheltered between the four enormous towers – Roundhouse, Boscastle, Shackleton and Lipson – credits zipped swiftly and invisibly between residents seeking everything from bread and milk, clothes and nappies, to stolen tech and sex and highs. Springer's car cut through the crowds, and faces turned towards his thumping music. Avoiding their eyes, Thea stared at his signet ring, so small and swamped by this big, brash Josh Springer, and she felt the exhaustion bedding in. She'd not seen it coming, what happened at the police station. It hadn't been a breakdown – not like the officer told Springer. Thea wasn't broken. She was furious.

Springer jammed the breaks outside the entrance to the Roundhouse, and the car skidded to a halt. He killed the engine and exited the car, swaggering around the bonnet towards Thea. Her heart sank. He'd waited until they got here, where everyone would see them. He was making the square his theatre, as it had been for FEB. In those days, the gallows were the focus, set on the steps at the far end and casting their long, lean shadows like sundials. Thea's parents hadn't been the only ones to die here – far from it – and yet the only remaining evidence was a small, pink plaque with a number, flush with the concrete slabs and trampled underfoot. She stared towards the steps without seeing, bracing herself for what she knew was coming next.

'Is that it, Thea?' asked Springer, opening the car door for her. He slapped hands with a passer by, flicking the man a greeting. In the distance, a police siren sounded, its short, sharp whoops firing then giving way to a drawn, sprawling wail that echoed between the towers and disappeared inside the night.

Thea held back a sigh. The moonlight was cool and grey, and she could feel the Gritstone eyeing her. There was a trap of a question, if ever she'd heard one. She rubbed her face into her hand. 'I'm tired, Springer.'

'Wouldn't have thought a thank you was unreasonable. You know they wanted to charge you with assaulting an officer?'

'Thanks, Springer.'

'Didn't need to bite him, did you?'

'He wasn't listening.'

'You never listen to me. What do you think would have happened if I hadn't come and got you?'

She climbed out of the car, avoiding his glare. He had propped himself against the wheel-arch, one hand absently stroking the iridescent metal and the other on his hip. Even before Laurel, Thea despised this version of

Springer; the one that flaunted his power as though it were jewellery, who wore jeans that cost a month of her wages, who hung around the square every evening, showing off his car and his watch and whatever new tech he'd wangled that week. She despised the residents who feigned interest and bolstered him. That stupid car. She spread her fingers and pressed her hand flat to the window as she slammed the door, leaving a print on purpose. It was some classic sports thing from before FEB – god only knew where he'd found it and what it had cost him – with hard lines, blacked windows and the most oversized sparkling silver wheels. Who drove themselves anywhere, anyway, these days? Only those who wanted to be noticed – who thought they were special – or who clung too hard to the past.

Thea would never have guessed that Springer would turn out this way. The boy she'd known wasn't interested in cars, clothes or what people thought of him. In that first frigid winter of FEB, they had sat together in this square for Re-education, shoulder butted against shoulder in a marquee so cold that ice stiffened the canvas, and it was Thea who had drunk every last word so thirstily, and Springer who'd moved his lips in time but not made a sound. *Collective progress supersedes the individual. Loyalty to the liberation is the only valid loyalty. The blood of the nation is what unites us. Love for your country is more vital than for family. Security can only be achieved through truth and sacrifice. Free and Equal is our one noble aim.* After the lessons, Springer teased her for believing. Couldn't she hear it was nonsense? Didn't she have a mind of her own? It was true that Thea only understood scraps of what she chanted, but the feeling the words left was perfectly clear. Terror. She couldn't shake it. At night, when she fell asleep on the worn out sofa, FEB's refrains repeated, like her father's snores. His skin smelled of mud from his work on the allotments. Her mother was warm and soft, though getting thinner. *Tell us what they do*, FEB whispered. *Tell us what they do if you want to survive.*

A fresh pang of loss struck for her parents – and for Laurel. If only Springer had thought before signing her away. She went to move past him, but he grabbed her arm.

'Hey,' he said. 'What's the hurry? Have you got somewhere else to be? That mystery man of yours, is it? I didn't see him come to the rescue tonight. Does he even know he's got a kid?'

Thea glared at Springer's hand around her wrist, and at the ridge of white scar on her skin that showed between his fingers. At the allotments all those years ago, the day when she'd tried to eat the beetle, he'd defended her for no other reason than because he was her friend, stepping in and stopped the beating, despite the risk. It wasn't like getting her the job at the Oakwood and never letting her forget it. Not like bailing her out and then fishing for gratitude where the whole world could see. Yes, she hated this version of Springer, all for favour and show. She snatched her arm back and shoved by him, ramming open the door at the base of the Roundhouse Tower and pounding into the stairwell.

Rubbish sacks were piled in the turnarounds, and the stink of them filled her nostrils. The acidic residue of synth smoke made her eyes sting. She gagged and pushed through the narrow gap left by two women whose conversation stopped abruptly, and she quickened her stride until she was jumping the steep concrete stairs two at a time. The gash across her belly burned.

She had met Henrik a year ago at the Oakwood Hotel, on an unforgivingly hot summer's day. His name, his looks and the lilt of his voice had been Scandinavian, probably, though she didn't know enough about these things to say for sure. There were only three types of foreigners in London: aid workers, businessmen looking to cash in on the 'Great Recovery' and a dribble of voyeuristic tourists, come to bow their heads at the monuments before ogling what was left. Henrik didn't tell Thea which he was, but she saw his rucksack with the UN EnviroAid logo hooked over the back of his chair at breakfast. That day, she'd felt terrible. Jemima had the flu and was absent from the Archive, and without someone there to rein in Thea, the hours had spiralled. She'd not been sleeping. She'd been so lonely. The first time his fingertips grazed her thigh, as she leaned across the table to pour his coffee, she'd thought it was an accident. He had smiled gleaming white teeth and watery blue eyes at her, and asked about where was best to keep cool in the city. As he chatted, he pretended to wipe his hands on his napkin, and Thea saw him slip a gold band from his finger and hide it in his pocket. When she returned for the refill, she'd felt him again, featherlight, creeping beneath the hem of her skirt and making her shiver. Plenty of other men had touched her at work before, some as handsome as Henrik, but her reaction had only ever been disgust. Nothing was different today, except Thea. She needed something selfish to lift her from her misery. He left his room number on a scrap of paper beneath his plate. She finished her shift with her body on automatic and her mind a tornado, then stripped away her uniform and stuffed it in the laundry, stole a yellow satin dress from dry cleaning and went to his room. She knocked with the conviction that she was meant to be there, and she didn't care what happened next.

When Thea discovered she was pregnant, there was no doubt she'd keep the child. She had tried halfheartedly to track him down, searching online for *Henrik* and *EnviroAid*, knowing nothing of any use would come back. She wasn't even sure she had his real name. She checked with Tamara on the Oakwood's reception desk, but the rooms were block-booked by a UN account. It wasn't as though she thought he'd come back and marry her, but she knew she'd need the credits for the baby. She had not known how much.

She reached the eighth floor and shouldered into the corridor, Springer at her heels. The fire door clanked shut, and the stairwell's stink and echo left, dropping them into a new version of quietness where conversations and televisions hummed behind closed doors. Thea fumbled in her pocket for her key, desperate to be alone with her thoughts of Laurel and away from Springer. She wanted to clamber beneath her covers and bury her head into her pillow, and scream until there was no sound left inside her. Then she could think of what to do next. At her door, she rammed the key into the lock, but Springer grabbed the handle, holding it shut. He stared at her, ruddy-cheeked and sweating.

'What's your problem, Thea?'

Her heart struck against her ribcage. She had asked him the same question – begged him for answers – in the same Roundhouse corridor, all those years before. In the first nights after the fever took his baby sister and then his mother, Thea and Springer had slept knotted together. He'd cried in a way that left her terrified and breathless, but she kept hold of him like he'd done for her when she was first alone, six months before. Then FEB came to the eighth floor and found him. After that, he stopped crying. He stopped visiting her flat. She watched him spend more and more time with the older Gritstone boys, the ones with *epa* tattoos, roaming eyes and extra rations. Without Springer as her friend, Thea felt even smaller. On the days when they were sent to the Hyde Park allotments, it was soon Springer who held the rifle while the others did the work. He wouldn't meet her eye.

'What's your problem? Why are you angry at me?' She had shouted at him one evening, and blocked his door like he was blocking hers now. Springer had shoved her off and wiped himself down, staggering back as if she was contaminated, and she'd realised then that he wasn't angry. He was petrified, like she was. FEB wanted boys who followed rules and didn't show emotion. Thea could uncover him in a moment, if she wanted. Reveal that he'd had questions and mocked her for believing. Told her not to listen. She could have exposed him as the kind, tolerant and thoughtful boy he really was.

She shook herself free of the memory and grabbed Springer's hand, wrenching it back from her doorframe and holding it up before his face so he could see the glinting ring where it squeezed against his knuckle. No chance of him being mistaken for kind and thoughtful now. She leaned forward. 'Your mother would be ashamed of you.'

Hurt flashed in Springer's eyes, replaced almost instantly with anger. He pulled away, the colour in his cheeks darkening further. 'I only wanted to know what happened.'

He looked at her, and she glared back, disbelieving. What did he want her to say? The police had given him her statement. He'd read it. He'd caused all this. He'd stolen Laurel. What right did he have to be her confidant as well as her keeper?

'You know everything, Springer,' she said, trying to stay calm. 'I went to visit Laurel, but she wasn't there.'

'That's it? She wasn't there?'

'No. Nothing was there. Not a baby, not a cot, not a nappy, not a thing.' She could feel her frustration growing, feel her heart quickening inside her chest. 'I went to Little Doves when I said I would. I had an appointment. They were expecting me. I've saved every credit I have and done everything they've ordered me to do, and they couldn't even manage to tell me they were moving, and I've no clue where they've gone or where to look. They've disappeared, Springer. Even the sign on the door. Completely gone.'

The words jammed in her throat. Everything about today made her feel dizzy. Laurel had to be somewhere. Was she safe? She squeezed her eyes shut. When she opened them, Springer had retreated to the opposite wall of the corridor. He wasn't speaking. What on earth was he doing, blinking repeatedly? She stared back, and it hit her – a look she recognised from their shared childhood. She felt a rush of it too, reflected back and magnified, being drawn into focus between them. Fear.

'What is it, Springer?' she asked. 'Tell me.'

He shook his head.

'You know what happened.'

'No. I don't. Not really.'

'You do.'

He glanced along the empty corridor. 'I might have heard something, that's all. I was speaking to Goldman.'

Thea's pulse spiked. Sean Goldman. Warden at the Boscastle. 'And?'

'We weren't talking about you,' said Springer. 'Just talking, you know? It was a while ago. Back end of last year. Goldman said he was getting trouble from a family in his tower. They'd given their baby to one of the homes, like yours, but when they'd gone to get him, he wasn't there. They were told he'd died, but the mother didn't believe them. Kept going back, over and over. Raised bloody hell for Goldman. Then one day, the home was just gone. The whole place, just like you said. Not a scrap of it left. I don't know if they found out what happened to the kid.'

Thea stared at Springer, horrified. Any questions in her mind about whether her worry was justified had been slapped down. Trampled. This *was* a crime. This was utterly deliberate. She knew it. Nobody had forgotten to tell her anything. Panic flooded through her, scalding hot. She stepped at Springer, jabbed her finger into the soft hollow of his neck. 'You knew. You knew it wasn't safe, and you signed her away.'

Springer's lips puckered. 'That's not true.'

'You didn't care what happened to her.'

'It's not like that, Thea.'

'You didn't tell me.'

'I didn't know there was anything to tell.'

Thea snarled and shoved him in the chest, and he thumped into the wall. At the end of the corridor, a door opened and Mrs Evans peered out; the five-foot-nothing, gossip-fuelled widow with the slobbering pit bull that crapped on the stairs. Her adult son appeared at her shoulder, staring without shame.

Springer straightened his sweatshirt and dropped his voice. 'Don't show me up, Thea.'

'Give me her name, Springer. The mother. Who is she?'

He shook his head again. 'I don't know it.'

'Find out.'

8

Dom and Tess waited in the sweltering office while Catherine ducked out to fetch the drinks. The windows were shut, magnifying the mid-morning sunshine so it stoked Dom's unease into something near unbearable, and he shifted and unglued his shirt from his back. Maya was sleeping on Tess's chest, her sweet face tilted upwards. He could hear breath sighing through her plump, open lips. Behind his eyes, the ache was growing. How peaceful Maya looked, blissfully oblivious to the heat and his tension, and how much he wanted to call her his daughter. He wanted to be the one to protect her. He wished he could shake the Box from his mind.

'Catherine will be back in a minute,' Tess said quietly. She rested her cheek on Maya's head.

Dom flicked her a nod. He knew what she meant.

The meeting was scheduled to be a brief one. Their donation – the standard request of 18,400 credits – had already cleared. It was an amount that had taken them two years to save. Catherine only needed to witness their electronic signatures on the Interim Custody Agreement before it could be sent to the Ministry of Children. She'd promised to have a word with her contact to get things processed quickly, and if they were lucky, Dom and Tess would be able take custody of Maya the following day. They'd not be allowed to leave the country until the final approval and visa applications came through but – until last night – this had been the milestone they were focused on. Final approval had never been refused to anyone whose ICA had passed. *Tomorrow.* In Dom's mind, the ticking clock was deafening. After five years of trying and failing for a baby – nineteen years of desire to fix his shattered family – tomorrow suddenly felt like too soon. He wrung his hands together to fight their shaking. He'd taken three pills already today. Catherine had said that when they'd finished the paperwork, Dom and Tess were welcome to spend the rest of the morning with Maya in the nursery. They should have been ecstatic. Instead, he felt exhausted, scared and confused.

If Catherine realised, she didn't let on. She breezed into the office with two mugs of steaming black coffee and set them on the desk by Tess and Dom, before turning to the window and raising up the sash. Fresh air drifted into the stuffy room, carrying with it the sound of cars hissing along Beauden Crescent and snippets of conversation from passing pedestrians. Dom breathed in, struggling to draw his thoughts into line. Catherine organised herself behind the desk and sipped from her water bottle. She was impeccably turned out, in her late fifties, Dom guessed, her white dress crisply pressed and perfectly professional, and not a strand of her thick, silver hair out of place. Each of her wrists was decorated in hot-pink bracelets, and two expensive-looking rings fitted together on her hand like wedding bands, one plain and one set with diamonds the size and shape of apple pips, but they were on her middle finger. As she moved, the stones glinted in the sun. She'd told Dom and Tess that her mother was British and her father was American. They'd lived in the English Cotswolds until her mother died and her father moved back to Colorado. She'd been visiting him when the election took place, and the guilt she felt for not trying to return through the FEB years – for the friends she'd lost and their children – had driven her back to open BlueSkies.

She unrolled her screen, powered it up and pointed a remote to the projector above them. The orphanage's blue-and-white cloud logo appeared on the wall. She noticed Dom staring at her and smiled, and he mustered what he hoped was an approximate reflection, then glanced at his watch and swiped *refresh*.

'Do you want me to run a check on Hilton-Webb?' Tim had asked, last night.

He and Katrina had called to hear about Maya, and Tess told them what happened at the fire station. Dom's response had been visceral, a *no* that came hard, sharp and without consideration. It was laced with disgust. There was nothing he and Tess wanted less than to find a rockslide on the road to Maya, and the way that Tim had used Catherine's surname already made her sound guilty. Besides, they'd done their homework. BlueSkies was five-star rated by the US Adoption Association. Catherine had spoken on the cultural challenges of international adoption at numerous major conferences and advised governments across the world on best practices. Tess and Dom had scoured adoption forums for comments from parents and never once saw BlueSkies mentioned with anything but glowing praise.

Tim shrugged. 'You never know, Dom. Sometimes our system throws up things that never found their way into the public domain.'

Dom bit his lip. He hated asking Tim for favours, especially anything that might cause him trouble. Running unauthorised background checks on private citizens was hardly model behaviour for someone on the fast-track to FBI sector head. Then he'd remembered the way that Officer Parks had shut the file down so abruptly. Reluctantly, Dom relented and told Tim OK.

Now, he tapped his watch again, willing his brother's name to appear on the screen. Tim had said he'd get back to them before the meeting began, and the longer he didn't reply, the more Dom's mind ran with grim possibilities. They had played and played in a loop, all night.

'Right.' Catherine's voice burst merrily into the quiet. On Tess's chest, Maya wriggled and snuffled before resettling. 'Are we ready? The law says we need to verbally confirm Maya's details and yours, and then we can pull up the ICA and get it signed.'

She directed Dom's view to the projection where her folders were neatly ordered and labelled in a line on her desktop. *Unallocated Children. Applications. BlueSkies Accounts.* She selected the one she'd titled *Currently Processing* and then a subfolder with Dom and Tess's names. She opened Maya's adoption report. Through the side of his eye, Dom saw that Tess had stopped watching. She'd shifted Maya upwards so their faces were touching and closed her eyes. Catherine scrolled through the form they'd already completed, and Dom murmured agreements as she asked him to confirm their names, dates of birth, occupations and address. She skimmed Maya's details, and his stare settled on the illegible black scribble at the bottom of the page – the signature that Fire Officer M. Parks had sworn did not belong to her. Sweat was pooling above Dom's lip, and he smeared it off, his stomach feeling leaden. Parks was right. A simple answer was probably the most likely one: the Box number mistyped at some early point before they started writing the location longhand, or some other clerical error. Catherine took a drink from her water. They could easily ask her. Why hadn't they asked her? What was the feeling he couldn't shake?

Dom dried his lip again, and his watch vibrated against his wrist. *Incoming Call.* He threw Tess a look, and she returned it instantly, knowing what he meant. Heart thudding, he rushed into the corridor, out of Catherine's earshot, leaving his wife to clutch Maya harder. In his haste, the door slammed, and the child's cry broke out.

'Tim?'

'Hey,' Tim replied. The picture on the watch was shadowy, but his brother's voice came clear down the line. 'I'm sorry I took so long. I was waiting for someone to get back to me. Listen, you were right. Catherine came up clean. BlueSkies too. There wasn't a mention. Records on Brits get pretty patchy when you start going back a few years and they don't always join up like they should, so I couldn't check her links, family or associates, but she looks OK to me.'

Dom let out a breath. Relief washed over him. 'Thanks,' he said.

'I wouldn't thank me yet,' said Tim. 'It's not all good news. I widened the search. Looked at international adoptions, UK adoptions . . . That sort of thing. I might have found something. I don't know. A British academic wrote a report a year or so ago. It claimed the UK adoption scene was full of shysters. He didn't mention any agencies by name but said that clients were being misled, especially international ones, which is why it ended up on our records. The Trafficking Team picked it up briefly, but they didn't pursue anything. I spoke to a friend in the department who said the guy turned out to be a crackpot, some ageing professor that churned out reports by the dozen and had aimed his ire at half the British establishment. The same month he wrote about the adoptions, he'd been gunning for the prime minister, calling out factory-grown meat and promoting conspiracy theories about hidden FEB-era gold.'

Dom pressed his knuckles into his temples. The ache in his head had grown to a stab. 'So why are you telling me?'

'I read his paper, Dom,' said Tim. 'It sounds far-fetched, but there was a line about falsified Box records that rang an alarm. I couldn't ignore it. You want me to send it to you?'

Dom paused. Did he? 'Catherine said we could take Maya to the hotel tomorrow. Tomorrow, Tim. That soon.'

Tim pinched the bridge of his nose, glancing off screen and choosing his words. 'You do what you've got to do,' he said. The wait thickened. 'Dom?'

'Mmm?'

'The professor works at UCL.'

The punch to Dom's chest snatched the air from his

lungs. Memories of he and Tim cowering in his mother's office bolted through his consciousness; how he'd focused on the titles of the books on her shelves to distract himself from the stampede of boots along the corridor. *Britain After the Romans. The Anglo-Saxon Chronicles. The Definitive Guide to the Sutton Hoo Artifacts.* He still remembered the order they came in, and the replica Saxon helmet that hung from the shelf-end like an eyeless, severed head. He remembered the yells too. *Spoonies! Fucking Spoonies! Find them!* Tim crying. The all-obliterating fear. He rested his forehead against the wall. Maya's scream had reached fever-pitch.

'You OK?' asked Tim.

Dom's thoughts spun. 'What's his name? The professor.'

'Levi Garber. I'll send you the link. Let you read for yourself.'

'Thanks.'

Tim cut the call, his face disappearing behind the photograph of Maya on Dom's home-screen. Dom turned and looked through the glass panel into Catherine's office, breathing slowly and deliberately to calm himself down. Catherine looked concerned, and Tess's smile was broad but empty as she reassured her. Tess was bouncing the shrieking baby on her shoulder. *Do what you've got to do.* Anxiety chipped through him. What he had to do sat in direct opposition to everything he wanted to do, everything he wanted for himself and that he'd promised to his wife. The ICA was visible on the wall, glowing brightly and waiting. He walked back to the office, cursing internally. They couldn't sign it. Not yet. Tess read his thoughts and absorbed them in silence. She looked terrified.

Catherine noticed the look as they exchanged it. 'Is everything OK?' she asked.

Dom shook his head. 'I'm sorry, Catherine. There's been a family emergency. We'll have to reschedule.'

He picked up his jacket and satchel from the floor, gripping the chair so his hands didn't shake. Tess watched him intently, and he stepped towards her – right up to her body. Maya was between them, and he kissed the baby's head. It was hot and damp as she bawled, and she smelled like freshly washed cotton. He whispered to both his girls as he scooped Maya away and handed her to Catherine.

'I love you. I'm sorry. I promise we'll come back.'

9

Thea climbed up the Boscastle's steep stairwell, holding her jacket tight around her body and with her stare fixed on her feet. It was as reeking as the Roundhouse's stairwell, as narrow and dimly lit, and her footsteps echoed. She gripped the cold, greasy banister, groping upwards through the sections where the bulbs had burned out and plunged her into almost complete black. Through the dark, her senses strained. An infant's cry came muffled through the wall, and she bit at an ulcer inside her mouth and quickened her step, counting away the turns back on herself and the fire doors that indicated each new floor. Springer had coaxed the address from Goldman, though neither man was happy about it, and the delivery came with threats. *Don't make trouble where there isn't any, Thea.* She'd almost laughed in Springer's face. She reached the ninth floor and broke into the corridor, squinting in its fluorescent brightness and splashing through a puddle of something rancid. She'd pluck every splinter of trouble from these towers, sweep up every shaving, hunt down each last shard. She'd collect it together and make the most enormous trouble, if it helped to find Laurel. She'd douse it with petrol and set it alight. The drones would see her trouble from space.

At Flat 9-44, she stopped and pushed her shoulders back. Drew herself taller. Her knuckles came down hard on the door, and a dog responded with a volley of barks from somewhere along the corridor, but the flat in front of Thea stayed quiet and still. She rapped again, and the dog's yawp escalated. The sound of an internal door being opened followed, and her blood thumped as she heard footsteps and then the chain scraped back. A brown-skinned man in boxer shorts opened the door, his ribs visible down his bone-thin, bare chest. He dragged a hand though his wiry black hair, standing it upright. His expression was thick with confusion and sleep.

Thea cleared her throat. 'Abbas Bakir?'

He looked at her, wary. 'Who are you?'

'Theodora Baxter. I live in the Roundhouse.'

'What time is it?'

'I don't know. Midnight, maybe. My warden gave me your address. Josh Springer.'

'Did he tell you to wake me up in the middle of the night?'

'It's about your boy.'

Bakir sharpened suddenly, vigilance replacing the dullness of sleep. She saw his shoulders tense and he stole a look along the empty corridor. 'My son lives with his aunt in Essex. Whatever kid you're ratting out, it isn't him.'

A woman in a nightdress appeared behind him, padding barefoot from a darkened room and flicking on the hallway light. She tugged a scarf over her head, pinching it beneath her chin with both hands and twisting. She looked scared. 'Who is it, Abbas?'

'Rania?' Thea inched forward, feeling a note of urgency rise. 'I need talk to you about your son.'

Bakir's voice lowered, and he lifted his thin arm and spread his hand like a warning, directing it first at Thea and then towards his wife. 'I told you. Hamid's not here.'

Thea stared at him. 'Not Hamid. Adil.'

Shock and fear rippled in unison across Bakir's face. His wife bolted to the door, and the scarf lifted and slid from her hair, dropping to the floor behind her. She grabbed Thea's wrist. Nails like talons, long, sharp and painted fresh-blood red, spiked from her fingertips and into Thea's skin. 'What do you know about Adil?'

Bakir put his hands on his wife's shoulders, firmly but not roughly, steering her inside. 'Go back to bed, Rania.'

'Abbas, no. She might know where he is.'

'He's dead, Rania.'

She shrugged him off. 'We don't know what happened.'

Her voice was growing louder. Along the corridor, a door opened, and a woman in a dressing gown leered at them. The dog in the flat beside them still bayed. A shout was followed by a crack and then a whimper. The animal fell quiet, but another door along the hallway had already opened, and the first woman was talking with her neighbour, their hostility plain. Bakir pressed his palms to his cheeks, squeezing his eyes shut momentarily as if to compose himself, then half raising a hand to the woman in apology. She folded her arms and scowled back, unmoved. Rania's eyes fired from her husband to Thea.

'You need to leave,' Bakir said to Thea. She heard his

voice shake, and he went to close the door, but she slid her foot forward, blocking him.

'Wait,' she said, speaking hurriedly. 'Hear me out. I was told that Adil went to a children's home. They said that he'd died, but you didn't believe them, did you? And then they were gone. My daughter – Laurel – she went to Little Doves. I was ill at the birth. They'd agreed I wouldn't be allowed to keep her before I woke up. I was told that I'd get her back when I was better, but now she's gone, too. The entire home has disappeared.'

Rania's taloned hand leapt to her mouth. 'Abbas, did you hear that?'

Bakir shook his head, and a look passed between them. His voice strained. 'We can't, Rania.'

Thea's stomach lurched. *They knew.* She looked at the woman, heat coursing though her. 'What happened, Rania? Why didn't you believe them?'

'My wife was in shock.'

'Abbas, please,' said Rania.

She gripped his arm, but he winced and recoiled as if she'd burnt him. He muttered something inaudible in her ear, and she gnawed her lip and slunk inside the flat, but her stare stayed fixed on Thea. Bakir turned to Thea, speaking slowly and deliberately.

'Listen to me,' he said. 'You're upsetting my wife. You're disturbing my neighbours. Adil is dead, and there's nothing more to it. We've wept for him. Leave us alone.'

Thea removed her foot from the doorway. 'Please,' she said quietly, looking to Rania. 'I'm begging you. Help me. I only want to find my child.'

The door clicked shut, and she let out a long breath. She

headed back along the corridor, her hand pressed to the wound in her stomach, and the spying neighbours threw her a tut before slinking inside. What now? Questions piled onto her. If Adil was dead, what did it mean for her Laurel? Sickness came in a wave through her body. Her mouth was watering. She shouldered through the fire door and into the darkened stairwell. Abbas and Rania were terrified. She could see it. What wouldn't they tell her? She staggered blindly down the concrete steps, her feet dragging and tripping. Above her, a door slammed. It echoed like a gunshot. She stopped, listening. There were footsteps too, moving faster and harder than hers. Running. Fear jolted into her. Abbas Bakir was chasing her. Closing in. She ran, too, but he grabbed her arm, and she yelped and struck out, falling into the wall as her punch landed. She squared up again, thrashing at the shadow, but there was a cry – a woman – and Thea froze, squinting into the gloom. The scent of perfume hit her, or freshly washed hair. Bright eyes solidified in line with her own. Long, sharp fingernails dug into her arm.

'Rania?'

Rania fumbled in the dark to find Thea's hands. She uncurled Thea's fingers from their fist and stuffed a piece of paper inside. It crackled like flame in the quiet stairwell.

'My husband's trying to protect us,' she said. 'They threatened my family. My boy, Hamid. They held a knife to his throat as he walked home from school. We don't know who they've got in the towers to watch us. They've started rumours. We're ridiculed. Everyone whispers. Don't be angry at Bakir. We just want to live quietly. Try to work. Survive.'

Her chest was heaving, and her eyes sparked, darting in their sockets and searing into Thea's despite the dismal light. Her words were tumbling, desperate and breathy, and Thea could see she was holding back tears.

'Who threatened you?'

'The men from the children's home. They hid Hamid in some Gritstone squat until night had dropped and I was wild with worry, then they dragged him home and left him in the square. He was tied like a hog, stinking of synth smoke, and covered in his own filth. That's why we sent him to live with his aunt. I could cope with the gossip, being called a bitch and whore and whatever else they wanted, but I couldn't cope with them touching Hamid. They broke into our flat, too. Took everything worth a credit. Warned everyone in the Boscastle not to talk to us. Not even the warden will come near us now.'

'Why would they do that?'

Rania leaned in, so close that Thea could smell the mint on her breath. 'I heard Adil cry,' she whispered. 'The day I went to collect him, he was still there. Inside their building. I know he was. I told Goldman I'd heard him. I told the whole of Boscastle. Half of London. The police. Hospitals. I told anyone who I thought had the faintest power or reason to care. I slept on the steps of the home for a week. I screamed at them. Swore. I don't know what they were doing, but I'm not mad like they say. Any mother could pick her child's cry from a hundred others. And why would they bother to threaten a madwoman? They needed me to leave them alone. They don't want people watching. Whatever they said, Adil wasn't dead. When I went back the last time, the home was gone.'

Thea's thoughts raced, bounding into each other, not joining up. 'So you dropped it?'

'What else could I do? You know the way we live around here. I haven't been to school since FEB, and neither has Abbas. We've no credits to pay for help. No smarts against devils like them. I'd nothing else to try, and who'd speak up for us if we asked them? Even those in London with good hearts have their own families to protect. Now, I need to keep Hamid safe. I can't lose him too.'

Thea's mind leapt to Laurel. Rania tapped Thea's hand with the tip of her nail. Thea looked at the paper.

'This is the name of a man who came to our flat. He worked at a university. I don't know which one. Abbas wouldn't let me speak to him, but I heard them talking. They were in the doorway, like you were. He said he'd read my statement to the police. Told Abbas that there had been others like it across the city – not exactly the same but near enough. He wanted to investigate. Asked us to make another statement for him, to see if we'd missed anything, or if the police had. Help him find patterns. He said he was certain it wasn't a coincidence. Abbas said no and sent him away.'

Rania's eyes clamped shut as though she was in pain. She took a deep breath and buried her face in her hands. Her shoulders rose and fell, and when she looked up again her cheeks was slicked with tears. Thea felt the swell in her own throat, too.

'Why are you helping me?' she said.

Rania dabbed away the wet with her palms. 'Adil has gone,' she said, sniffing. 'It's been more than a year.

Whatever those people did, he's not coming back. I know that, but hearing you speak – it makes my old wounds new again. I need to know what happened to him. I want someone to pay for it. I'm sick of being invisible. I can't do nothing. I hope that you're cleverer than I was, or braver or luckier or stronger or *something*. I want you to find a way to not give up.'

Rania stared, black eyes boring into Thea, and Thea couldn't speak – couldn't find the words for anything as overwhelming as her feelings – and so when Rania hugged her, she fell into her arms instead.

10

The ceiling lights spat in the empty tube carriage. Tess's shoulder bumped against Dom's, and he stared at his reflection in the window as it disappeared then leapt back into view. A thread hung from the button of his jacket, and he twisted it around the tip of his shaking finger, pulling and feeling the series of pops as it worked towards release. Even from this distance, he could see the shadows beneath his eyes. He looked as exhausted and unhappy as he felt. Tess was still beautiful, her long blue-black hair obscuring one side of her face as she looked down at her lap. She was leafing through a glossy brochure for BlueSkies Adoptions, scanning page after page of smiling infants, as though it might offer some previously unseen clue. She glanced up, caught Dom's eye and stuffed the brochure into her handbag, giving him a slight smile and a reassuring nudge. They had hardly slept last night, instead poring over every detail of Professor Levi Garber's paper, by turns gutted, terrified and tearful, and then disbelieving that a word of something so extreme could be true.

Whether the report proved to be fact or fiction, it made for a gut-wrenching read. Garber started with a potted history of international adoption, highlighting its dramatic rise at the end of the twentieth century, driven by increasing infertility levels, the gap between rich and poor nations and high-profile celebrity cases that fuelled copy-cat demand. There had been a lull when the Zero Virus impacted the wealth of traditional adopting countries, but now, in the UK at least, numbers were on the up. Cash-strapped, infertile couples had realised they could get a child from Britain cheaper and quicker than virtually anywhere in the world, with the added feel-good factor of a rescue mission. The scale of the boom had caught everyone off guard, especially the regulators, and whilst there were children with a genuine need for parents, demand began outstripping supply. In response, organised criminal gangs were custom-building orphanages, combing the poorest communities in search of perfect, healthy newborns, overwhelming vulnerable birth mothers with lies and false promises in order to get them to hand over their children. Garber called what followed *laundering* – like what happened with money. The crooks bribed low-level government officials into creating paperwork that said the children were abandoned and eligible for adoption. They would be given new blood registrations, and their real identities – if previously recorded – were erased. It wasn't that the children's files were falsified as such, rather that false information was keyed into legitimate government systems, making them legal. It also made the children's pasts untraceable. By the time the crooks were finished, it was impossible to know which children were genuine orphans and which were not.

The carriage lights flickered again, the train rocked,

and Dom pushed down the unease in his gut. The problems with Garber's report were clear. It was unlike any academic paper he'd read before. In place of expert quotes there were anonymous sources; in place of hard data, approximation and speculation. No proof. Dates conflicted, and the handful of police complaints that Garber mentioned from mothers weren't in the public record, Tim said. Garber peppered his narrative with strident personal opinions on the unchecked legacy of FEB that had enabled his theories and dragged the reader on tangential hypotheticals. Combined with what Tim had told Dom and Tess about the aggressive nature and prolificness of Garber's writing, it was hard to take him seriously. Yet, the details were still too hideous to ignore. They couldn't not check.

A recorded voice announced that the train was approaching the station. Tess stood up, rolling her screen and tucking it into her back pocket, giving Dom another encouraging half-smile. He wiped his hands down his thighs and stood too. For all the horror of Garber's report, it had given him a single guilty reason for relief: he'd been able to distract himself from where they were heading today.

'Do you remember how to get there?' asked Tess as they emerged from Warren Street Station and into a crisp and bright August morning. The night's dew was burning off in a haze.

Dom nodded, the nerves sitting heavily. Memories he hadn't known he possessed dug between his temples, and the sunlight felt blinding, making him wince. He had walked this route from the station to the university campus too many times to count. There had been a deli across the street where there was now a pawnshop, and he remembered the sausage rolls he'd eaten there, so hot and greasy that the paper bags turned opaque. He would argue with Tim at the crossing about who pressed the button and inhale the sweet, soapy scent outside the launderette on the corner. Drag his parents into the newsagent and whine for football stickers. High-five Mr Charles, the six-foot, seven-inch Ghanaian security guard who worked the gate. He took Tess's hand and turned along the thoroughfare, following the route his mother had always taken with him, feeling with each step that he had slipped back in time. Had Garber worked here when his mother was alive? Perhaps he'd known her. Perhaps he'd been here that day too. He had to know what happened, at least. The pavement beneath Dom's feet seemed to be shifting; he had the sense of watching himself walking. He could hear that Tess was speaking but not what she said. They turned again, and the entrance was on top of them, the rust-coloured Cruciform building towering over the road, the angles of it crooked to the street as if they'd recognised Dom and were turning away. Bicycles were chained to the railings like they'd been before, and for a second it struck him that they might have been the same ones, left for nineteen years by the people who'd not come back. The sound of his pulse in his ears was deafening. Maybe it hadn't been good that he was distracted. He should have been preparing. He didn't feel ready. There was a shout, and his heart leapt as if it were a gunshot. The colours around him were becoming more lurid, the air thinner, the noises louder and more intense and harsher, until his senses were overwhelmed.

He stuffed his hand into his pocket, grabbing his pills and taking two out. He swallowed them, and Tess linked his arm, her free hand holding tight to his bicep. When she'd called ahead to make an appointment, the woman on the desk said there wasn't a need. Garber didn't teach on Tuesdays (or any day, they gathered) but he was always in his office. Never left it. Just knock, she'd told them. Simply come to the campus and wander inside, find his room and say hello. She made it sound easy. On automatic, his feet led him through the main courtyard. In his mind's eye, he could see the pathway to the History Department where his mother had her upstairs office, to the door where she'd written *Wilcume! – Welcome!* in old English. She'd browned the page with tea and burned the edges with a candle so it looked like it was torn from one of the Anglo-Saxon manuscripts she so loved.

There had been a cafe in the lobby of Humanities. That's where Dom had found her body, and his father's. She had left to grab the boys a cup of hot chocolate each, with marshmallows and whipped cream, before her lecture. Said she'd only be a minute. It was two weeks after the election, and Cat. One and Cat. Two population regulations were coming into effect. FEB had ordered the universities to shut and their resources were reallocated, but many staff and students continued to turn up in protest. There had been rumours of FEB's militia using violence at other dissenting universities, but nothing inside London, and his parents hadn't seemed concerned. They'd received their letters with CATEGORY TWO as the header a few days earlier, and his father binned them. No one reasonable would listen to such nonsense, he said. It was the end of the day, and his mother's last lecture. Dom and Tim would wait with their father until she was finished, and then they'd go home. It was Tim who heard the commotion first, and he looked from her office window to see the black-clad, balaclavaed men with guns. They fanned across the courtyard, spreading like an oil slick towards the building Dom was in. Their father was out of his seat immediately, sprinting to warn their mother, ordering the boys to stay put. For what felt the longest time, Dom obliged. Gunshots reverberated from downstairs, and the corridor ran with boots and screams and cries of 'SPOONIE!' He cowered with Tim beneath the desk, not moving. Then someone kicked open the door and threw in a canister, and the tremor gas forced them choking outside. Thick white mist and the unbearable burning in his eyes left him staggering, half blind and in desperate search of air, dragging his shrieking, vomiting brother beside him. His tongue was so swollen that he couldn't shout for help. On the staircase, he could feel his strength dissipating, his muscles beginning to contract uncontrollably. His legs gave way, and he fell the last few steps. In the lobby at the bottom, the cafe had been ransacked. There must have been twenty bloodied bodies before them, but he picked out his mother and father instantly. They were sprawled behind an upturned table. Their eyes were open, their faces somehow at once slack yet frozen. His muscles spasmed so hard that he couldn't look away from them, couldn't reach to grasp for his brother, as incapacitated as he was and wide-eyed with terror, just a few feet away.

Dom slumped to the bench in the centre of the courtyard, lights strobing through his vision. He was shaking now like he had done that day, wasn't he? So violently from his core that he couldn't make it stop.

'Jesus, Tess. I can't breathe.'

He sunk his head into his hands, his throat constricting. The pressure in his chest was hammer against anvil, each strike radiating outwards so hard and fast that he thought he would explode.

Tess dropped beside him. She wrapped her arms around his body and pressed herself into him. 'You're panicking, Dom,' she said. 'Slow down.'

'Nothing's changed. It's the same. It's exactly the same.'

'Everything's changed,' she said into his neck. 'There's no one here who wants to hurt you. You're safe.'

He heard a noise leave his lips, like a dog that had taken a boot to the gut.

'We don't have to do this,' said Tess. 'We'll go to the hotel and call Garber instead. Have him meet us somewhere else.'

She gripped him harder, and he pressed his eyes shut, ramming his thumbs into his sockets, willing the black to expunge the images that were branded behind his eyes. He did want to leave. He would have run if he thought his legs would carry him. It felt like Tess was holding him together. But where would he run to? The memories would follow. He wouldn't know about Maya. He couldn't leave without knowing. He gasped and peeled his eyes open, forcing himself to focus on the tree across the courtyard. The strong, thick trunk. The bright green leaves. He counted to one hundred. Two hundred. Three.

The hammer-blow of his heart began to wane, fear giving way to a shiver of relief. He counted higher, well past one thousand, then planted his feet, and hauled himself up. He followed the path he remembered around the buildings, leaning on his wife as they passed the Memorial Fountain, and then the East Cloister. At the Faculty of Social Sciences, they signed in at the desk and were given a pass card. They took the lift to the third floor and found Garber's office. S324.

'It's open,' said Tess as they approached along the empty corridor.

She was right. All the other offices appeared closed, the seats outside them vacant, but Garber's door was ajar. She dropped her voice and knocked. Dom's throat was still tight, and he breathed slowly and deliberately, trying to stay calm. The quicker they finished this, the quicker they could leave. There wasn't a reply, but Tess nudged the door, revealing the disorderly room. The sight of it did nothing to soothe him. They stood at the threshold, taking in the chaos. Bookcases lined the walls from floor to ceiling, but they overflowed, and chest-high stacks of books teetered on the floor too, leaving only a trail of grubby carpet visible. It led to a desk that was strewn with papers and coffee cups. Food cartons and fruit peel spilled from the bin, the smell of them overly sweet and mouldering. Garber had tacked newspapers over the windows, and they'd yellowed with age, casting the room in a sickly light. A strip was torn down one edge, and sun sliced into the room, dust hanging thick in its glowing blade. Tess stepped towards a bookcase, reading the spines.

'Look, Dom,' she said, pulling one out and turning

it over to read the back. 'He has books about adoption. Dozens of them.'

Garber had books on seemingly everything, Dom realised. He followed Tess inside, scanning the shelves. Adoption. Immigration. Drone regulations. One on security coding that he recognised from his work in DC. There were photographs amongst the books too. A middle-aged man with a neatly cut beard and a group of grinning students, with a hand-scribbled note tacked to the corner that said *Chernobyl 2019*. The same man appeared again, older and whiter-bearded, wearing tinted spectacles and a dark blue skullcap before what Dom thought might have been the Wailing Wall. The room was the physical manifestation of Garber's article on adoption, cluttered and disordered, leaping between concepts without coherence, unnerving and compelling at the same time. There were qualifications in frames. *Esteemed Fellow of the Institute of Behavioural Economics. Recipient of the Chase-Tracker Award for Outstanding Contribution to Understanding the Psychological, Cognitive, Emotional, Cultural and Social Factors Involved in Human Decisions. Honorary Member of the Psychologists for Economic Science.* A stack of books he'd apparently authored. *Are Humans Really Rational? Decision-making Dissected. Predicting the Unpredictable in Human Behaviour.*

A shudder powered through him. Garber studied *people*. He stepped behind the desk to look closer and saw that the drawers were open – every one of them. They were messy, as though someone had been searching hurriedly. His senses sharpened. There was a sandwich on the desk, unwrapped but uneaten. One of the coffee cups was overturned.

'Tess? I think we should wait outside,' he said, stepping forward. He couldn't put his finger on why he thought it so keenly, but the dread he'd felt in the courtyard was resurging. His mind was still in somersault, not processing clearly. Tess looked up from her book, and as he rammed Garber's chair aside to get to her, he froze. On the wooden rim, next to his own hand . . . what was that? Blood? It looked like blood, didn't it? Bright red and fresh, smudged like someone had tried in haste to wipe it off.

'Shit.'

'What is it?'

He kicked the chair back and leapt towards his wife, meaning to steer her through the maze of books towards the exit, his heart pounding, but as he looked towards the corridor, a woman was blocking them. She was baring her teeth and staring them down.

11

Thea stood in the doorway to Professor Garber's office, and the man and woman stared back from inside. The moment Thea saw them, she knew they shouldn't have been there. The woman was holding a book, the man was standing behind her, and when they looked up, they both wore the same startled, shame-faced expression of a child who'd smashed a glass after being told *don't touch.* Unease bore through Thea's stomach. Even without that look, it was clear they were intruders. He wasn't the professor. She felt certain of it. There was a blazer slung on a chair beside the window, but this man already wore a jacket. His hands were shaking, and the room was more than messy. She'd spent enough of her life walking the line between control and chaos to recognise the difference between something intentional and something otherwise inflicted. You might not clear a mug away to the kitchen, but if it fell, you'd stand it up. The newspaper on the window had been tacked precisely over the glass. No sheets overlapped, no corners were peeling. Anyone so meticulous would have never left such a large rip unfixed. Rania's parting words rang in Thea's ears. *Be careful.* The woman put down the book – too quickly. Who were these people and why were they here?

'Where's the professor?' she said. It came out like a spit.

The man shook his head, not meeting her eye. 'I don't know.' He sounded American and looked chalk-pale, ready to run. He fumbled with his wedding band and then put his hand on the small of his wife's back. 'Excuse us, please. We were on our way out.'

Thea planted her feet harder, not moving. She hadn't expected anyone else to be here, and the run-in had thrown her. She wasn't sure she'd even expected to find Garber. She'd never set foot inside a university before, hadn't been ready for the sprawling scale of it, and there was something about the smell, leather and wood like the museum's Archive, that left her feeling unsteady. The couple were well-dressed, their clothes clean, smart and not worn thin like hers were, and she was aware that she'd drifted beyond her depth. Despite the disorder in the office, these people fitted. At the Roundhouse, Thea would have called them out for their intrusion and asked what they were playing at. Here, she slunk back, making way for them to leave. Places like this weren't for people like her. The woman headed for the door, squeezing sideways through an aisle of clutter and lifting her handbag ahead of her, to fit through the narrow gap. Fear seized Thea at the sight of what she was holding. Protruding from the top of the woman's bag was what appeared to be a booklet, and the Little Doves logo was printed on the top corner of the cover. It wasn't exactly the same – the bird was missing – but the cloud was identical, its three soft puffs fading from top to bottom, powder blue to white. Thea's memory flashed to the steps of the deserted townhouse and the pigeon ruffling his feather on the railings. The quiet. Her panic. The sign that was gone. Words tumbled out before she realised what they'd be. 'Do you work at Little Doves?'

The woman paused and looked at her, confused. 'Where?'

Thea pointed. 'The children's home.'

She glanced at her ashen husband then dipped into her bag, drawing out the booklet. Thea stared at the group of laughing children on the front.

'This?' The woman shook her head. 'No. I mean, I don't know Little Doves. This is a children's home, though. BlueSkies. I don't work there. We're adopting.'

Thea's thoughts spun. 'Adopting?'

'Yes. Well, we hope to adopt. A girl. Four months old. We wanted to know more about Professor Garber's research. We read a paper of his and saw that he had concerns about where some of the children came from and it's just—' She cut herself off, clutching the booklet and eyeing Thea anew. When she spoke again, suspicion laced her tone. 'Are you one of his students?'

Thea pressed herself against the wall. She couldn't answer. Her mind raced, grasping for scraps of the story that Rania had told her, slotting them into what this woman was saying and trying to force a fit. Adil hadn't died. Rania heard him. So what happened? Could they have put him up for adoption? Thea scanned the couple, with their spotless clothes, foreign accents and credits to fly all the way from America. An idea smacked into her.

What if the home had sold Adil? What if people like this had *bought* him? Rania said there were more police reports, didn't she? What if Adil wasn't the first child sold – nor the last? What if Little Doves had taken Laurel and sold her too? The room pitched. *We're adopting. Four months.* Every muscle in Thea's body was twitching. What if this couple had bought her baby girl?

The woman stared at Thea, waiting for her response. When it didn't come, she glanced anxiously at her husband. He gave her an almost invisible nod and they went to leave, huddling together and slipping past Thea with their eyes turned away. Rage shot through her. Her hand whipped out, snatching hold of the woman's wrist and wrenching her back. The woman yelped and yanked her arm away, holding it against her body. She looked at Thea, clearly afraid. Thea let go, aware of the force with which she'd made the grab, and of the leaps she'd made on so little evidence, and the facts she might have missed. She needed to act more cautiously. Keep her wits and her cool.

'I'm sorry,' she said and she stepped backwards, lowering her voice and forcing herself to lift her hands in fake apology. 'I didn't mean to scare you. You think there's something wrong with your baby?'

The woman glared at her. 'I didn't say that.'

'You were going to.'

Silence.

Thea dipped her head and found the woman's eyes. 'I can help you.'

The couple exchanged a look. 'Do you know about the professor's research?' asked the man.

Thea nodded and stood up straighter. She had to take

the risk. 'He told me about the kidnapped babies being put up for adoption, yes.'

'Jesus.' The man rubbed his temples with a trembling hand.

The woman shook her head, pained. 'But there wasn't any evidence.'

Anger swelled again in Thea's chest. No evidence? Wasn't Rania's voice or Adil's absence evidence? Wasn't Laurel evidence? Christ, wasn't *she*? The woman was examining her, her tears clearly threatening. Thea glared back. She needed to know. She wanted to scream it. Her voice quivered with the strain of holding herself in.

'Do you want me to tell you if you've got a stolen child?' she asked them.

The woman's eyes widened. 'Garber said they were untraceable.'

'Show me your documents.'

The man touched his wife's arm and leaned in, whispering pointlessly. 'I don't think we should, Tess. Let's wait to speak to Garber.'

The woman ignored him and pulled her screen from her back pocket, unrolling it, bringing it to life and turning it to face Thea. Thea's eyes skidded urgently down the file.

Name: Maya Doe
Status: Abandoned
Estimated birthdate: Late March
Ethnicity: Caucasian
Eyes: Brown
Hair: Black

Sickness flooded through her. They had changed the baby's name – of course they had – but she knew it was Laurel. In her bones, she knew. She could feel her fury rising. She gripped the screen.

'Have you got a photograph?'

The man glanced at his wife, hesitated, then relented. He tapped his watch and held it out so Thea could see. His home screen showed a photograph of a gorgeous, grinning baby. It forced the breath right out of her. Long lashes framed the child's dark, shining eyes, and a shock of black hair spiked from her head. Podgy fingers held the blanket beneath her chin. A cry broke from Thea. On the way to Little Doves, she'd been scared she'd not remember what her daughter looked like. Now, every detail was clear as diamond in her mind. This girl's features were the same as Laurel's, but the way they pieced together wasn't anything like her. The disappointment was complete and overwhelming. Thea fell to her knees and threw up on the floor.

12

'Right. Today's the day! Let's get this done.'

Catherine Hilton-Webb tucked herself behind the desk in her office, motioning for Tess and Dom to sit too. The BlueSkies logo was already projected on the wall, and when Catherine tapped her screen, the Interim Custody Agreement leapt into its place. She scrolled partway down the document, finding where they'd abandoned it. Her smile was broad and eager as she looked from Tess to Dom.

'You must be so excited,' she said.

Dom lowered himself into the seat beside his wife. He managed to haul the shape of a smile to his lips, but neither he nor Tess could summon a verbal response. They had tried again to contact Professor Garber this morning, dragging themselves reluctantly back to UCL but finding him still truant. There was a damp patch in the corridor where the carpet had been scrubbed. Dom stared at the projection, trying to keep the oversized words from slipping out of focus. Another night of sleeplessness had left him feeling slow and more confused than ever. Tess had told the university's receptionist what happened – left their details – but no one seemed concerned. There wasn't so much as an eyebrow raised for the absent academic and his haphazard office, nor the smudge that may or may not have been blood, nor the odd, bedraggled girl who claimed to know him. He wrung his hands together. The girl had shaken them. The look of her was feral. When she'd bolted, he'd not known whether to make chase.

Catherine saw Dom's smile slip. She reached across the desk and squeezed his forearm. 'It's overwhelming, isn't it?' she said gently. 'Becoming a parent? Please don't be embarrassed. A lot of our couples feel the same way. There are so many complicated emotions involved in adoption, and I can only imagine the extra challenges you face by coming back to the UK. I'd like you to know that you're not on your own, Mr and Mrs Nowell. You're welcome to stay with Maya in the nursery while the ICA processes. My contacts at the Ministry know that it's coming, and it'll only take a few hours to complete. You're then free to take her with you, as we discussed, but you can visit us any time before the final approval and visa pass. My staff have plenty of experience and will happily help with Maya, or talk things though. You only need to ask.'

Dom extricated his arm from beneath Catherine's hand and looked at Tess. She was staring, blank-faced, at the form on the wall. Catherine followed Dom's eye-line and paused, the last traces of her own smile dissipating.

'I have to admit,' she said, speaking carefully, 'I was relieved when you called. You left in such a hurry the other day. I'm not sure I've ever seen that from a client. I do hope everything was OK? I was worried you might not come back.'

She tacked a tinkly laugh to the end of her sentence, but it was clear that none of them felt it was a joke. Tess sniffed and scrubbed at her nose. They had discussed it. Last night, Tess asked Dom if they could bring themselves to walk away from Maya. Should they? What would their life be like if they did? Dom reached across and linked through her fingers. She flicked a nod at him. *Ask.* He knew she was right. The possible answers were terrifying, but what else could they do? He squeezed Tess's hand and looked at Catherine.

'Where did Maya come from, Catherine?' he asked her.

Surprise rippled through Catherine's calm expression. She looked back, a smile suspended on her painted red lips but discomfort sparking in her eyes. 'Pardon me?'

'We went to Kensington Fire Station.'

'You didn't tell me you were visiting.'

'We hadn't planned it.'

'Was there a problem?'

Dom shifted. He could feel the damp collecting between Tess's palm and his. 'I'm not sure,' he answered truthfully. 'We met the woman who registers the children at their Box. She couldn't find any record of Maya.'

A noise part way between a laugh and a cry burst from Catherine. 'She must have made a mistake.'

Dom shook his head. 'I don't think so. We saw the records ourselves. There was no baby found on April 3rd or any of the dates close to it. We showed her Maya's documents and the signature on the handover that should have been hers – it wasn't. She couldn't tell us who it belonged to.'

Catherine hesitated, the tip of her tongue smudging

the lipstick in the corner of her mouth. She looked hot, flushed, and suddenly older. Her finger dabbed at her makeup where it met her the dampening line of her hair. Silence hung in the room.

'Catherine?' Tess sat forward in her chair. 'Is there something about Maya we need to know?'

Catherine replied too quickly. 'No. Of course not.'

Tess placed her hands on the desk, as if steadying herself. 'Please,' she said, glancing at Dom. 'Tell us. We can't take her otherwise. Why wasn't she listed at the Kensington Box?'

Catherine stared for a heartbeat longer then her composure collapsed. She hid her face in her hands. 'Maya didn't come from the Boxes,' she said, her voice cracking.

Tess gasped and seized Dom's thigh. The woman from Garber's office lunged into his consciousness. *Kidnap*. He felt a punch of rage and pain. 'You took her?'

'What? No!' Catherine shook her head furiously. 'I would never do that.'

'What happened, then?'

'Her aunt brought her to me when Maya was six weeks old. She said that her sister had died at the birth and Maya's father wasn't interested. The aunt had offered to raise Maya, but instead he'd sold her to a brothel. A brothel! Somewhere utterly hideous in Lambeth. I tracked it down. You wouldn't believe. The woman said she'd spent every credit she had finding Maya and buying her back before she came to harm, but she was too afraid to keep her in case her brother-in-law returned.'

'Dom!'

Tess's eyes were wide with horror. She dug her

fingernails into him. He shook his head, addled by shock. Anger raced through him. A baby in a brothel? *His* baby in a brothel. Could it possibly be true?

'Why didn't you call the police?'

Catherine pulled a tissue from her sleeve and stuffed it against her nose. 'The aunt made me promise that I wouldn't go to the police. Maya was blood-registered, and the father worked for a government office. He was respectable, she said. He would tell everyone she was lying. She couldn't risk him being traced and Maya sent back. That's why she came to me instead of a Box. They'd have tested the child straight away and known.'

'And the aunt? Where she is?'

Catherine shook her head. 'I don't know. She wouldn't give me her name. I'm so sorry, Mr Nowell. Mrs Nowell. I have never lied about a child before. I didn't know what to do. This woman . . . she was terrified. You should have seen her. She begged me to keep her secret – to give Maya a new identity and find her somewhere safe. I made a fresh record for her. Changed her name. Jasmine. That's what her mother had planned to call her. I said that we'd received her from the Boxes, and I paid someone I know at the Ministry to have her re-registered. I didn't think anyone would check.' She sniffed again, smearing her mascara with the tissue. 'Are you going to report me?'

Dom felt nauseous. 'I think we need a moment.'

Catherine muttered an agreement and dragged herself up, stumbling around the desk and smoothing her crumpled skirt. Her water bottle toppled and fell to the floor, but she didn't pick it up. In the doorway, she paused. 'Maya needed help,' she said quietly. 'Perhaps you don't understand how bad it is in Britain. I will never turn away a child in need.'

The door swung shut behind her. Two fat bluebottles threw themselves against the window, buzzing.

'I feel sick, Dom,' said Tess. Her pupils were enormous pools of black.

He slumped forward, clawing his hands through his hair. *Jasmine*. 'Do you believe her?'

'I don't know. Do you?'

He pressed his thumbs into his temples, feeling the blood throbbing beneath his skin. It felt unlikely that Catherine would invent a story so extreme, but if she knew she'd been rumbled for something bigger, extreme would be the card to play. Did he understand how bad it was in Britain? Guilt for having run away rubbed at him again.

'What do we do?' asked Tess.

He shook his head.

'If we call the police and Catherine was right . . . Dom? What if they sent Maya back to her father?'

'They wouldn't do, would they? Not with the aunt's story.'

'But we don't know who she is or where she is. You'd risk that?'

Dom's head pounded. It didn't bear thinking. 'But can we take her? Catherine's already admitted that she lied. She's not trustworthy.' He dragged his hands down his face and looked at his wife. He wanted so badly to see her holding Maya again, to see them both happy. He wanted to be a family, to move forwards with the future that he'd waited so long for. It made him ache. He closed his eyes, trying to think it through rationally.

'Tess? If we knew for sure that Catherine was telling us the truth, we'd take Maya with us, wouldn't we?'

'Yes. I think so.'

'What if we knew for sure that Catherine was lying again? What would we do then?'

Tess stared at him. He shunted closer to her, taking up her hands, an idea grasping for purchase against the slick of grief.

'Listen,' he said, lowering his voice. 'Whether or not what Catherine has just told us is true – whether or not Garber's theories are true – we know that Maya is not who we thought. I mean, she might be abandoned – god knows right now that sounds the best option – but if Catherine got hold of her in some way that she shouldn't have done – some way she'd never tell us – I don't know if it's safe to leave Maya here.'

He cupped Tess's face in his hands and held her dark, anxious eyes with his own. They could sign the ICA and get it processed then take Maya with them. It might be weeks until the final approval came through. That was time they could use to work out where Maya came from. Keep her safe. His stomach twisted. To fall deeper in love. Beyond the door's glass panel, Catherine twitched in the corridor, still snivelling but trying to get herself together, tipping her head back and struggling to wipe her ruined makeup. Tears were collecting at the rim of Tess's eyes too as Dom held her. He watched his suggestion melt in.

'I don't want to leave her, Dom,' Tess whispered.

'We're going to do this?' he asked, his eyes searching into her.

She nodded.

'Alright,' he said. 'Then let's call Catherine in.'

13

Thea lay on Jemima's sofa and stared without seeing at the wall ahead. She had been so certain that the child was Laurel. When the couple had squirmed with their hangdog expressions, when she'd pieced together what it was that was happening, when she'd scanned the baby's details on their documents, she had known it with every spark of her heart. Her chest still felt tight, like someone had bound her with rope and was pulling. How could she possibly have got it so wrong?

Jemima returned to the living room with two mugs of steaming chicken soup, and the little folding table rocked dangerously as she placed them down. She lowered herself beside Thea, dropping the last few inches with a groan.

'These are for your head,' she said, putting two white pills into Thea's palm and closing her fingers around them. 'And that scar of yours. OK?' She gave a gentle smile and rubbed Thea's thigh with her hand. It felt hot from the mugs.

Thea didn't move. It was desperation that had convinced her, she knew. Having no other options. That's why she'd been so ready to believe. Her fingers hung limp around the pills. She hadn't been entirely wrong. One of her leaps had landed. The Americans might not have been adopting Laurel, but with all she'd learned from Rania, their reactions and the absent professor, there was one clear truth that shone from the mud.

'They're stealing a child, Mima,' she whispered.

'They're adopting a child, Thea.'

'One that might be stolen.'

'True, but from what you've told me, they're trying to make sure that's not the case. They wouldn't have been at the university – wouldn't have said what they said to you – if they didn't care.'

Thea felt her scowl thicken, and she sat up, looking at Jemima. She didn't give a damn if they cared. This wasn't about intentions. It was about the outcome. They were as guilty as whoever it was that thieved Laurel. They wanted a baby. Thea's girl was missing. You only needed to see the Roundhouse's booming economy to know that where there's demand, someone always supplies. She shook her head. 'You should have seen them, Mima. They had credits. I could tell they did. It was obvious. They came to Britain for a quick and easy fix.'

It was Jemima's turn to shake her head. 'You're making assumptions, Thea. They said they were adopting. Nothing more.'

'Then why not stay in their own country? It's because all adoption amounts to is moving a baby from a poor family to a richer one. That's why. They're here because they think they're better than us, and because when you've got credits, it's easy to pretend you're helping and not a thief.'

She doubled forward, sinking her head into her lap and wrapping her arms around her shins. Her stomach ached, and not only from where they'd wrenched out her child. She not been prepared for how physical this grief would be, nor how exhausting. It left her feeling weak to her bones.

'Careful, Thea,' said Jemima. 'That's the Salter in you talking, if ever I heard it. It won't help.'

Thea's lips pinched. 'That's not fair.'

'It's as fair as it is true, sweet pea. I'm not attacking you. The FEB did a number on us all. No one can claim that none of it stuck. Our biases are sometimes buried deeper than we can dig out. The only way to stop them causing trouble is to remember they're there.'

She rubbed Thea's back, and Thea buried her face harder into her legs. She might have been a Salter to start with – she might even have been proud of it – but she wished those days as far into her past as could ever be possible. Jemima's accusation rubbed in the way that only happened when it contained a grain of truth.

'I've let her down, Mima,' said Thea.

Jemima leaned into her, circling her arms around Thea's body and holding her tightly. 'You've done no such thing, Theodora. Oh, the guilt you pile on yourself, little one. It'll flatten you. You need to stand up. Face forward. Look to where you want to go.'

Thea closed her eyes. She wished she could face forward in the way that Jemima had done. Her friend's start in life had been no better than Thea's. Jemima's parents divorced when she was an infant, and the series of family illnesses, tragedies and abandonments that followed left her in the care of the state before she was five years old. She spent her childhood in and out of foster care and children's homes but drove her way through, kept herself focused despite the chaos and earned an education, found a job she loved in a big, bright library, bought a home with a garden, met a man and fell in love. When her husband dropped dead less than a year after their wedding – an undetected heart defect finally making itself known thirty-two years into his life as he ran for the bus one sunny October morning – she never remarried. There was a photograph of Joe on the mantlepiece, raising his pint to the camera and grinning in the courtyard of an overcrowded pub. The pressure in Thea's head intensified. How did Jemima have the energy left to help her? Thea had asked her the question once but didn't understand the answer. *You're helping me, Thea. It's you who's helping me.*

'What do I do, Jemima?' she said. Her voice cracked. 'I don't know where else to look.'

Jemima peeled herself back and heaved Thea upright. 'We need to find the Americans,' she said, cupping Thea's face in her hands and staring into her eyes. 'Talk to them properly. Tell them who you are and what's happening. They might know something that can help us. Think, Thea. Where will they be?'

Thea shook her head. 'I don't know.'

'When they showed you their screen . . . Did you see where they were staying?'

'No.'

'Did you get their names?'

'The man called the woman Tess.'

Jemima closed her eyes and licked her lips, thinking.

Thea's head pounded. She'd not seen anything on that screen of any use. All she remembered was the photograph of the baby that wasn't Laurel, and her own fiery panic, and the man looking grey-skinned and the woman's frightened face. The woman's face. *Their faces.* Heat bled through her. It wasn't a name or an address, but a face was something, wasn't it? It was somewhere to start if she was able to be brave. She could show the police, perhaps. Try to force them into action. Show the US Embassy. Someone who might know. She sucked a breath. 'I drew them,' she whispered.

Jemima's eyes opened. She looked at Thea, confused. 'You drew them?'

Thea paused. She'd done it on the bus on the way to Jemima's. She'd not been able to help herself. She'd needed to draw the baby, to see how the child's eyes and nose and hair could be precisely the same as Laurel's until they all came together, but her pencil had continued to sprint across the page. It was like an expulsion, like if she scribbled them into physical being, it might ease the burden on her memory. She edged her hand into her pocket. She was shaking. Whenever she drew, it was always an expulsion. At other times, she bit her tongue to stop herself from speaking. She could squeeze her eyes shut and hold her breath to not cry. Yet when she gripped a pen, she couldn't control it. Pain came as a flood. She withdrew her hand from her pocket, pulling her notebook with it. There was something about her drawings that felt too intensely revealing. They held a mirror to herself more than to her subjects. She'd not shown them to anyone.

She gritted her teeth and opened the book, flinching at Jemima's intake of breath.

'Thea, you drew these?'

Thea stared at the floor, embarrassed. The woman she'd drawn was terrified, trapped in the moment when Thea seized her wrist. The man looked shocked too, his revulsion and disbelief directed at Thea with excruciating precision. Jemima shook her head, and Thea felt her skin burn. Her friend had already called her out for her prejudice, and now she'd know how cruel and selfish she could really be. Thea hated that part of herself, those whip-crack reactions. Where Jemima summoned words and found ways to move forward, Thea bit, scratched and fought like a cat. The dark, cold cell at the police station came back to her. She'd tried to stop. She wanted to be different. Yet the damage was buried as deep as the bias. Nothing she did could change that. Now Jemima knew it too.

'I didn't mean to frighten them,' she said quietly.

Jemima turned through the pages, and Thea squirmed, wishing she that could take back her notebook but unable to move. Images of the man she'd drawn a thousand times stared back at her, with Laurel squeezed into every scrap of white between him, smaller and softer than he was, again and again, her perfect face butted against his brutish one, overlapping at their edges. Past and present, melding together. Her misery rose. Each flicked leaf felt like a layer of skin stripped. She'd scribbled record numbers from the Archive in the corners of the pages, with the dates that she'd searched. Not only was she selfish, she was desperate too.

'Oh, Thea.' Jemima's voice was a breath.

Thea pinched at the skin on her forearms, her whole body searing with shame. What would she have done without this woman? How many times had she come to Jemima and asked for her help? She pressed her eyes shut as the memory of her parents' death tore through its cage. The night before it had happened, she'd argued with them. Thea had sworn, called them traitorous bastards. She'd only been eight. There was a rally planned at the Gritstone, part of the FEB Hearts and Minds Tour, and rumours were circulating that the FEB Five themselves might even show up. The man in her memory had come in advance of them. In preparation, he'd taken over the running of the Gritstone's communal kitchen a week before, and her parents were working especially hard. Thea had been so excited to see the leaders. It was like the election. There would be another party. Everyone would be happy, like they were before. How she missed seeing her parents smile. Yet when she got back from her allotment duty that evening, it was chaos. Someone had stolen the chicken that had been brought for FEB's leaders. The man from the kitchen was shouting at people, demanding searches and making threats.

Thea never found out if her parents took the chicken themselves, but she knew at least they'd been involved. In the middle of the night, her father woke her, instructing her silence with a finger to his lips. She sat, fuddled by sleep, and in the dark corner of the bedroom saw her mother crouched by the camping stove that they'd bought to take on their trip to Dawlish. She was beneath the slightest slit of open window, fanning the smoke into the cold night air. Fear slapped Thea.

'What are you doing?' she hissed at her mother. She glanced to the door as if expecting FEB militiamen to charge in. Her father lifted her from the bed and carried her rigid body across the room.

'Eat, sweetheart,' said her mother. She peeled a hunk of grey flesh from a chicken bone and held it out. In the flame's blue light, she looked old and thin and not anything like she used to. Thea recoiled at the meat's scent, hunger walloping, but she couldn't take it, could she? It was treason. *Free and Equal. Community first. No secrets. Self-sacrifice.* Didn't her parents remember the lessons? What were they doing? She shook her head and tried to wriggle away, but her father gripped her tighter, forcing a finger between her lips, pushing his nail between the rows of her teeth and prising them apart, so hard that it hurt, and then he stuffed the chicken in. Thea gagged, but her father held her, begging apologies into her hair, saying they needed it, holding his hand clamped over her mouth until she was forced to swallow. When she finally gulped, he released her. She crumpled to the floor and scampered back from him, sobbing.

'You're traitors,' she screamed at her parents in a whisper. 'Don't you care about the liberation? Don't you care about Free and Equal?' She ran to the bathroom and bolted herself in.

When they were caught, her parents denied it. In the square between the towers they pleaded their innocence, and when that failed, for mercy or reprieve. It made no difference. It was the man from the kitchens that decided their sentence. The FEB Five had indeed arrived for the rally, at the very worst time – or perhaps the most perfect – and Thea had watched him tell them about the chicken and grovel an apology for the lack of a feast. *Are you going to let them get away with it?* one of the FEB Five said to him. *Aren't you going to show the people that the days of selfishness in Britain are over? Free and Equal does not tolerate greed.* The man bobbed his head in agreement. He ordered her parents to be hanged. Their stomachs were removed with a foot-long machete. The entire Gritstone Estate watched as they bled out on the concrete. Thea had stood beside Springer in abject shock, paralysed, not knowing which feeling consumed her more powerfully; the terror that reached inside her chest and crushed her heart so hard that she was sure it would stop beating, or the dizzying relief that it hadn't been her. The night before, she'd called her parents selfish. Yet who would feel relief at their parents dying? Who would watch in silence? Who wouldn't fight against it? Thea was far, far worse than them.

She stared at the man's face in her notebook, her parents' nameless executioner, and nausea rolled over her, the guilt as thick and smothering as that day. She understood now. They'd been starving. The liberation was a con. How she wished she could have changed what she'd said to them, slept that last night in their arms, not on the cold bathroom floor. From the notebook in Jemima's hand, the man glared back. Afterwards he'd left the Gritstone, and she'd never seen him again. Disgust hammered into her, her own guilt plain in every variation of his face for Jemima to see. There was something more there too that she couldn't find words for – that she groped for through the darkness but never dared to look at – but its angles and its grain and its edges were jagged, and they cut the same as the absence of Laurel, and the sum of it all was impossible to bear. It was something like debt, like some wretched unfinishedness. Her hand leapt to the notebook.

'Please, Mima. Stop.'

Jemima closed the notebook. She looked at her.

'I'm sorry,' said Thea.

'What are you sorry for?'

Thea flicked her head, pained.

'These are astonishing, Thea. Can't you see it? Why aren't you showing the world? Sweet pea, with your talent, the high blue sky is the limit.'

She reached out and threw her arms around her. Thea's chest seized. Her mind was racing. *The high blue sky.* The university's corridor exploded into perfect clarity around her.

'Oh, Mima,' she said. 'I know where they are.'

14

The cab ride back to the hotel was a blur. Tess and Dom sat on either side of the car seat in which Maya lay dozing, her tiny fingers gripping Dom's. His hand shook so hard that he worried he'd wake her, and he dared not reach into his pocket for his pills. Grief crushed his chest like a boulder. His stare drifted from the dishevelled vista of his childhood to his quiet, sad wife and the beautiful, defenceless child who was now officially in their care – so nearly their daughter – and he swallowed down the misery that backed up in his throat. How he wished with all his heart that this was different. They had waited so long and with such aching patience to be parents, fantasised endlessly about what this day would look like. He could see now, too, that the wait had been a form of desperation. Parenthood was about more than he and Tess as partners. Dom needed Maya. She had been his chance to finally move forward. His new beginning. He was going to give her everything that he'd missed so hopelessly, everything he could never give to Tim, though heaven knows he tried. He was going to love her completely, and Tess, and never leave them. Building a family of his own was going to fix him. The boulder pressed down harder. Perhaps he wasn't for fixing. Perhaps it wasn't possible. Their moment of joy at becoming three had been robbed.

Tess caught him looking at her and gave a half-hearted smile before returning her attention to the window. She was clutching Maya's bag on her lap, a linen tote with the BlueSkies logo that contained everything Maya would apparently need for her transition into this new world: two baby-grows, two grey muslins, a spare nappy, an empty bottle and a carton of ready-made formula milk. It seemed so inadequate. Of course, Tess and Dom had everything they'd need for Maya waiting at the hotel, but the absence of anything remotely personal pained him. He had nothing to show Maya about who she had been in the months before they knew her. When he'd been evacuated from London as a child, at least he'd had his memories. He'd had his brother who shared them, and together they bound him to an identity, albeit one that he wasn't sure he wanted. Maya's loss felt unbearable by comparison. What would he tell her when she asked, when she was older? The aunt. The father. Catherine? Reality thumped him. He might not be able to tell her anything. He might not know her. She might not be his.

He ran his thumb over the back of her silken hand. Had they done the right thing, taking her with them? The cab slowed outside the entrance of the Yeandle Hotel, and Dom tapped his watch against its screen to pay. He wanted to believe that he had taken her only for the reasons he'd told Tess. Even in the most favourable of accounts, the British Police Force were notoriously understaffed, inefficient and ineffective, yet was it best for Maya to not involve them at all? Dom couldn't shake the feeling that he might instead have been motivated by prolonging his denial, semi-consciously gifting himself another week or two of pretending their family had a future and that none of this was real. The cab's door unbolted, and Tess unclipped Maya's seat, lifting it out into the bright afternoon sun. The baby wriggled and screwed her face up as the light hit her, rubbing her knuckles into her eyes and whinnying. They climbed the steps and plunged inside the cool, shaded lobby. If only he'd been able to talk to Garber, even if all it achieved was to dismiss him as a crackpot. The young woman from the university office pierced back into Dom's consciousness. Her rage and desperation had infused him. He shook his head, disgust rippling deep. Was this about what was best for him and Tess, or best for Maya? God, he wished he could say for sure.

'Mr Nowell?'

A voice called from across the lobby, and Dom looked up to see the hotel's concierge skipping from behind his podium and making a path towards them with his hand raised in a wave. It was almost 3 p.m. – check-in time. The space was crowded, and as the man weaved between the guests and their upended suitcases, it was a beat before Dom realised that two more men were trailing him. His stomach leapt. Police.

Tess turned to him, her fear evident.

'It'll be alright,' he said, unconvincingly. 'We haven't done anything.'

The concierge stopped short and stepped aside, letting the two tall, uniformed officers past, then he nodded an embarrassed acknowledgement to Dom and Tess before retreating wordlessly back to his work. As they approached, the officers removed their caps and tucked them into their elbows, like in some old-fashioned movie.

'Dominic Nowell?' said the first, giving a swift, professional smile. He looked between them. 'Contessa Nowell?'

Dom straightened and made an attempt at smiling back. He felt sure they must have seen his heart thrashing beneath his shirt. His hand slipped protectively to the small of Tess's back. Had Catherine called them in a crisis of conscience over Maya, or something worse? 'Is everything OK?' he asked.

'We hope so, sir,' the policeman replied. 'I'm Officer Whittaker. This is Officer Holt. We'd like to have a chat to you about the disappearance of Professor Levi Garber.'

Relief crackled through Dom's body. Garber, not Maya. By extension, not him. Yet no sooner than it had flared, the relief extinguished. *Disappearance.* An image of the smudged fingerprints bolted through his mind. The woman who ran. The policemen's eyes were on him, not hostile but measuring, and he could feel the scrutiny of the lobby too. He pressed his hand more firmly into Tess's back and tucked the other into his pocket, not wanting anyone to see how he was shaking.

'We've never met the professor, I'm afraid,' said Dom, groping for the answer that he hoped would satisfy them quickest. 'I mean, we tried to a couple of times at the university, but he wasn't there.'

Officer Whittaker nodded, but his smile had gone. 'All the same, sir, we do have some questions for you.' Maya was starting to grumble, and he bounced a look at her.

'Perhaps you'd like to discuss this in your room?'

He gestured to the elevator, and Tess moved automatically. The people before them parted without instruction, and Dom, Tess, Maya and the officers stepped into the lift, travelling silently up to the fourth floor. They waited as Dom unlocked the room and saw them in.

The door thunked shut, and Maya's complaint erupted to a scream.

'Take your time,' said Holt. He raised his voice above the wail, but gave Tess a reassuring look as she planted the car seat down and fumbled to extract the bawling child. 'Sort your little one out first. We'll wait.'

Tess released Maya and scooped her up, holding the baby against her body and pressing her face in the curve of the child's neck, as though she thought someone might snatch her away. Dom upturned the tote and spilled its contents onto the bed. He opened the formula and poured it into the bottle, focusing on the act as hard as he could, and not the crushing tightness in his chest. Tess took the bottle and dropped onto the end of the bed, her eyes fixed on Maya with the same determined focus. Maya grasped without aim and gulped at her feed. The BlueSkies logo stared up from the crumpled bag, as lurid as the projection in Catherine's office. Dom took the baby-grows from where they'd fallen and covered it up.

Maya quietened, and he turned to the waiting police. 'I'm sorry,' he said, rubbing his chin and trying to fake a calm that he didn't feel. 'Professor Garber. What can we help you with?'

Whittaker took a screen from the holder on his belt, unrolled it and swiped it to life. He tapped a microphone symbol in the corner and placed it on the sideboard. Tim's voice sounded in Dom's head, warning him not to say anything without a lawyer, but wouldn't that make them look guilty – or at least obstructive? He didn't have any secrets to keep about Garber. The police would see that, wouldn't they? They'd not see the rest. He wrung his hands behind his back.

'We were given your details by the reception staff at University College London's Faculty of Social Sciences,' said Whittaker. 'We understand that you raised concerns with them about not being able to contact Professor Garber?'

Dom nodded. 'That's right.'

'Could you tell us what happened?'

'We went to his office yesterday. He wasn't there. We tried again this morning but didn't have any more luck. We left our number and the name of the hotel so that he could call us instead.'

'You had meetings arranged?'

'No.' Dom shifted, glancing at Tess. 'We were just hoping he'd be there.'

'The receptionist said you seemed worried about his welfare?'

Dom felt heat prickle beneath his skin. The receptionist hadn't been concerned. She'd brushed him off. What changed? 'I suppose so.'

'Why were you worried, Mr Nowell?'

He paused. 'The room, I guess. Garber's office. It was a mess.'

'You were concerned about the dirt?'

The red fingerprints pressed themselves again into

Dom's mind. Why didn't he mention them? More and more, he felt as though he had something he needed to hide. No, not hide. Protect. He cranked a smile to his lips. 'It sounds like an overreaction when you say it, doesn't it? I expect it's my error. The receptionist told us that Professor Garber was always in his office, but he wasn't, and something about the room felt . . . I don't know.'

Whittaker raised an eyebrow. '. . . felt *messy*.' He turned to Tess. 'Why were you visiting Professor Garber yesterday, Mrs Nowell?'

Tess kept her gaze on Maya, and Dom could see that she was making the same calculations as him. 'We're in the UK to adopt,' she said. 'This is our new daughter. We'd heard that the professor was an expert on international adoption, and we wanted to ask him about it. Hear his thoughts on helping Maya learn about her heritage. That sort of thing.'

Dom let out a breath, hoping it didn't show.

Tess looked up at Whittaker, her eyes wide and steady. 'The university said that the professor wasn't missing. They weren't concerned when we spoke to them. Has something happened?'

Holt and Whittaker exchanged a glance. 'Your enquiry caused the university to look into his attendance,' Holt replied. 'It transpired that he'd not been seen all week, and when a colleague checked if he was ill, they found he wasn't at home either. Apparently it's extremely out of character. They've filed a Missing Persons Report.'

'That's terrible,' said Tess.

'It might not be,' said Holt. 'It might be nothing more than a grown man taking himself on a little getaway without thinking to tell his colleagues, but we need to follow the process and check.' He tapped something into Whittaker's screen. Whittaker's eyes skirted the room. 'So just to confirm, you visited Professor Garber's office on two occasions – yesterday and this morning – looking for advice on matters of adoption, but he wasn't present and you didn't see anything suspicious.'

Tess shook her head. Dom's stomach turned. *Kidnapped babies.* Why hadn't he chased the woman, asked her what she'd meant and why she looked so terrified? And when she'd seen Maya's face on his watch . . . what was that? Confusion, perhaps. Disappointment? Mismatched pieces of a jigsaw floated. The woman had been looking for something. For someone. Fear hacked into him. He needed to snatch the pieces from their orbit, sort and order them and see where each one fitted. See if he was a part that was missing. He swallowed hard and shook his head too.

The officers shared another look, seemingly satisfied, and then Holt tapped off the screen and passed it to Whittaker, who rolled it up and tucked it away.

'Thanks for your time, Mr and Mrs Nowell,' he said, heading towards the door. 'If you think of anything else, let us know.'

At the threshold he paused, holding out his wrist, waiting for Dom to bump his watch. Dom obliged, feeling the vibration as the contact details of Officers Holt and Whittaker zipped onto the glass and logged there, feeling as much like a threat as an offer.

Holt smiled at Maya, who had hushed and was drawing

down the last of her milk. 'Congratulations, by the way,' he said, 'and good luck.'

The door closed, and Dom listened to the officers' footsteps retreat along the corridor.

'What on earth, Dom?' said Tess. 'I don't like it.'

He slumped beside her on the bed and lay back, staring at the ceiling. He didn't like it either. There was nothing to say they should have been so secretive, but for whatever reason, they'd both felt the need to hold back the complete truth. The word *kidnap* beat in his head, like a metronome. Tess stood and placed Maya in the bassinet they'd prepared for her earlier, tucking her beneath the soft cotton blanket and reaching for the stuffed yellow elephant that they had left on the sideboard.

'What's this?' she asked.

In the mirror, Dom saw her holding an envelope. She flipped it over and tore at the opening, and he watched her tug at the folded paper. Her hand shot to her mouth, and she leapt back and dropped the letter, yelping as if it had scalded her. He jumped from the bed and snatched it up. The print was black and bold, with long, thin letters that crawled like cracks in ice.

Dominic and Contessa,

We're losing patience. You've got what you came for. Why aren't you happy? If you don't want to be fishing her tiny body from the river, we suggest you wait quietly for your final approval. No more snooping. Pack your bags while you're waiting. We expect to see you GONE.

15

Jemima had her hand on Thea's elbow as they stood in the fourth-floor corridor of the Yeandle Hotel. Thea stared at the door before them. From inside the room, she could hear Dominic and Contessa Nowell's conversation – not their exact words, but their drawn American accents, the lilt of their questions and the silences that followed where the answers should have been. It wasn't an argument, but they didn't sound happy. She felt her hackles rise.

'Easy,' said Jemima. Thea was shivering and Jemima tightened her grip. 'You need to stay calm.'

Thea nodded. She knew her friend was right, and she was trying to breathe deeply, but her adrenaline was spiking. They'd been simple enough to find, this pair. The BlueSkies logo was so similar to the one for Little Doves, and once Thea had remembered, an address for the children's home followed quickly. BlueSkies and Little Doves were connected. They had to be. She and Jemima had sat on a bench along the street from the home in Beauden Crescent, watching and waiting for someone to leave. It had taken all Thea's restraint not to batter down the door and storm in, but Jemima warned her that they needed to be patient. Until they could be sure where Laurel was, they couldn't risk anything to scare the crooks away. Instead, they held back, then followed a cleaner when she left on her lunch break, accosting her in the alleyway that cut through to the shops. It didn't take many questions nor many credits to extract the name of the mixed-race American couple with the almost-complete adoption application, nor many more to coax her into finding out where they were staying. Now Thea was here, her restraint was slipping. Jemima insisted that the odds were in favour of the couple being honest. If they wanted to speak to Garber, they were looking for truth, like Thea. But what if Jemima had misjudged them?

Thea knocked on the hotel room door. The voices inside halted. There was a pause, then footsteps. Dominic Nowell opened the door. His wife leapt from the edge of the bed. She was clutching a baby to her chest.

'Dom,' she said. There was fear in her voice. 'It's her.'

The man's eyes jolted from Thea to Jemima and back again, his face slapped with confusion and rage. Thea looked past him, her vision fixed on the child as it gripped a hank of the woman's hair and tugged. It was the girl from the photograph, the almost-but-not-at-all Laurel. Thea's adrenaline surged, and her legs felt weak. This might not have been her daughter, but the couple were thieves regardless. Jemima's counsel sounded in her head, and she braced herself, rooting her body through the soles of her feet, stopping herself from exploding in and seizing the baby back.

'I need to talk to you,' she said, staring him down.

Nowell's scowl flared, and he snapped from his stupor.

In his hand was a sheet of crumpled paper, and he lifted it up and thrashed it at her. 'To talk to us or threaten us?'

'I haven't threatened you.'

'Did you send this?'

'I don't know what you're talking about.'

'Who are you?'

'Who are *you*?' Thea fired back. She pointed beyond him, into the room. 'And that child. Who's she?'

'*Theodora*—' Jemima muttered in warning.

'That's our daughter,' said Nowell.

'Like hell it is.'

He turned to his wife. 'Call the police.'

The door slammed shut, and Thea threw herself at it, beating her fist against the wood and shouting at him. Jemima yanked her back.

'They're thieves, Mima,' said Thea, pulling free from Jemima's grasp but letting herself be steered to the opposite wall. Her hands fell by her sides. 'That kid isn't theirs. You know she isn't.'

Jemima pressed a finger to her lips, and stroked Thea's hair. She gave her a kind, knowing look, then knocked on the door more gently. 'Mr Nowell?' she said. 'Wait, please. We haven't sent you anything. I swear it. We only want to talk. Thea, here – my Thea – her baby was stolen. We think she might have been sold for adoption. We're trying to find her and bring her home.'

Thea wrapped her arms around chest. Her stomach was cramping. Jemima watched her, pinning her back with a firm stare and knocking the door again.

'Mr Nowell? Please. We need your help.'

They waited a moment, and then the handle clicked

down. Nowell looked at them, ashen. His voice had dropped. 'Someone stole your child?'

Thea raised her chin at him. She could see the woman with the baby in the background, glaring. She didn't trust herself to speak.

'What happened?'

'Thea was sick when her daughter was born,' replied Jemima. 'The hospital said they were taking Laurel to a care home until she was better, but now she's gone.'

'And you think we have her?'

'You have someone's child,' said Thea.

Jemima's hand shot up, quietening her. She turned to Nowell.

'No,' she said, shaking her head. 'We know that you don't have Laurel, but you might know something that can help us track her down. Thea was told that Professor Garber had heard of cases like hers. Other missing children. That's why she was at the university. She wanted to ask him. When she ran into you and your wife, she panicked. She's sorry she frightened you. She was frightened herself.'

Thea hugged her body harder. Was she sorry? It was true that she'd been frightened. She was still frightened. She looked at Jemima, so calm and confident. *My Thea*, she had said. It made her ache.

Nowell dragged his hands down his face and let out a long, ragged breath. He opened the door wider, stepping aside. Jemima took hold of Thea's hand and led her in.

On the far side of the room, the woman pressed herself against the wall. She hoisted the baby to her shoulder, rubbing their faces together and looking anxious. 'I'm sorry about your daughter,' she said quietly.

Thea felt like her legs were going to give way. She fumbled in her pocket for her notebook, pulling it out and opening it to the drawings of Laurel that were squeezed into the scraps of space between drawings of the man that she also couldn't find. Her body burned. She held the notebook out to the couple, avoiding their eyes.

'Have you seen her?' she said. 'At BlueSkies, I mean? Do you recognise her face?'

Nowell looked, and she felt the shock register, but he shook his head. 'We've not seen any of the other children from the home,' he said. 'We've only been in the office – or the nursery when it was empty. I'm sorry.'

Disappointment strangled her. 'Can you help me find Professor Garber?'

He glanced at his wife. 'The professor's missing. The police were here earlier to question us about it.'

'To question you?' asked Jemima. 'Do you know him?'

'We've never met him. We heard about his research and wanted to talk to him, too.' He paused and looked again at the woman, and she nodded. He took a heavy breath. 'We came to Britain – I came back to Britain – to adopt a child in need, but something's not right. We don't know what it is, but you've only confirmed to us that we've not been given the full story about our daughter.' He paused, and Thea saw how violently his hands were shaking. 'If she's really ours to take.'

Silence hung thick, and Thea stared at the baby. 'Her name's Maya?' she asked. She couldn't help it.

The woman nodded. As if she knew her name, Maya turned, focusing her enormous, dark eyes on Thea. Thea's heart clenched. She stuffed her notebook back into her pocket, wishing herself alone and unseen in her grief. She turned and walked towards the door, touching her fingertips to the throbbing wound in her belly.

'Thea?' said Jemima, moving after her. 'You can't leave. We're not finished.'

'They can't help us, Mima.'

'We've not asked the right questions.'

Thea stopped. She knew of a question they hadn't asked. She swung back, looking at Nowell. 'You said I threatened you.'

In his hand, he still clutched the paper. He flipped it over and examined it for a moment, then passed it to Thea. Jemima read over her shoulder, her hand leaping to her lips to catch her cry.

Thea's head spun. She stared at Nowell. 'Who wrote this?'

'No idea,' said Nowell. 'We've only just found it.'

'What are you going to do?'

He shook his head. He looked beaten.

Jemima took hold of it and clicked her heels on the carpet. 'Get your shoes on. I know where we can start.'

16

The rush-hour tube carriage was full to capacity. Bodies were pressed against Dom, radiating heat, the smell of them stale and unpleasant. He gripped the greasy hand-hold tighter, planting his feet and bracing against the train's lurch, wishing for a glass of water to help the heat and the ache in his head. Thea was sitting a few feet away with her friend, Jemima, and through the crush of people he could see that their hands were clasped together. They each stared ahead, not talking and not moving, lost in thoughts the other seemingly already knew.

Can we trust them?

At the hotel, Tess had hissed a whisper into his ear as he'd snatched up his bag and yanked on his shoes. Thea and Jemima had been waiting in the corridor, but the door was open, and he could see that they were also in deep, hushed discussions. Jemima had said that the records at the British Museum might help with the letter, but she was coy with the details, and he didn't see how. The train jolted, and he bumped into the woman beside him, who looked up from her watch to throw him a scowl. He wanted to *trust*, but the word felt thinner and more slippery than it had done before. Two days spent reevaluating the limits of what he dared to believe was even conceivable, let alone truthful, was testing him. He no longer trusted what he'd ask himself to do, either. He and Tess had taken Maya from BlueSkies on an impulse so unlike them, giving little thought to what came next and having no concept of precisely what actions they could possibly take to unearth the truth, if indeed there was a truth that needed to be unearthed. What followed this afternoon only compounded Dom's anxiety. The letter had fired a bullet right through him. Though he wouldn't tell Tess, the threat that something terrible might happen again to his family, might be inflicted upon them, left him feeling like he was thirteen again, running blindly along smoke-filled corridors, panicked beyond panic, feeling his muscles weaken to putty and his vocal cords fail. Inside, he could feel himself collapsing. He wasn't sure how much longer he'd be able to hold out. He glanced along the carriage. Were Thea and Jemima behind the letter? If they were, it didn't follow that they'd lie about a baby. All he knew for certain was that he couldn't look away.

He took his screen from his satchel and pulled up Maya's application on the Ministry of Children's portal, tapping in their personal passcode. Grey sand ran through the image of a timer, and then FINAL APPROVAL PENDING appeared in block print. Dom knew that their status wouldn't have changed in the hours since they left Catherine, but he felt time was passing too quickly, as though, grain by grain, that sand was mounting and threatening to swamp him. He needed to know what he couldn't ignore. He minimised the application and stared at the icon for Professor Garber's report instead. He didn't need to open it. He'd read the words so many times that he knew them by rote, if not each one in their exact order then in their purest, darkest essence at least.

The conditions required to enable epidemic levels of child-laundering in Britain today have occurred as a direct result of FEB-era policies, in particular the deliberate, systematic and all-encompassing dismantlement of established society, both at an institutional level and in relation to individual emotional sovereignty.

A shiver rippled through him. He remembered well the slogans that were plastered across the city and on endless door-dropped leaflets in the run-up to the election. They were the same ones that were later spray-painted in bulbous blood-red letters on the walls that edged the playing field, and on the bus stops in the high street, and in the underpass by his school. *Self-Sacrifice Unites Us. Free and Equal is the way to Liberation. Put the People First.* Through clever misdirection, hollow sympathy and snappy catchphrases, FEB's leadership had made the nation think they cared. What wasn't ever spoken or written, but which quickly became apparent, was that to FEB, *The People* was a unit, a vast, solid and inflexible mass whose overall submission was infinitely more important than the sum of its component parts. Maintaining the integrity of The People – keeping it mute and impotent and docile – was the way they'd retain power. Those who jeopardised The People were dispensable. Individual life was cheap.

A hot poker jabbed between his ribs. When he'd slammed the door on Thea earlier, she'd called him a thief. Over the years, he had used that word a hundred time to describe FEB. He never said it out loud – he knew he'd sound self-pitying – but in his mind he believed on some fundamental level that they'd stolen his family and the life he should have had. So ingrained had this idea become that he'd almost stopped feeling the emotion that came with it. Years had passed since he'd been consciously angry or afraid when he remembered what had happened. He'd thought he was past that, but being in Britain was teasing old emotions from where he had balled them up and buried them. Strand by strand, as fine as spiders' silk, Maya and Garber and Thea, and Billy Slade's trial and the greenness of the trees and the accents of the people and the scent of the city, were all drawing out feelings that he hadn't known he still had. In London, his parents were everywhere, yet nowhere.

The carriage lights flickered, catching Thea's cheekbones. She was painfully thin but nothing like fragile, all sharp angles and rigged with wire instead. She gave off the sense that she might have been electrified, as though she barely kept control of the current flowing through her, and one touch might set loose ten thousand volts. He dug his teeth into his lip. Where was Thea's family – not just her daughter, but the rest of them? He recognised that pent-up, misfiring voltage. She'd not had people on her side to diffuse her. Of all FEB's destructions, he knew without question that this was the most catastrophic. Buildings could be rebuilt and code could be rewritten. Laws could be repealed, reworked and renewed. Institutions could be forged from the still-scalding embers of the past. But family? Nothing could come close to replacing those losses. Even if he managed to rightfully keep Maya, even if he went on to adopt other children who would take his name and grow and marry and have their own babies, there would still be a part of him irreplaceably stolen. Was he a thief? He had the queasy feeling that the question extended beyond Maya's origins. Legacies often stretched further than people liked admitting. Thea stared across the train into nothingness. He hoped Laurel was safe and sleeping like Maya, with her own version of Tess staying up and keeping watch.

They pulled into Holborn, and the carriage doors slid open. He staggered out, swept along by the crowd's exodus, and followed the back of Thea's head as she disappeared and reappeared amid the people.

Could he trust her? What choice did he have.

17

When they emerged from Holborn Station, the sun had dropped behind the buildings. It had taken with it the sky's lustre, and the day's warmth and comfort, and Thea rubbed her hands along her goose-fleshed arms. The clock on the corner of Southampton Row and High Holborn said the time was 8.40 p.m. The Archive closed at nine. She cast a look to Jemima, who gave her a nod and reached out to squeeze her elbow, and they crossed the road without waiting for the lights. Dominic Nowell had been fumbling with his Tourist Ticket at the station's barrier, and he lagged behind, calling for them to wait. Thea turned to see him dart into the four-lane traffic, skip-stepping from the path of a Driverless Express, then dipping his head and raising a hand in apology to the disgruntled passengers as the car rammed its brakes. Resentment bubbled in Thea's stomach. Though she trusted that Nowell and his wife were genuinely shaken, she wasn't stupid enough to mistake their self-preservation instinct for proof of good character. Despite his American accent, Nowell was British. It had taken Thea a while to realise that he'd said it, and she felt as though he'd hidden it.

Tricked her. A fact so important should have been branded on his skin. *I came back to Britain*. It was almost laughable. How benevolent. Jemima would have upbraided Thea for even thinking such a thing, but without a doubt, this man was Cat. Two. Salters like Thea's parents were meant to be the future of Free and Equal Britain, but they suffered the worst of it. Only the Spoonies were able to escape. She kicked through the gate of Bloomsbury Square Gardens, cutting across the weed-addled grass and past the pink plaque embedded in a tree stump. Wilting flowers and burned-out candles clustered between its straining roots, and she shot Nowell a glare so she wouldn't have to look at them. *Shift yourself faster.* If only she and Jemima could have taken his letter and done this alone.

Jackson was on the security desk outside the British Museum's Reading Room. Thanks to Jemima, Thea knew everyone who worked at the Archive, if not to greet them directly then at least by name and sight. Jackson was one of her least favourite guards. Whilst many of the regular staff would let her stay beyond closing, if only to save her work, settle her mind or wait for Jemima, Jackson was uninterested in anything beyond officiousness. He watched the clock as though it might flee.

Jemima paused in the lobby, turning her back on him. She unstrapped her watch and passed it to Nowell.

'You take this one inside, sweet pea,' she said to Thea. 'I'll take care of Jacks.'

Thea nodded and headed away. She doubted that Jackson was the type of man to be charmed, but if anyone could buy them time, it was Mima. At the Archive's entrance, the terminal's light glowed green as Thea tapped her watch against it, and the glass gate slid aside. She started for a screen on the first row of tables, removing her backpack and slinging it beneath the chair before realising that Nowell wasn't with her.

'What are you doing?' she asked, spinning back.

Using Jemima's watch, he had passed himself beyond the glass threshold as Thea had done, but then he'd stopped in the centre of the double doorway. Like a rock in a stream, he blocked the trickle of exiting people so their paths split either side of him. Oblivious, his gaze floated around the room.

'I'd forgotten it,' he said, as though she'd know what he meant. He was speaking slowly and quietly, melting each word into the next like he was trying to tease back a memory without it disintegrating. The Archive's lights had been dimmed for the evening, and through the windows of the soaring domed ceiling, dusk coloured the clouds in purple-tinged grey. Thea followed Nowell's stare as it roamed from the canopy to the book-adorned balconies and along the leather-topped desks. He settled on the sculpture that stood at the hall's centre. Wisp-thin silvery ladders stretched towards the ceiling, twenty of them or more, each covered with silver figures no bigger than a finger. In their hundreds, the miniature people clambered skywards, some with children strapped to their bodies, some reaching down to heave up the ones behind.

'That's new,' he whispered.

Thea felt herself squirm. The sculpture had been at the Archive from the day it first opened, but she'd long stopped noticing it. She was trying to haul *herself* up. She didn't have time to notice. Outside, a cloud shifted. The figures gleamed.

'We need to hurry,' she said, dropping her voice and slinking back to the desk. She woke the Archive screen and logged in, waiting while her homepage loaded. It was cluttered with her open documents; Archive Update Bulletins and Search Guidelines, notes she'd made for herself on things that might have been memories or she might have invented, and the face of the man she'd examined here last. She hurried to close the windows so that Nowell couldn't read them, regretting having done so when he saw what was behind them.

'Is that your family?' he asked.

The picture of five-year-old Thea at the Dawlish campsite stared back at them. Andreas and Rose were beaming behind her, their hands on her shoulders, their hair whipped by the wind atop the sun-swept Devon cliff.

Thea scowled and pulled up the Archive's menu, covering the image. 'Have you got the letter?'

Nowell reached into his jacket pocket and passed it to her. Through the side of her eye, she saw his face redden. Her scowl set, and she scrolled through the navigation options. Every other time she'd been to the Archive – on thousands of occasions, perhaps – she'd only ever searched the photographs. She didn't have the name of the man she was looking for, nor any image of him she hadn't drawn herself, nor a strand of his hair to extract his DNA from, nor his fingerprints, nor any details of his history. She didn't have any of the things that relatives usually came armed with, to allow them to search the Archive in its entirety within minutes. Memory was her evidence: incomplete, unreliable and slow.

She found the Handwriting Database and swiped it open, selecting *Scan* as Jemima had instructed her to do and flattening Nowell's crumpled letter against the screen. There was a surge of white light, making the paper translucent, and she could read its words backwards. *Tiny body. River. Why aren't you happy?* She stuffed her fear for Laurel to the pit of her stomach and replaced it with anger, as purposefully as she could. Fear caused paralysis. Anger galvanised. It was safer. If she'd had a letter like this, a copy of her parents' execution order, she'd have found the man already. She'd have been able to move on. At her side, Nowell wrung his trembling hands together. Harder, she pressed the paper to the glass. Pathetic. She could smell his clothes. They were freshly laundered. *I came back to Britain.* How old was Dominic Nowell? Older than Thea, but not by much. Early thirties? What right did he have to be sat here, quivering? How quickly and easily had he been able to move on?

The screen flashed, indicating the scan had finished, and Thea thrust the letter back at Nowell. She tapped *Start search*, and in silence they watched the Archive's database leap into action. A progress bar appeared, a green spot unfurling into a dash and then a line, creeping from left to right across the screen. There were 37,856,003 handwriting samples to check, it said. Thea knew that to have such a large quantity of data in any record was astonishing, even by Archive standards, but FEB's mistrust of technology after the Zero Virus was matched only by their love of competitive diligence – of keeping score of 'achievements' and alike. Almost every confession from the

FEB years could be found here, handwritten. There was every order given, every report issued, every plan made, every word committed to paper by those who worked for FEB and those who endured it, copied into digital immortality when the regime fell. As well as providing evidence of the strength and depth of FEB's depravity, the Handwriting Database had become invaluable for many of those searching out the fates of their loved ones. Even a partial writing sample, something grabbed from an old shopping list or birthday card, could be compared against an unnamed confession or an order, and a fate uncovered. If whoever it was that threatened the Nowell couple had lived through the FEB years, the chances were good that they'd be identifiable here. They'd get a name, and maybe something else to work with. It could lead Thea to Laurel.

A woman's recorded voice came over the Tannoy, announcing the museum's immediate closure and asking all remaining guests to leave. Thea pressed herself deeper into the chair. They'd have to drag her out. Around them, the last of the Archive's visitors had disbanded, and she could see that Jackson was losing patience. He'd emerged from behind the security desk and had one hand hooked on his hip, whilst the other raked his beard. Jemima chatted and blocked his way, but he was watching. On the screen in front of Thea, the counter sped upwards. Her stare inched sideways, to where a sliver of her breezy campsite holiday was still visible. There was the streak of citrus yellow from her t-shirt, and the green grass was luminous. The sky was clean, crisp blue – or was that the ocean? A wave of grief crashed through her. How different her life would have been if she could have left like Nowell. If her parents had escaped, she would have never birthed Laurel. She wouldn't have learned what it was to love a child so desperately – but she wouldn't have lost her either. Thea would never have known it was possible to experience such pain and still not die.

She covered her nose and mouth with her hand, feeling her breath damp and ragged against her skin. Across the room, Jackson broke free of Jemima and marched towards them. They weren't going to finish. She couldn't come back. This wouldn't wait until morning. Where was Laurel? She wanted her. No.

'Oh my god,' said Nowell.

Thea shifted to face him. 'Mima won't like it, but we need to try and pay him. You need to pay him. We're not leaving.'

Nowell shook his head. 'That's not it, Thea. Look.' He rammed his chair back from the table.

Thea turned to the screen. The search had finished. Three people were listed, three possible matches. The first two were names that she didn't recognise; a woman and a child that might have been Italian. At the third, a siren went off inside her head.

18

Dom, Thea and Jemima stood on the steps of the museum's South Portico as Jackson clanked the bolt on the door from inside. Night had fallen fully, and the spotlights were blinding. They stared at the little printed docket in Dom's hand.

PROFESSOR LEVI MATTHEW
ZACHARY GARBER

Arrested for dissidence, 8 May. Trial by Jury at Central London County Court, 29 May. Confession in full. Unanimous verdict. Imprisoned, Wormwood Scrubs. Executed by chemical injection, 12 June.

Dom's head swam. His vision was spitting. The record was listed in the year that FEB came to power, almost two decades ago. Garber wrote the letter. But Garber was dead.

Across the plaza, the museum's last visitors were exiting through the gate to Great Russell Street. The guard opened and closed the metal threshold for each of them in turn, nodding a 'good evening' as they disappeared from view. Thea snatched Dom's wrist and yanked him down the steps. Jemima scurried at their side, clutching her cardigan around her body.

'We need to get away from here,' Thea whispered at the ground. 'We don't know who's watching.'

She let him go, and he twisted his wedding ring around his finger, feeling it tug his skin. It hadn't occurred to him that anyone might be keeping tracks on them, but it was obvious, wasn't it? He glanced behind then followed Thea across the road, around the corner and along the darkened route they'd travelled in daylight less than an hour before. The evening was warm, and Bloomsbury was busy, the pavements scattered with people making their way home or to dinnertime meet-ups, and the tables that overspilled the cafe were full. Nobody caught Dom's eye, but he knew that meant little. The first chance he had, he'd ring Tess and check she'd locked the hotel door and put the chain on. Tell her not to open it for anyone. He'd keep them on screen until he returned.

At the corner of Bloomsbury Square Gardens, Thea stopped. The square had been padlocked for the night, and she stole a look along the street before vaulting from a bench to the top of a rubbish bin and over the railings. She turned back and held Jemima under her arms as the old woman clambered after her, then took her weight and eased her down.

'What are you doing?' Dom asked.

'We need to discuss this where no one will see.'

He sucked his cheeks, climbed the railings and chased after them, letting himself be drawn to where the trees were fullest and the bushes high and dense with summer growth. Thea pressed herself into the shadows and dropped her voice so low that Dom needed to lean in.

'We have to find Garber,' she said. 'He's not some bearded old crank who made up a paper. He knows what's happening. He can lead us to Laurel. He's involved.'

A car passed down the road on the opposite side of the trees, faster than it should have done. Headlights flashed through the leaves, mottling the three of them in yellow and black camouflage. Dom shrunk backwards, further from sight. His thoughts were clattering together, rusted metal against rusted metal, powdering away before they made sense. 'But he's dead.'

Jemima tugged at her gold hoop earrings, her eyes roaming the park. 'I'd have said that someone resurrected him. It happened often enough. The years after FEB fell were chaos; millions of people missing or displaced, digitised records lost with the virus . . . There were plenty of folk looking for a new start, and to bring a man back to life wasn't difficult. All it took was a few credits to someone with the right official access.' She shook her head, frowning. 'But it can't be someone *pretending* to be Garber. The handwriting wouldn't have matched. Besides, to steal a name is one thing, but to assume a full identity? Too much risk.'

Dom pushed his fingertips into his eye sockets, as if the pressure might somehow make logic align. 'Why haven't the police worked it out?'

'That he's back from the dead, or where he is now?'

'Either. Both.'

'Perhaps they have,' said Thea. 'Or perhaps they don't

care. The police are lazy, ruthless racketeers. You said you found the letter after they'd gone?'

'You think they left it?'

'I wouldn't rule it out. '

Voices surged from the pavement, teenagers half singing and half shouting along to the music that blasted from their watches. Dom waited for their footsteps and the laughter to pass. 'Why would Garber threaten us?' he said. 'He was trying to uncover the adoptions, not suppress them.'

'Maybe it wasn't a threat. It could have been a warning.'

The last traces of music dissipated into the evening, and quiet hung beneath the trees. Nothing about the note had felt benevolent. He remembered the blood on the chair at Garber's office.

'So how do we find him?' said Thea. She was staring at Dom, waiting for an answer to which he had no clue.

He tensed, bracing against a shudder. Instinct told him to hold his family close and run in the opposite direction from the author of the letter, but Thea was right: Garber was the one link they had to discovering where Maya had come from too.

'Alright,' he said, working through his thoughts. He dug into his bag and pulled out his screen. 'If we can't go to the police, then we can't go back to UCL either. The only place we have to look for Garber is in his work. My brother singled out his adoption paper, but the link he sent was to an academic library. All of Garber's papers were there. There were scores of them. The professor may have been discredited, but it didn't stop him publishing. Tess and I skimmed the titles, but we didn't go any further. We should see what else he wrote recently. Perhaps it'll throw up an idea as to where he might be.'

Dom brought the screen to life and swiped in his passcode, pretending not to notice the diligence with which Thea clocked the pattern. His homepage loaded, and he felt a flash of embarrassment – like someone had caught him naked – at the sight of the photograph he'd pinned there. It was from three summers earlier. He was holidaying at the Grand Canyon with Tess and Tim, Kat and Sasha; they were sweaty from their hike and coated in orange dust but smiling in the sun. Dom and Tess had found out the week earlier that his sperm count was officially 'non-viable' and had booked the trip on a wave of heartbreak, desperate for anything they could fool themselves was escape. Tim's family had come as a distraction. Dom had hoped that the warm, cheerful company would buoy them, but mostly it only confirmed they were missing out. The trip had been punctuated by happy moments such as this one but was overall the saddest time of his adult life. He'd only put it up because Sasha had asked him – called it the best holiday ever ever *evvvvver* – and he'd not the heart to say no or change it back. Thea was staring at the photograph, the same way he'd stared so plainly at her family. He was glad of the dark to hide his grief.

'That's my brother and his wife,' he said, not looking at her. 'And their daughter, Sasha. They have a son now too, Finn.' He paused, hoping his voice would steady. 'I'm sorry that I asked about your picture. I shouldn't have done.'

Thea didn't respond. Dom crouched, propping himself against a tree trunk and balancing the screen on his knees. He opened his email, hiding the Grand Canyon and scrolling to the message he needed. Thea and Jemima crouched beside him as he selected Tim's note and pulled up the academic library, skipping the paywall with Tim's FBI link. He tapped Garber's name into the search bar and tapped the box marked *Author*. The page reloaded instantly, but it was not as he remembered. Before, the screen had been filled with a list of results. Now it was blank. The knot in Dom stomach's tightened. He deleted *Garber* and double-checked the title of the adoption paper from his desktop, tapping that in beside the icon of the magnifying glass instead. He hit *OK,* and the screen refreshed. Empty. He stabbed *illegal adoption* and *child laundering* and *child trafficking UK* into the search bar. A handful of matches came up, and he sped to the bottom, his eyes raking through the authors. Nothing had Levi Garber's name.

'What's the matter?' asked Thea.

He shook his head, confused. 'Garber's research,' he said. 'It was here, but it's gone.'

He emptied the search field and retyped the professor's name, this time unchecking *author*. A new list appeared, longer than the previous one. He scanned it, finding *Garber* highlighted in snatches of text that showed the paper's relevance, but it was always in the references that the name appeared, never as the writer of the paper itself. There was research on refugee migration patterns and the privacy implications of Artificial Intelligence-led transportation, and all manner of other disparate areas. They were all citing Garber's expertise in behavioural economics, and all dated from before FEB. There didn't appear to be anything about adoption. Dom tapped through to the second page of results, then the third and fourth. This was deliberate. Someone had systematically and thoroughly erased Garber's work.

'It's all disappeared,' he said again. 'It's been removed. Everything.'

'Why?'

'I don't know.'

Thea looked over his shoulder. 'They've missed one,' she said, pointing. 'Haven't they?'

Dom glanced down, realising she was right. The paper was titled 'The Benefits of Positive Patient Behaviour in Chronic Disease Control', and Garber's name was written below. He was listed as the third author, not the first, and the screen had cleaved him in two. Only Prof. L. Ga— was visible. Dom's pulse quickened. Behavioural economics. Garber's field. The date of publication was more recent than the others. The professor was dead by then – or he wasn't – but it was after whatever it was that came before.

He tapped, downloading the paper and opening it instantly.

'What's it about?' asked Thea.

Dom skimmed an abstract that made little sense to his tired, novice brain. 'It's something about encouraging patients to manage their own medication. Take their drugs on time and things like that. It's almost a decade old, though.' He scrolled, skimming the words without taking them in, willing a solution to leap out and slap him and feeling more disappointed with each passing page. 'I don't think this is going to help.'

Thea reached over. 'What's Grateley Profiles?' she

asked, touching the corner of the page to zoom in. A bright blue letter *G* with a florid silver *P* hanging from its curve grew on the screen. Beneath the logo were the words *Research funded by Grateley Profiles*.

Dom shook his head. 'Don't know.'

He opened another window, searching online for Grateley Profiles. He tapped the top match – a pharmaceutical manufacturer in Fodenrock, Colorado – and an elderly man smiled up from his hospital bed in a sunlit room. The image morphed into a woman examining a test-tube, then to a group of handsome young men with stethoscopes around their necks. They were grinning at an upward-trending graph. Below, there were headers like *Pollution Inoculation*, *Next-generation Antibiotics*, *Pathogen Protection* and *Fertility*. He dragged his stare from the beaming couple and their dough-featured newborn to the section beneath: *Meet Grateley Profiles' Board*. He tapped again, and a grid of nine adjoining images filled the screen. Seven of them were photographs of men in generic grey suits, one was a red-haired woman. The last square contained just a featureless black outline where a face should have been. Dom touched the greyed-out figure, half expecting to see Garber's face appear. Instead, the blank picture remained, and a name and biography materialised above it.

Dr. Thomas Fox, BSc, MSc, PhD. Specialist in medical repercussions of biological warfare. Cooperated with, or consulted for, various public and private organisations in the healthcare, pharmaceutical, technology, fertility and warfare sectors, including the British government.

Dom felt a jab of discomfort and pulled his hand away. He scrolled further, pausing on the media reel near the bottom of the page. His eyes were drawn to the video in the centre. *Grateley Profiles proud to be awarded Federal support for development of pioneering fertility treatment. Funding gratefully accepted by Board.*

Dom opened the video without wanting to, setting the clip from some Colorado-based news stream into motion. The reporter was standing to the side of a large stage and parroting what sounded like a marketing campaign for Grateley Profiles' contribution to combatting growing levels of global infertility. She turned, and the camera panned to the stage where a bespectacled politician was handing an oversized cheque for some obscene number of credits to a woman in a sea-green dress. Behind her, a group of men watched on, clapping keenly. Dom recognised the woman from the Board's photographs, her auburn hair stacked in curls on the top of her head. He counted the men watching – there were eight. The camera closed in on them, and Dom's chest seized. At one end of the crowd, he found the face that was missing from the photographs. Thomas Fox was hanging back, smiling like the others but clapping less eagerly. His eyes flitted sideways, as though he was waiting to leave.

'Jesus Christ,' said Dom. He rewound the video. Paused it. Gawped. Fox was older, bearded, thinner, and his hair was dyed darker, but he was still unmistakable.

Jemima looked at Dom. 'What is it?'

'Carl Hamilton,' Dom whispered. She stared at him, disbelieving. He turned the screen to her. 'It's Carl Hamilton. Look.'

'My god,' she said, though a spike of breath. 'It can't be. Can it?'

Dom dropped the screen into the grass, disgusted. Hamilton – the FEB Five's own mad scientist – was alive. He was in Colorado, of all places. Not even hiding. Working for a pharmaceutical company and claiming to be an expert on biological warfare medication when half the world's worst weapons were developed on his watch. Surely Dom couldn't be the first person to recognise him? Someone else had to have realised who Thomas Fox was. He dry-retched into his fist. The ground was pitching. 'He should be in jail.'

Thea looked at him, rigid.

Dom glared back. 'You don't understand.'

Jemima shook her head. Her eyes were filled with pity. 'Oh, love. You've got nothing to be ashamed of. I've seen your hands, and it isn't nerves. Hamilton Shakes, those. Aren't they? I know what that stuff does.'

Dom pressed his palms together, staring at his fingers and trying to force his heart to keep pace.

'Did they get you in the riots?' she asked gently. 'The tremor gas?'

'UCL attack,' he said. 'My parents died.'

Thea made a sound like paper ripping, a cry stifled before it left her throat. Her eyes had grown wide, and she was dragging her fingernails along her arm. She looked smaller than she had done, fragile suddenly. When her voice came, it was strangled. 'How old were you?'

'What?'

'When it happened. How old?'

'Thirteen,' said Dom.

She flinched. 'That's why you're in Britain?'

'We can't have children. I can't. The gas—' His words shattered, and he couldn't collect the pieces. His breath was racing, and colours danced in his vision. Panic surged, threatening to engulf him. He tucked his hands into his armpits, squeezing.

Jemima leaned over and wrapped herself around him, like Tess had done at the university campus. He could feel the tears threatening. Jemima held him tighter.

'I'm so very sorry to hear that, Mr Nowell.'

19

Thea sat in the dark on the floor of her apartment, her spine pressed to the end of her parents' bed. Rose and Andreas hadn't slept between the sheets for seventeen years, but if she closed her eyes and willed it hard enough, she could almost smell the scent of their bodies deep in the fibres. Feel their lingering warmth. Between her fingertips, she worried the frayed edge of the quilt. When they'd been alive, Thea had spent her nights being cradled by the sunken, velvet sofa. It had taken her more than a year to summon the courage to step back into her parents' bedroom, let alone sleep in their bed. She'd never call this room anything but theirs, but now, at least, it was the place she felt most safe. She butted her watch against the charger on the bedside table, watching the battery leap to a hundred per cent. The screen lit with the surge of power, and a stream of messages from Springer appeared in quick succession, sending vibrations against her skin. She swiped them away, unread. She'd not had the energy to close the curtains, and the bright, full moon and London's unerring glow steeped the room in a hazy grey. Shouts came from the square beneath the towers as the drunken participants of a night out shared their long and laughter-filled goodbyes. She pulled her knees to her chest, clear thought as distant as their carefree voices. Amidst an ocean of half-truths, she felt tiny and unmoored. There were miles and miles of the unseeable beneath her. Frothing white-tipped questions were advancing, rearing up then crashing down on her; wave after wave of them, thumping without relief.

The day had been beyond exhausting. They'd found one man deceased who had been so clearly living. Another alive whom the world had wished dead. Hamilton had been gone for so many years that it was an easy wish to make. Easy, too, to believe it had come true. Thea had not personally given Hamilton anything but a glancing thought in the past decade, but now she wished for his death too. If Hamilton was selling fertility drugs to the men he'd made sterile, it wasn't a leap to think that he might be selling babies. Selling Laurel. From what Thea had learned of Garber, it was unlikely the professor had any idea that Hamilton was alive and still dealing in misery, much less that the man had once indirectly funded his work. Surely, Garber would have never dared to write the adoption paper if he'd known. It was impossible to imagine Hamilton letting any form of slander lie, even if it wasn't aimed at him explicitly. Besides, Hamilton couldn't have ignored that which might unearth him. She picked at the crescents of dirt beneath her fingernail. Yet the paper was written more than a year ago . . . Was the letter a threat or a warning to Nowell? Garber could be hiding, or he could be in trouble. Thea felt a fresh surge of grief for her daughter. What had Dominic Nowell stirred up?

Dominic Nowell.

She tapped his name into her watch and projected the search results onto the damp-dappled wall. There wasn't much that was clearly him; a professional profile on the website of what looked like some low-key US government department and a couple of news pieces where he'd been called on to comment about Code Restoration. She scrolled halfheartedly. It didn't matter. All she really needed to know about him became clear beneath the trees of Bloomsbury Square Garden. Looking at his screen and discovering Hamilton, his face had been the perfect mirror of every unbearable emotion that Thea had tried to crush, to obliterate, deep inside. She felt sure she could trust him. FEB had stolen from him too.

She hesitated. Deleted Dom's name – that's what he'd said to call him – and tapped in *Carl Hamilton*.

Photographs of the man from Grateley Profiles flickered onto the wall – not Thomas Fox as she'd seen him lurking awkwardly earlier, but a younger man, suspended in snapshots of history, many of which she knew well, at least in their essence. There was Hamilton standing shoulder to shoulder with the FEB Five on the day of the election, how she'd seen him herself as part of the Trafalgar Square mob. There was Hamilton clinking his beer glass with Slade and Easton outside the Houses of Parliament. Hamilton visiting an army regiment. Hamilton practising at a gun range. Hamilton in a lab coat. Hamilton signing documents. Hamilton standing before a row of ordinary terraced houses, with a battered, bloodied corpse in the street. He examined it, blank-faced and from a neutral distance. Sitting on the wall behind, a group of children looked on. Hamilton in a suit at what must have been his wedding, the woman on his arm looking fit to burst with pride as they cut their cake. She was wearing a headdress, a delicately layered wreath of green that rested on her head like an idol's crown. Oh god, were they laurel leaves? Thea paused, zoomed in. Exhaled. Yes, definitely laurel. Numb, she continued scrolling through the images. There were hundreds of them. His face was captured from every conceivable angle, and the reel of images was so complete and continuous that Thea felt he could see her. He was present in her room, looking down on her. Alive. There were endless references to the gas attacks, too. She tapped on an old bulletin from *London Daily*. The reporter's brisk, authoritative voice announced the completion of a major research project by Harvard University. It had concluded that exposure to hamilditiophosphate caused almost complete infertility in pubescent males. It cut to a campaigner arguing for nation states with stocks of tremor gas to surrender it for destruction, and another arguing that de-arming was the preserve of the weak and naive.

The bulletin ended, redirecting to *London Daily*'s homepage, where reports and analysis of the day's main and only news was writ large. Thea stared at the courthouse, front and centre. She'd been avoiding the trial since long before Billy Slade reached the dock, purposefully averting her eyes from any screen that showed his chiselled, sun-browned face. If she didn't see it, she wouldn't have to remember. FEB could stay where it belonged – in the past. Without thinking, she stabbed her finger into him, and the courtroom scene leapt onto the wall. Slade was wearing a navy suit and a clean white shirt, with two pens poking from his pocket, red and blue. His hair was neatly parted, yet he looked less sure of himself than she remembered. Dirtier. His eyes still had their urgent glint, but from behind his glasses, they appeared magnified into something that might have been bewilderment. His adam's apple bobbed in his throat. From time to time, he gripped the edge of the dock momentarily. Judge Lyons was addressing the room, admonishing Slade for his obstructiveness in the measured, authoritative way that had made her so famous and respected. She returned the floor to the UN prosecutor, who proceeded to talk about the executions, about how Slade had toured Britain's prisons on a loop, about his obsession with personally signing every order as though he wanted to keep score. In London alone, in four years, with tens of thousands of prison-based executions, Slade's signature was on all but a handful of orders.

But when asked about his guilt, again and again, he blamed his dead and absent comrades. He was only a passenger in the FEB Five – himself a prisoner. Those men made FEB into something that he'd never signed up for. He never saw it coming. They used him. If he'd not done what they wanted, then his own death would have followed. Wasn't it obvious? He didn't have a choice. Thea tensed against the bed, feeling pinned by his presence. As he spoke, his words were forced through gritted teeth. FEB wasn't in the past. Of course it wasn't. How stupid of her. She'd barely managed to pretend before.

They made us do it.
We only followed orders.
We had to protect our families.
Kill or be killed.

Slade was spouting the same thin excuses as the rest of Britain, rebounding his own shame and culpability onto everyone who'd survived. *Everyone.* In FEB, guilt went beyond pulling a trigger. It was not sharing food and ignoring the sirens. It was making sure you chanted louder than your neighbours at lesson-time, and tattling on a friend before they tattled on you. Had anyone but Thea truly believed what FEB told them? Did everyone follow orders? The blame was only bearable when you shifted it elsewhere.

She clambered onto the bed, wriggling beneath the covers and pulling the quilt up to her chin and around her body, gripping it in her fists. Kill or be killed. Betray or be betrayed. Sometimes even that was not enough. Slade's protestations mounted on her like boulders. What difference did choice make?

'I'm so sorry,' she whispered into her parents' pillows.

She wanted to scream it. Perhaps everything that had happened to Laurel was inevitable, born as she was to a mother like her. But – *oh* – how Thea loved her. How it hurt to love her. The courtroom continued to play, Judge Lyons insisting that Slade should answer the question, and Slade beginning another dogged rant. *Where was my choice? Show me your evidence!* Thea's vision centred on his lips as they moved. There was nothing like regret about the way he held his body. His hands were raised, but it wasn't in surrender. He was casting himself forward, towards the prosecutor, leering over him from his position on the stand and jabbing a finger until Lyons intervened again. A forgotten feeling struck at Thea's consciousness. The courthouse onlookers listened in eerie quiet. Slade didn't pause for any semblance of reflection. *Did Thea have a choice?* She dragged herself to sitting. She was shaking. Her head was filling with drawings of Laurel so vivid and complete that they must have come from somewhere. No. They weren't Laurel. They were real. Reflections, not drawings. Herself. It was Thea. She lunged towards the window, feeling the ice that held her memory shatter, covering her in glass-sharp, freezing shards. She looked down at the concrete square between the four towers, at the steps where they'd built the sundial gallows. She was eight years old again, in the warm shade, trembling. Sickness punched, doubling her over. She gripped the worm-eaten windowsill and howled.

The alarm sounds. Thea thinks that it's lunchtime. She drops her hoe in the allotment mud and runs back towards the Roundhouse. Her stomach is eating itself from the inside. She hopes there's bread today. When she reaches the square, the trestle tables are still flat-stacked beneath the tarps. No food is waiting. Instead, the towers have emptied and her neighbours wait around her, as confused as she is. Officials from FEB are on the steps they use as a stage, beside the A-frames. Nobody's speaking. She feels a fizz of fear. Her parents see her, and her mother waves, beckoning Thea through the crowd. Thea's eyes are still raw from a night of crying, her muscles stiff from trying to sleep on the bathroom floor. She can taste the stolen chicken on her tongue, rotten as though it had festered in the sun. She narrows her glare and stays where she is. The crowd shifts, and Thea gets a better look at the officials, realising they are nervous too. Beside them, she spots the man who has taken over the kitchens in preparation for the rally. He's furious. And then she sees them – the FEB Five already here.

Billy Slade, James Easton, Edward Wade, Eric Simmons, Carl Hamilton. They are watching quietly, but this isn't a celebration. The kitchen official begins shouting and pacing. A chicken has gone missing. A chicken! Stolen! Thea thinks that her heart has stopped.

Who took it?

He yells at the crowd and her stomach yanks to knots.

The thieves have taken from the people here to save them.

They've stolen from us all.

You see that, don't you?

Only traitors would steal from their country.

Only someone who didn't believe in Free and Equal.

Who hates our country?

Who wishes us all to failure?

Come, traitors. Answer your fate!

No one in the square dares to respond. No one moves. The official thwacks his cane on a railing by the steps. It smashes. Thea can hardly breathe through her terror. She tries not to think what the government will do to her. She's loyal to her country. She's loyal! She doesn't want this. She believes with all her might in Free and Equal. She feels a trickle of liquid down her thigh. What have her parents done? Bile climbs in her throat. The official is stamping down the steps, grabbing children by their wrists and biceps, wrenching them from their families into a line.

Have you eaten stolen chicken, boy? You look fatter than yesterday.

Purple-faced, he spits the words at the first child. In his neck, veins bulge and pulse like worms beneath his skin. The boy shakes his head, his skinny body convulsing. The official slaps his face and moves on to the next child.

Has your family thieved from their protectors, from FEB?

Have you deprived our nation of solidarity?

Are you a traitor? Tell me what you've done!

Thea chokes back a scream. I'm no traitor! Believe me! Her eyes cut across the square, finding her parents. They're rigid. The official stops at Thea. Her stare tears back to him. He curls his fingers around her throat, not tight enough to hurt, but it stops her moving. Her heart is exploding. She's dying! What would he do if he thought she was disloyal?

What about you, girl? Is your belly stuffed with chicken?

Through the corner of her eye, Thea sees her mother shifting. In her eyes, there's a desperate flame. Thea feels her hands crunching into fists. To have a stomach stuffed with chicken would have been a blessing, if it weren't at the price of her nation's liberation. If it weren't treason. Rage lashes through her. Her parents had told her the Liberation was everything. On the day of the election, they'd said FEB would save her future. What had changed? Didn't they love her enough to save her, any more? They didn't love FEB. That was for certain. They'd never have done this if they did. Beneath the man's tightening grasp, she gasps and wobbles. It's not possible for her heart to beat any faster. Is this what FEB meant when they told her that they were the only truly loyal ones? Her real family? She knows they're her duty as much as her protectors. They're the only ones who will ever really care. Her mind stings from trying to pick apart the reasons. The official shouts at her, threatening and cursing, and his spit lands in her eyes, on her cheeks, her lips. Her whole body burns with hunger and panic. She sees colours, and she knows she is crying. She can't stem it. If she tells the truth, it will prove that she's loyal. She'll secure her future. And officials have been known to raise rations for loyalty. They'll be happy with her. Proud. She'll be safe. They'll look after her. He'll not clench his fingers. He'll not stop her breathing. She'll not die.

She gasps again, and urine puddles around her sandals. He notices the liquid, and his pupils flicker. His fingers release, just slightly. Lowering his mouth to her ear, he asks again. Whispers.

Did your parents take the chicken, child? FEB has eyes, you know? We'll discover it.

Thea doesn't look to where her parents are standing. She drops her head and weeps the answer.

Yes.

20

Dom perched on the end of the hotel's bed, his heart thudding and heels jittering on the worn carpet. Maya slept soundly in the bassinet beneath the window, watery moonlight spilling onto her blankets through the split in the curtains. The bathroom door was ajar; he could hear the water running over Tess's body as she showered and smell the shampoo she was rubbing in her hair. The bedroom lights were dimmed, but the glow from Dom's projection cast the room in blue-tinged brightness. His brother's face was life-sized on the wall.

'It's Hamilton, isn't it?' Dom said, unable to keep quiet any longer. He studied Tim as he rewound the video, watching again and pausing it at the same point that Dom had paused too. Tim leaned in closer, squinting and pressing his fingers to his temples. Though Dom couldn't see Tim's screen, he recognised the moment when the unbelievable became true.

'Jesus, Dom,' he said. 'I think you're right.'

'The company makes fertility drugs.'

'You're kidding me.'

He shook his head. 'Nope. Hamilton's weapons made a

generation of British males infertile, and now he's cashing in. His bio says he's an expert in chemical warfare.'

'That's brazen.'

'It's madness.'

'And you think Hamilton's selling children too? Like Maya?'

'It's not inconceivable, is it? The man's proved he's a mercenary.'

'God knows.' Tim hesitated. Sasha's cat, Pirate, jumped to his lap, and he nudged the disgruntled moggy to the floor. 'I don't like this, Dom. Whatever you're on to, you know I'll help in any way I can, but I think you should get back to the US. We can talk about what to do when you're here. When you're safe.'

Dom stretched his arms above his head, slotting his fingers together and cracking his knuckles, resisting the urge to collapse back on the bed. The adrenaline that accompanied Hamilton's discovery had passed, and he felt exhausted. 'We can't leave. Maya's application isn't finalised. She doesn't have her visa.'

Tim dragged his hand though his hair. Dom knew what he was thinking. This was bigger than Maya.

'We're not leaving her, Tim,' he said. 'She's not safe either.'

His brother's frown intensified. 'Will you go to the embassy at least? Let me call them. I'll tell them you're coming.'

'No. We can't risk them stopping the adoption. We don't know what will happen to her if they do.'

'But the letter, Dom. That needs reporting.'

'To whom? For all we know, it came from the police.'

'But you can't ignore it.'

'I'm not. I'm going to find Garber. Talk to him.'

'Talk to the man who threatened you?'

'It might not be a threat. Thea thinks it could be a warning.'

'I'd be taking a warning from a dead man just as seriously as a threat.'

'I am taking it seriously.' Anger pierced Dom's exhaustion. 'It's my family, Tim. Don't you get it? I'm not letting Hamilton screw my family again.'

Across the room, Maya whimpered, stretching her own chubby arms above her head and kicking her blanket from her feet with a yawn. Tim slipped back in his seat and took his eyes to her, keeping them there as she resettled and sparing Dom the rebuke he deserved. Dom rubbed his face, watching her too.

'I'm sorry,' he said.

Tim gave a shrug, small but sodden with regret. 'I feel bad about Sash and Finn, Dom. You know that, don't you?'

Dom nodded, one shame unleashing the next. 'I'm sorry about that too,' he said. 'You shouldn't have to.'

He dragged his stare back to the projection. Tim looked as drained as Dom felt; not in the immediate, urgent way that the last few days had thrust upon him with their lack of sleep, anxiety over Maya and a mind that was raking through old memories incessantly, but in the way that had bludgeoned him too since seeing Hamilton. This was the type of tiredness that didn't end with sleeping. It hollowed him out to the marrow of his bones. The feeling wasn't new, however. He'd known it in some form for as long as he remembered. Most days, he could steel himself enough to stand upright – to go to work and chat and smile so that no one would notice his slow collapse inwards – but it emptied him to do it. Each day became harder. Today had been an onslaught. When he looked at his brother, it made his chest ache. Dom had tried to protect Tim, and he thought he'd managed it. He hadn't realised Tim felt the deep exhaustion too.

There was a pause, and Maya's snores steadied back into their regular rhythm.

'How are you going to find Garber?' Tim asked.

'Don't know.'

'Are you OK, Dom?'

Dom let out a long, ragged breath. What would his parents have done in his position? Would they have known what to do? 'Hamilton's been hiding in plain sight,' he said. 'I don't understand it. How have we been the first to see?'

'We're not the first,' said Tim. 'No way.'

'But who'd shield him? Who could possibly think he should be free and not in jail?'

Even before the words had left his lips, Dom knew he'd asked them with his heart, not his head. Tim gave him a look, one that walked the wire between sympathy and pity, confirming the same.

'You've no idea what deals he's made in the last fifteen years, Dom,' said Tim. 'Grateley Profiles might be covering for him, if he's making them credits. Or there could be some old FEB-era backer with a personal interest in keeping him out of the dock. It might be New-FEBers. Some of them have the funds to turn eyes elsewhere.'

Dom wrapped his arms around his body and tucked his hands beneath his arms. Periodically over the last decade or so, New-FEBers had poked their heads up from whatever dank hole they hid in – whenever a politician got caught doing something they shouldn't have done, or big business announced big profits – spouting their rot about the need for a return to FEB-principled governance, to give the masses back what was stolen from them and avoid a resurgent political class of self-interested elites. They were vile extremists, hell-bent on causing offence and disruption as much as anything else. The media – and Dom – had always dismissed them as a few inconsequential loons. They'd never come to power.

Yet 'never' in politics had been wrong so many times. A chill ran through him. The possibility that New-FEBers could be protecting Hamilton was terrifying, but less than a week in Britain had shown him how the conditions that incubated FEB were as prevalent as before. FEB's success was born from anger. They didn't storm the streets with weapons – not at first, at least – and in the run-up to the election, when it became apparent they were gaining momentum, the mainstream media had derided their supporters as nut-jobs too. The press told families like Dom's of FEB's appearance as though they'd sprung from nothing, like the Big Bang. Nothing, then a flashpoint, and then everything at once. But they hadn't, of course. Not anything like it. FEB candidates may not have previously held office, but they'd been there for years, in the towns where the factories had closed and the high streets had fallen into disrepair, and schools had struggled with overflowing classrooms, and the hospitals had no beds.

FEB had been present, building slowly, plucking up the politically homeless: those people ignored, disenfranchised and disillusioned, those who desperately wanted a job but couldn't find one, who didn't have the money for the bus fare to the interview, didn't have the money to buy their children breakfast, much less a degree or a down payment on a home. Westminster politicians didn't register their existence. They weren't worth considering, let alone helping. The value they added – their inherent worth – was nil.

For FEB, this made for easy pickings. They simply listened when no one else would. Hamilton and the FEB Five took the voters' fears and weaponised them. In debates, they rubbed salt into red-raw emotions, moralising their opponents' perceived shortcomings. They evoked idiocy and narcissism, not just differing opinions. They knew that FEB supporters were less concerned with ideological specifics than with flipping the finger to the status quo. Messages of injustice, churned out repeatedly, galvanised support in a way that traditional politicians' pleas to think of the economics never could. By twisting rage into moral indignation, FEB made it flammable. After decades of neglect, these people didn't have to be victims. They weren't powerless. They belonged to a crusade. FEB didn't destroy the pillars of British democracy. They were already crumbling. They simply nudged them over and crushed them to dust.

Dom only needed to look at Thea – the way she clenched her jaw, the way she watched him through the side of her eyes, the tension through her body as though at any second she might pounce – to see that anger and injustice ran as deep as they'd ever done. The thought that Hamilton was still out there, perhaps even biding his time to capitalise, was horrifying.

He stared at Tim, emotion backing up in his throat. 'Do you remember that night at the British Museum?' he asked. 'Mum and Dad took us. I don't know when exactly, but it was winter sometime, and I can't have been older than ten because we were both at the same school. Dad picked us up from the playground, and we met Mum at the tube. It must have been Tottenham Court Road. We had our sleeping bags and backpacks, and we went to see the displays first – the Anglo-Saxons it was, Mum's favourite – some new exhibit of their weapons, I think. We saw the Viking ship from Sutton Hoo, too, the burial boat. It smelled like mud and burning. And then we stayed when the museum shut. There were other families there, and we each picked a spot on the floor in this gigantic round hall, and the museum staff brought us hot chocolate, and a woman stood in the gallery and read us a bedtime story, and then we climbed onto these inflated mattresses they'd laid out and slept the night. I remember seeing the sky glowing through the windows in the ceiling, and the whispers all night and padded footsteps, and feeling so grown up and happy – and just being together. I'd forgotten it all, but Thea took me to the Archives, and I remembered. Every detail. It's in the old Reading Room. That was where we slept. It didn't look any different. The smell of it was the same too – the dust and the books. It was a good feeling, Tim. Remembering. It's been so long since remembering didn't feel like a sucker-punch that it caught me off guard, you know? Finding something happy in the middle of all this.'

A smile had cracked at the corner of Tim's mouth. 'I remember,' he said. 'Mum forgot her wash bag, right? In the morning her makeup was smudged so big and black around her eyes that we said she looked like she needed a trip on the burial ship too.'

Dom laughed. He waited as the memory's warmth lingered and left, feeling himself solidify in its wake. The sound of Tess's shower finished, and he heard her moving about the bathroom, clattering the glass panel aside and towelling off.

'I'm going to get him, Tim,' said Dom, staring at his brother.

Tim nodded. 'I'm already thinking about how we can do it. If Hamilton's in Colorado like it seems, there'll be FBI protocol and someone at the office who knows the best thing to do. I'll ask around.' He paused and glanced sideways, in the direction Dom knew to be the kitchen. Through the wall, Dom could make out the muffled joy of breakfast time; Sasha laughing, crockery chinking, Finn's lighthearted shriek and Katrina's singsong scold. Tim dropped his voice and shifted closer to the camera, the weight of his responsibility lining his face. 'I'm not sure how to play it, Dom. If someone's covering for Hamilton, it's going to be someone powerful. There's nothing to say the FBI *wants* to know about this. The worst thing that could happen is Hamilton getting word. I'm not going to lie, Dom. I'm scared.'

Dom shook his head. 'Don't tell work. You have to keep this to yourself.'

'Jesus. No. Don't be stupid. You've found Carl Hamilton.'

'You said it yourself; he wasn't lost. We can't tell anyone that we know where he is until we know who we can trust.' Until he could protect Maya too, Dom thought, but didn't say.

Tim was shaking his head now. 'And how are you going to find someone to trust, Dom? There's no way you're going to be able to do this on your own. How would you even begin? Let me help you.'

'I don't want your help, Tim. I don't want you to do a single thing that might endanger your children. You saw Garber's letter.'

'And I told you to report it – like we need to report this.'

'And we will, but not yet.'

Tim itched at his stubble. 'This is insane.'

'Do you promise?'

'But you don't know what you're doing.'

Dom looked at Maya starfishing in her bassinet. 'I might not know *how*, but I know that it's possible. I'm going to get Hamilton. I want him to answer for what he did . . . what he's still doing. You watch me, Tim. I'm going to put him in the dock.'

21

Thea staggered down the Roundhouse's dark stairwell, her feet tripping, hands grasping at the banister and great howls of grief bursting out. Tears were streaking down her face, blurring her vision, and the pressure in her head made it fit to explode. She tore around the corner and onto a new flight of stairs, slipping at the top step and landing painfully on her tailbone. She dragged herself up and smeared the tears and streaming snot across her face, holding out her shaking hands and staring at them as she sobbed, not knowing what to do with the glistening wet. She rubbed it on her top, panicking she couldn't dry it, then stumbled on downwards. Glancing back, a dim light flickered. There was nobody above her, but the noise in the black was louder than a riot. Every ghost of Thea, every version of herself that had needed to cry in the last fifteen years but couldn't, was hounding her down the stairwell, howling too.

On the ground floor she threw herself through the exit and into the empty, moonlit square between the towers of the Gritstone Estate. The night hit her skin, cool and moist, and she gasped, tumbling into it, desperate for air.

She hadn't known what would happen. She hadn't! She'd thought her parents would be punished – demoted from their privileges in the kitchen, maybe whipped or beaten – but she swore to the heavens that she hadn't known they'd die. If she had known, she would have stayed silent. Of course she would have. Wouldn't she? Another cry broke out. She had wanted them punished. Blood scorched beneath her skin. She was blistering on the inside. She'd been so afraid, so small and so stupid, and she understood suddenly why the word *grief* had always felt inadequate, so little as it was, too neat, contained and simple for feelings as boundless and engulfing. She had no right to grieve for her parents. The uneasy feeling that she'd carried without knowing where or how it had seeded, nor what it fed from and what it meant to grow into, had a name now. It wasn't grief. It was guilt. Betrayal.

She fell to her knees in the square – at the base of the concrete steps where the makeshift stage had been with its A-frame – where she'd stood in her own piss and gawped at the official as he held her by the throat. *Yes. They stole the chicken. They did it. Yes.* From the centre of a paving slab, a rose-gold disc glinted. She mewled and smeared her eyes again, trying to see the plaque more cleary, trying to focus on the crumbling ground at its edge. She rammed her fingernails into it, as if prising the metal up would somehow remove everything that had happened here. Erase the terrible thing that she had done. Her fingernails ripped, and she cried out in frustration, clawing harder and more frantically, seeing the pads of her finger turn red and slippery with blood. *Gritstone Estate,* it read. *182.*

'Thea?'

Her head snapped round. Springer was standing a few feet away.

'I killed them!' she cried, looking up at him.

He glanced towards the Roundhouse. She followed his eyes as they skimmed up the tower. A handful of windows were lit, and faces peered out. Springer took a step further away from her, as though the heat of her confession might burn. He was wearing tracksuit bottoms and a t-shirt with a hole above the seam, and trainers without socks. His buzz-cut scalp was shining in the moonlight. His expression hung somewhere between revulsion and fear.

She crawled towards him, skinning her knees on the rough ground. 'My parents,' she said. He flinched as she grabbed his trousers. 'That day, with the gallows. I said they'd done it. When the man asked, I said yes . . . Josh? It was me! Didn't you hear? Say something. I killed them.'

Springer leaned over, peeling Thea gently from his legs. 'I heard you, Thea,' he said. He was directing his face away from her, pointedly driving his eyes to where she wasn't. She wriggled beneath him, catching their line, wanting his reaction. Loathing? No, pity. She didn't deserve pity. Or was it something like confusion? A new realisation skewered her. Springer rubbed a hand to the back of his neck. He wasn't quiet and confused because he didn't believe her. He was quiet and confused because he already knew.

She fell back, releasing him. Of course Springer knew. He'd been there. She remembered. He had run from the allotments by her side when the alarm went, stood at her shoulder in the square. He couldn't understand why she didn't know too. A second realisation hit, another crippling stab of it. Her parents hadn't cooked a whole chicken. Nothing like it. Springer's mother and her own were best friends. They'd have shared it. There were probably others. Her eyes skidded back to the Roundhouse, to the lit windows that were growing in number. Their ogling inhabitants. Panic seized her. Everyone who lived in the Gritstone had been there. They'd all seen it. How had she blanked this, coloured it so black that she couldn't see the slightest glint? It was as bright as the sun now, every detail white-hot and burning. She looked at Springer, desperate.

He dragged his hands down his face and let out a sigh, kneeling beside her. His arms slipped beneath her body.

'You didn't snitch,' she whispered into his chest as he scooped her up.

He didn't answer, and in her mind's eye, Thea saw Springer with his mother and sister, huddled around a stove in the dark like her parents, as hungry and scared. She looped her hands around his neck, letting him carry her inside, out of view of the towers, up the stairs and along the corridor where they lived. The door to her apartment was ajar, and he nudged it further open and set her down inside. She leaned against him, feeling his warmth and the pulse of his heart through his t-shirt, willing him to bandage his arms about her body and stop her feeling of disintegration.

'What did I do, Springer?'

'You didn't know what would happen.'

'You did.'

She pressed herself harder into him, feeling her tears and the sticky stream from her nose soak into his clothes. He smelled of sleep and sweat, but against his chest she felt a wisp of relief. She missed her friend, perhaps not as he was now but as he had been then, the boy who was her protector despite what he knew of her, despite what she knew of him and could have done. She stared at his hands where they hung at his side, at his mother's gold ring where it was wedged above his knuckle.

'I'm scared, Springer,' she said.

'I'll help you, Thea.'

She could feel the tears stinging anew, threatening to spill again. 'I need Laurel, Springer. We need to be a family. I can't breathe without her.'

He nudged a hank of her hair from where it had fallen over her eyes and tucked it behind her ear, but she saw the slightest pinch of his lips and felt him tense. A bubble of frustration popped at the base of her stomach.

'What?' she asked.

'Nothing.'

'You don't think I can do it?'

'Do what?'

'Be a mother.'

'I never said that.'

Springer's face hardened, and Thea stepped away, ready to close the door on him and be alone, but he grabbed her wrist and pulled her back, planting his hot, wet mouth over hers. Their missing years flared, and his hand was on her spine, hauling her into him, and suddenly she realised. *You didn't know what would happen.* It wasn't a leap too far, was it? *You don't know what's good for you.* She drove her teeth into his lip and shoved him back.

'Hey! What are you doing, Thea?' He reached to his mouth, checking his fingers for blood and scowling at her.

'Oh, Springer. You bastard.' She wiped her mouth in disgust. 'You did it on purpose, didn't you?'

'I don't know what you're talking about.'

'Laurel. You saw what I did to my parents. You thought I wouldn't care for her.'

'Don't be ridiculous.'

'You don't trust me.'

'I'm looking out for you, Thea. Like I've always done.'

'Bullshit.' She spat the word across the corridor. 'You might have done once, but not any more. You track my watch. Follow me. You're a jailor, Springer, not a warden.'

Rage sparked in Springer's eyes, and he glared at her, dabbing at his lip and squaring up as though he expected her to shove him again, but Thea wasn't moving. She was looking towards him, but her eyes weren't seeing. She could hear that he was speaking, but not what he said. Instead, the courtroom scene she'd watched on the news earlier was swirling in her vision, reforming, replaying and crisping into focus. Her fury had been extinguished by a thought more important than anything Springer could say. *You're a jailor.* Slade had toured the jailhouses, hadn't he? He'd signed the death orders. The prosecutor in Thea's projection had said that, in London, Slade had approved nearly all the executions in person. Her heart pounded faster. *All but a handful.* Who approved the others? She snatched her keys from their hook and pushed past Springer. He called her name as she sprinted down the hallway. What if Slade hadn't been at Wormwood Scrubs to sign for Garber? What if Hamilton had signed the order instead?

22

The tap on the door was almost inaudible, but Dom was awake, and his mind was alight. He stiffened at the sound, his eyes darting through the black room and finding the sliver of yellow-grey light that ran beneath the wood. It came again, sounding more fingernails than knuckles. A shadow shifted, and he slid from the bed and across the room as quickly and quietly as his nerves would allow. It was hardly a knock. Far too late for housekeeping. Hamilton's men? Whoever wrote the letter? With his hand on the bolt to check it was fastened, he peered through the spy hole. Relief. Thea glared back.

'Get dressed,' she said as he opened the door.

'What's happened?'

She fixed her stare at him, hooking her lips above her teeth and hissing like a cat. From the bed came the rustle of linen as Tess wriggled and rolled away. Dom shot Thea a look and raised his hand in appeasement, then crept back into the room to grab his clothes from where he'd tossed them on the chair. He glanced at Maya in her bassinet. She snored on, oblivious. He pulled his jeans over his boxers and made for the exit.

Thea pointed at his satchel. 'You're going to need your screen.'

In the alley behind the Yeandle Hotel, Thea made for the bikes. There was one in the rack and one sprawled on the ground beside the bins. As she wrenched the upright one free and thrust it at Dom, he saw that the chain its owner had used to secure it had already been cut. It clanked against the railings.

Thea picked up her own bike and climbed on. Dom paused. 'You've stolen a baby, and you're worried about a bike?' she said.

She kicked off, accelerating up the alley and disappearing around the corner. Dom swallowed his misgivings and followed her. When he hit the main road, Thea was already a streak away, and he stood on the pedals and pumped his legs, feeling the lactic acid collect in his thighs. It was past 3 a.m., and the streets were deserted. He could hear the thump of blood in his ears, the rip of the air as he cut through it. At the junction, Thea bumped the kerb without slowing and skidded left. He chased her harder along the riverside, her dark hair loose and whipping in her wake.

'Where are we going?' he asked, breathless.

'You were right,' said Thea, not looking at him. 'The letter was a threat, not a warning.'

Dom's fingers clenched around the handlebars. He'd left Tess alone with Maya, without even a note to say where he'd gone, or when he'd be back. The hotel door should have locked automatically as he shut it. Did he check? When they stopped, he would message Tess and tell her to double-bolt it. Ask her not to leave the room.

He rammed the feeling of dread from his mind. 'How do you know?'

'Garber's working with Hamilton.'

'You're sure of it?'

'I will be.'

She sped beneath the end of a bridge as it spanned the Thames, then down a ramp that led to an underpass. Dom followed, squinting in the surge of harsh electric light. The underpass stank of urine, synth smoke and liquor, and bundles of puffed-up sleeping bags lined the base of the walls like giant grubs. By the time they emerged from the long, snaking tunnel, he had lost his bearings. He could no longer see the river but felt sure they couldn't have passed beneath it. They were somewhere residential, weaving through rundown streets of low-rise blocks and shoulder-to-shoulder houses. Thea slowed and pulled into the garden of a narrow, single-storey terrace. She dropped her bike on the neatly trimmed grass and darted to the window at the front of the house. Dom hung back, watching her tap the glass, his chest heaving. A face appeared at the edge of a curtain, scared at first, then awash with relief. She gestured something that might have been *hang on,* then hurried away. The door opened.

'What are you doing here?' said Jemima as she ushered them inside. She cast an anxious look along the street then closed the door, turned the key hurriedly and tucked it into the pocket of her pink nightdress. She pulled Thea into the living room. The women lowered themselves to the sofa, their hands knotted together, knees touching and faces close. Dom stood in the doorway, unsure of what to do.

'We need to see Garber's execution record,' Thea told Jemima. 'I watched a news report today that said Billy Slade made a point of approving almost every order made under FEB, especially in London. Garber's docket said that he was held at Wormwood Scrubs. We need to find out who signed off his death.'

'You think it was Slade?'

'I think it was Hamilton. I reckon he was one of the few that Slade didn't touch. They made a deal, Mima. I know it. There was something the professor said or did, or something Hamilton wanted, that made him spare his life.'

At the room's threshold, Dom tensed. 'Control,' he said quietly.

Thea and Jemima looked up, confused, as though remembering he was there.

'Control,' he said again, the thought solidifying in his mind. 'Hamilton was obsessed with it. He understood how to build a weapon better than anyone FEB had, but a regime needs more than force to keep power. Garber was a world leader in behavioural economics. He understood *people*. He'd have known what to say to the masses to tap into their fears, to keep them afraid and docile and compliant when FEB wanted, and how to summon their rage if they needed that too. He'd have known how and when to intimidate without using chemicals. He'd have known the ways in which people react under pressure, how they'd run and how to trap them.'

He shivered and leaned against the doorframe, believing Thea's theory and its reasons fully as he spoke them. Memories of the lengths to which FEB went in the name of control came rushing back. Jemima gave him a sympathetic, pinched-lip smile and shuffled up the sofa, making space for him. He slipped into the living room and sat beside her. She patted his knee. Thea met his eye – he felt himself measured – before she returned her attention to her friend.

'Do you know anyone who can help us, Mima?' she said. 'How can we find out?'

'Can't we check the Archives?' asked Dom.

Jemima shook her head. 'The Archives won't give you everything, Dominic. They'll tell you who's dead and maybe how it happened, but they won't ever tell you who did it. The names of anyone who gave an instruction, made an arrest or fired a bullet on FEB's watch aren't kept on those files. The government says it's so that future trials can run without prejudice, but honestly . . . Can you imagine what would happen if that information was available to the public? One trial is all they've managed in fifteen years. If folks had names, they wouldn't wait.'

Jemima's hand tightened around Thea's. She rubbed Thea's knuckles with her thumb, and Thea wriggled, frowning. Dom felt the weight of something unsaid.

'So why are we here?' he asked.

'I worked in Whitehall during FEB,' said Jemima. 'I know my way around the records. Chances are I typed the things you need to know into those computers myself.'

'And you still have access?'

'Heavens, no.' She turned to Thea. 'I'm sorry, sweet pea, and I don't know anyone who works there now. It's been far too long. I'm sure the information's logged, but I can't get you in.'

Thea sagged into the sofa, wincing. Dom felt it too; the pummel of repeatedly running into dead ends. He licked his lips. His mouth was drying. The conversation he'd had with Tim swilled through his consciousness. Dom was going to put Hamilton in the dock, like Slade was. Tim was right, at least in part; crimes against humanity was more than enough to do it. Dom didn't need to put himself and his fledgling family in more danger than he'd already done, albeit accidentally. All he really needed to do was tell someone in power, someone trustworthy, that he'd found him, and they'd do the rest. Tim could help with that, if only Dom would let him. Any crimes involving the children would stop by default. Yet what Dom had not been able to articulate to himself was that he didn't really *need* to do it. Looking at Thea, his understanding crystallised. He *wanted* this etched on Hamilton's record. He wanted history to register the full extent of Hamilton's depravity. He wanted everyone who helped him to be stopped from causing misery. They had to answer. He paused. Wet his lips again. Considered it. But could he break the law to do it? Both the UK and US governments had imprisoned people for much less.

'I might be able to do it,' he said.

Thea sat upright. 'Do what?'

'Get you into the system that holds whatever information you need.'

They stared at him.

'I work in data security for the US government. Tech infrastructure. I run teams that design and build computer systems for countries affected by the Zero Virus. We test them for weaknesses. Places they might break.'

Thea's eyes widened. 'You're a hacker.'

'No. I manage risk.'

He pulled out his screen and unlocked it, focusing on the prize of Hamilton and his family's safety, not on what he planned to do. He passed the screen to Jemima. 'Which ministry would hold the records? Can you find it for me?'

She nodded, and her wrinkled hands sped across the screen, pulling up a page for the Ministry of Justice, then handing the screen back. It wasn't a glossy, public-facing page, but rather a grey window that was blank except for the ministry's name, logo and a retina-scan login box.

'They'll be somewhere in here,' she said.

Dom looked at the top corner of the screen, noting with grim satisfaction the familiar padlock icon. USAID SECURED was watermarked across its centre. The British government was running GoldLock 6.1. It was an outdated version of a security software he'd worked on, and one he knew the Americans had pulled and replaced when flaws were found. The UK probably hadn't had the budget to upgrade. He opened a new window, calling up Exploit Database, a publicly available archive that had caused him more than a handful of headaches over the years for listing every known vulnerability for every known security software application in the modern world. The operators argued it helped engineers to harden their systems, but it was a hacker's dream. He tapped *GoldLock 6.1* into the search bar, locating the description of its error-riddled code and the instructions on how to break in. He checked them twice, working slowly and carefully, and his heart skipped as the system let him in. In less than a minute, he'd navigated his way to GoldLock, creating himself a new profile with full administrative rights. He gave the screen to Jemima again and wiped his damp palms down the leg of his trousers, exhaling.

Jemima gave a determined nod, opening a menu and swiping swiftly, flitting through options she clearly knew. She found the archive she was looking for, typing *Levi Matthew Zachary Garber* into the search. The summary information they'd already seen from the Archive came up, alongside a mugshot of the young, skinny man that Dominic had seen in photographs at the UCL office. Beneath that, there was a scan of a handwritten form. Jemima scrolled past the details they knew, beyond the boxes for *Next of kin* and *Address* that had been left blank.

'Thea.' Jemima pointed at the name that was scribbled but clearly legible. 'Look! You were right.'

Thea nodded. Like Dom, she already knew. Carl Hamilton.

Jemima glanced between them. 'What now?'

Dom was already capturing a screenshot, saving it and swiping away, navigating through the back channels of the British government's records, using his new privileges to sidestep the mesh. 'Now we follow the only link we have between Garber and Hamilton,' he said. 'Grateley Profiles might be registered in the US, but it looked big, didn't it? Global, maybe. Hamilton and Garber are both British. It's not unlikely that it's registered here too, or at least has a presence. Where should I start, Jemima?'

'Revenue and Customs. Tax records.'

'What are you looking for?' said Thea.

'Inspiration,' Dom replied.

He found his way into Revenue and Customs and

tapped the company's name into the search. The system listed four files: three years of tax returns and a document titled 'Organisation Overview'. Dom opened it, seeing the UK contact details for Grateley Profiles at the top of the page. The registered address was in Kensington, London.

'Is it an office?' asked Thea, reading over his shoulder.

'Don't know. Maybe.'

Jemima slapped her knees and heaved herself up suddenly.

'What are you doing?' asked Thea, as Jemima marched towards the bedroom.

'I'm going to get ready,' Jemima replied, without looking back at them. 'You can piss off if you think you're going anywhere without me.'

23

The address in Kensington wasn't an office. Thea stood on the pavement between Dom and Jemima, halfway along the broad, sleeping residential street that was St George Court. Opposite them, the first wisps of an apricot dawn touched the rooftops above a vast, white townhouse. The early morning air was cool and damp, and she caught herself shivering. Curtains were drawn at each of the enormous bay windows, and the sycamores that lined the road were reflected in the glass, their leaves shivering too. Thea drove her hands to the bottom of her pockets. She couldn't have been more than a mile or two from the Roundhouse, but she'd never been to this part of the city. She had known that it was here, that houses like this existed, but only in the way she knew that foreign countries existed: sprawling, soft-sand beaches, snow-capped mountains, pyramids filled with gold. They were there, but not for people like her. As the sun strained higher and the sky's colours intensified, the shadow cast by the townhouse's wrought-iron railing shifted. The quiet pulled at her, strong, steady and unnerving, like an ocean retreating before the wave.

'What now?' asked Dom. His voice was a whisper, as if he was afraid he might wake someone.

Thea didn't know. Momentum had carried them here, not rational thought. They had come because they could, and because there was nowhere else left to go. They hadn't paused to think what they might find, or what they should do.

'We could knock,' said Jemima. It was more a question than a statement of fact.

'But we don't know who's inside,' Thea replied. We don't know how this will take us to Laurel, she wanted to say.

Silence resettled, and she peered harder at the house, watching a trail of weak white steam escape from a ventilation flue and dissipate into the air. A security camera was positioned underneath the eaves. It pointed at the doorway, where bushes trimmed to perfect orbs flanked the blue-tiled steps. Through an open window a few houses down, she could hear a crying baby. The sound faded, and doubt crept over her. Someone had swept that child up. Rocked it. Fed it. Loved it. She imagined a bedroom filled with toys and books and happiness. Thea had said to Jemima that adoption was moving a baby from a poor parent to a rich one, as though that was something terrible. Yet now she was here, she felt small and dirty and worthless. She picked at the crud at the base of her pocket. Was Laurel living on a street like this one? Did someone love her? Would they give her the things that Thea could not? She would have lost her job at the Oakwood Hotel, for certain. She'd not even thought of work for three full days, let alone shown up. Chef would be livid. Perhaps

Springer was right. Perhaps they all were. An image of her parents flitted through her consciousness. She couldn't be trusted. She wasn't responsible. Disappointment sat like a rock in her gut.

She turned to Dom. 'What will you do?' she asked him.

'What do you mean?'

'Afterwards,' she said. 'When we don't have anywhere else to look.'

He fiddled with a button on his jacket. 'There will only be an afterwards when we've answered everything. As long as there are questions, there are places to look.'

'The baby—' She winced and forced the words out. 'Your baby . . . Will you try and find her family?'

His expression was serious. 'Yes. I won't destroy a family like Hamilton and FEB destroyed mine.'

'But what if her mother was like me? You could give her a better life.'

'Wealth doesn't trump love.'

'You don't love her?'

'If we have the right to do so, Tess and I will love Maya with everything we have.' He paused, and when he spoke again, she heard a crack in his voice. 'But if she has a mother anything like you, they deserve to be together. Look at what you've done.'

Thea stared at her feet, feeling as though the lump in her throat might choke her. She wanted to tell him what she'd done, and to tell Jemima, to confess like she'd done to Springer and have them see her for who she truly was. Guilt chipped at her insides. 'I'm sorry I said you stole her,' she said. 'And I'm sorry about your parents.'

Dom gave her a small, warm smile. 'Thank you for coming to get me, and for telling me about Garber. You didn't have to.'

She didn't answer.

'What about you?' he asked. 'What will you do when there are no more questions?'

'Leave,' said Thea.

'I left. It doesn't work like you think it will.'

Jemima looped her arm around Thea's shoulders, pulling her in and planting a kiss on her forehead.

'She's not leaving,' she said. 'She's going to be an artist. You've seen what she can do, haven't you? She's going to put that ridiculous talent of hers to use, draw her pictures and sell them for millions of credits, and end up with a house on a street like this.'

Thea pressed her eyes shut. 'Don't, Mima. Please.'

'Don't *you*, Theodora. Why do you think I've helped you for all these years? I've always known you were a fierce one. The first day you turned up at the Archives, it was written all over you. You were used to doing things for yourself, like me. Heaven knows the world isn't short of a lonely soul, but you were different, too. You might not have known where you were going or how you were going to get there, but you marched into that room like they'd built it just for you. You'd have burnt the museum to cinders before you'd give up. And the hours you've put in there? I've never seen drive like it. I knew if I could only help you find something better to channel all that smartness and stubbornness into than the past, then you'd see that you're brilliant. It's why I gave you all those books about goodness knows what and his buddy. I didn't realise you already had something you loved. We could have saved some time.'

She smiled again and squeezed Thea tighter, casting a look to the house across the street.

'Dominic's right,' she said. 'Look at what you've done. Look at where that clever head of yours and that fire has brought us. When my Joe died, I wanted them to bury me with him. It took me years to feel like I could do anything again. Be anything. You're made of something I always wished for, Thea. It's special. I feel like I can do better when I'm with you. You know what you want, and you deserve to have it, sweet pea. Please don't give up.'

Jemima hugged Thea harder, and Thea felt the tears backing up behind her eyes. She didn't want to give up. She wanted to be trustworthy and responsible and smart and successful and everything that she wasn't but Jemima thought she was. More than anything, she wanted her baby. She wanted to protect Laurel like she hadn't managed for her parents. She couldn't do it, though, could she? She might have brought them to this street, but it hadn't fixed anything. It was chasing shadows. She looked at the townhouse beyond her friend's shoulder. In a downstairs window, a curtain was twitching. A thud followed, and one of the sash's panes slid up. The trees' reflections disappeared, and the sound of a radio drifted out; and Thea saw the face as the face saw her too.

She leapt from Jemima's embrace, disbelieving. The beard was thicker and whiter than in the photographs at his office, and his skin was darker and more weathered than she'd seen it on Dom's screen. Still, it was Garber. She was positive.

Garber hesitated, his surprise evident as he examined the three of them watching the house from the semi-lit dawn. Then, as if someone had spoken to him, he glanced behind and disappeared from sight.

Thea's heart skipped. Before her mind had engaged a thought, her feet were sprinting across the road. Dom and Jemima were chasing her, hissing whispered warnings as she rammed open the townhouse's gate and bounded up the steps, all traces of doubt abandoned behind. Garber was here. Garber, who knew what happened. Who was part of it! He would take her to Laurel. She'd make him do it. She wouldn't let him go until he did.

At the top of the tiled staircase, Dom caught her wrist and pulled her back, but not before she'd slammed the knocker against the polished black door. It opened instantly.

'You need to leave,' said Garber. He glowered past her, jabbing a finger at Dom, then fired his eyes furiously up and down the street. He was wearing a dressing gown, grey pyjamas and slippers. There were crumbs of bread on his fleecy lapel.

Thea ripped herself free of Dom's grasp and shoved past Garber, throwing him against the doorframe. She cast a desperate look around the hallway, as if expecting to see Laurel. 'Where's my daughter?'

Garber yanked himself upright. 'You're a bloody fool, Mr Nowell,' he said, the tendons in his neck straining. 'I told you to drop it.'

'You threatened my family.'

'And you should have listened.' An overfed Siamese cat scurried down the staircase, skidding on the creamy marble floor as it reached the bottom, then it rounded the corner and disappeared from sight. Garber dropped his voice and bared his teeth at Thea. '*Get her out.*'

Dom didn't move. Thea stepped back, further into the belly of the house and towards the kitchen into which the cat had fled. The rage on Garber's face intensified. He stamped after her but he was old and gaunt, and she was ready to tear his skin off, to claw out whatever information was hidden inside. Through the corner of her eye, she saw an apple on the countertop, sliced through its core. She snatched up the knife beside it, brandishing the blade at him. It was no longer than her littlest finger, but it looked as sharp as broken glass.

Garber stopped dead. Dom and Jemima reared up behind him, their faces panicked.

'Tell me where she is,' Thea said.

Garber lowered his voice further. It was so quiet that she could barely hear him.

'Look,' he said, opening his palms and speaking to her as though she were a child. 'Even if I knew who you were, and even if I knew who your daughter was, I couldn't tell you *where* she was. There must be more than forty thousand adopted kids on the Ministry of Children's post-FEB records.'

Thea tightened her grip on the knife's handle. 'But you knew what I was talking about, didn't you? When I asked about my daughter. You know she'd been stolen. *You* stole her. She was at Little Doves Children's Home. In Lambeth. Where have you taken her?'

Garber shook his head and took a step forward. 'You need to leave.'

'Not without Laurel.'

'I'll call the police.'

'Bullshit.'

'Put the knife down.'

'We know you work for Carl Hamilton. For FEB.'

'For God's sake, keep your voice down.'

'Give my daughter back, you thief!'

Garber growled and lunged at Thea, reaching for the knife and snatching her wrist with unexpected speed and strength. Thea kicked his shins, trying in vain to wrench herself free or turn the blade on him. Dom burst forward, ramming an arm between Thea and Garber and forcing his body between them like a crowbar, prising them apart. Jemima's arms were around Thea's waist, heaving at her, twisting, pleading as she did it, and trying to drag her towards the door.

The flash of light came before the sound. There was a sudden thrust of weight, Thea's legs buckled, and terror surged as she fell to the ground. She shrieked and thrashed, shoving at the mass that was crushing her, realising as she did that it was Jemima. Her friend thudded onto the marble, and Thea scrambled back. The old woman's eyes stared at her, wide but sightless. Blood pulsed from the wound in her forehead, pooling on the floor and shimmering in the sunlight that spilled through the open door. Thea looked up, unable to breathe, seeing the masked, black-clad figure as it bound down the staircase and turned the gun on Dom.

'Dom!'

The flash came again, accompanied by a blunt, semi-muffled sound that she wouldn't have recognised if she hadn't seen its origin. Dom lurched towards the door, and the bullet missed him, splintering into the wall. He ducked and flinched away from the impact, hesitating just long enough for the gunman to catch hold of his shirt. He wrenched Dom back, raising a thick arm into the air and bringing the gun-barrel down hard on the back of Dom's skull. Dom collapsed in the doorway, and Thea scrambled over him, her ankle tangling on the strap of his satchel. The gunman grabbed her hair, and she thrashed against him, struggling to free herself of the bag-strap. As she kicked, she caught the gun with her foot. It skittered across the floor, and the gunman released her, scrambling after it. She clambered over Dom's limp body and through the door, tripping on the top step, thumping down the tiles and smacking her head on the railings. She hauled herself up and looked towards the house, dizzy. The gunman was standing over Dom as he returned to semi-consciousness. Dom looked directly at her for a heartbeat then grabbed the man and pulled him down. They struggled on the floor, grunting and writhing before the third bang came. Thea shrieked, scrambling to get away from them, looking over her shoulder. The gunman stood up and fixed his cold stare on her. She threw open the gate, and ran and ran and ran.

24

Thea sprinted through the London streets, not daring to look behind. With blood thudding in her ears, her lungs searing and the rising sun in her eyes, she ran without any conscious thought to direction; away from Jemima and Dom's lifeless bodies, away from the Kensington house with its dawn-tinged frontage, away from the sneer of the bearded professor, away from the muffled crack of suppressed gunshots, towards the blinding light as it splintered in her vision, towards the white-hot promise of oblivion, towards anywhere that wasn't *here*. They'd only been on that road because Thea had found it. They'd only been inside the house because Thea charged in. Around her, the city was waking. An increasing number of cars, buses and bicycles threaded along the tarmac, but the pavements were still comparatively empty. She tore down them unhindered, spotting a glint of the river between two buildings and turning towards it. At the end of the alley, the sky opened above her, watery blue but bright and cloudless. She gasped as the breeze hit her, then slowed and staggered across the Victoria Embankment. The Thames was high against its limits, the scent of it oily, salty and animal, and she clambered to the top of the wall and wrapped her arms around the lamppost, peering down into the familiar green-grey murk. Could a jump from here be lethal? The water would be shallow by comparison to the centre of the river, and she was hardly high to start with, but if she threw herself with enough determination the mud might grab her legs and drag her down. She didn't want to die, but the pain was unbearable. She wanted Laurel – and her parents and Jemima. The years were pushing into her, forcing her forward. On her cheek, the metal lamppost felt icy. She peeled her body back from it. How simple it would make things if the wind blew her over. The relief she would feel to just disappear.

'Are you OK?'

A voice sounded and Thea slipped as she turned, crashing from the wall to the pavement, scraping herself on the rough brick. She scrambled up, and the expression of the teenage boy who was watching her changed from concern to terror. He leapt back, his hands up in surrender, and Thea realised that she still had the knife from Garber's kitchen. She was holding it at hip-height, gripping the handle so hard that her hand hurt, and directing the blade at the boy's stomach. He was stiff with fear, and she stumbled backwards, pinning him in her sight for as long as she could before doubling back across the road and throwing herself into the alleyway. She slumped behind the bins. Jemima's blood covered her t-shirt and the bare skin of her arms. She rubbed at it furiously, trying to scrape the red away. Her fingers turned pink at their tips. Was the colour real? Her vision was clouding. The alley slipped from focus. Thoughts slurred into one another. Jemima.

Her fault. Oh god, her friend's scream. She opened her mouth to scream too, but her breath was too deep and fast and ragged. Instead, she collapsed, her head cracking against the floor. The boy from the riverbank was peering into the alley but apparently not seeing her. Thea wanted to call out, to wave him over and beg – *please, please help me* – but her limbs were leaden and she couldn't raise a sound. The boy looked Asian, like Dom's wife. Dom's widow. He raised a hand to shield his eyes but still couldn't find her, then glanced behind and walked reluctantly away.

Pain surged in Thea's head, and she squeezed her eyes shut. She needed someone to find her. To fix this. She'd left them! The vomit came without warning, doubling her like an uppercut before she could stop it. She retched again, trying to scramble to her knees but shaking too violently. There was a thud as something fell from her back, tipping her off balance, and she leaned against the bins and wiped her chin on the bone of her wrist, staring at Dom's satchel where it lay on the floor. It had been around her ankle when she tried to clamber over him. When the man had hold of her. She must have snatched it up.

She wiped aside her sticky hair and threw the bag open, wrenching out Dom's screen and unrolling it, pressing the button on the top edge, holding her breath. It lit, and she hammered in the same passcode that she'd watched Dom enter twice before. At Jemima's house, he'd hacked the government's system with ease. Effortlessly, he had slipped from the Ministry of Justice to the Ministry of Commerce, found Garber's records and then Grateley Profiles. The professor's voice sizzled in Thea's mind. Dom said that everything the government did was linked. It all webbed together behind the wall. If that was true, how hard would it be for Thea to slide sideways again, like he'd done? If she could navigate to the Ministry of Children, she could pull up the adoption records. She could narrow them down. Trace Laurel. Opportunity fired through her. She was halfway there already. Dom had already broken her in.

The passcode worked, and Dom's home screen loaded, flooding instantly with messages from his wife. Thea swiped them aside and opened the Internet, adrenaline spurring her on as she saw Grateley Profiles' tax record reload, just as they had left it. Copying Dom, she tapped to the corner of the screen, trying to call up the menu that would act as her map. Instead the page went blank. *Your session has timed out. Please login to continue.* A retina scan window sat beneath the text.

She dropped the screen in her lap, feeling sick and stupid. It was a ridiculous idea anyway. Garber had said there were forty thousand adoption records. Even if by some miracle she'd found her way into them, Laurel wouldn't be called Laurel. Even if only a fraction of those forty thousand children were stolen, how would she know where to start? Even if she uncovered the list, sorted the children by age, date and gender, it could still mean she was looking at thousands of names. Then what? Would she write to every adoptive family? Save or steal a lifetime's worth of credits and travel the world to knock on every door? In the distance a wail of sirens sounded. Police cars. She couldn't tell the police. She couldn't tell anyone. What would she say? Where was the start of her story? There were too many moments of her own culpability that made it impossible, and whatever she did, Garber would be on her: Garber, Hamilton and the man with the gun.

The realisation drove itself into her, one needle at a time until her body was hot and stinging with truth. If Laurel was even alive, Thea wouldn't find her. How many years already had she spent looking for her parents' killer at the Archives? Here was a task as big. Bigger. Laurel would grow, change and have no memory of her mother. No reason to look back. Already Thea's mind was forgetting her child's details too. Laurel had smelled of talcum powder, but so had every baby at Little Doves. Her lips were pink and plump and steep in the middle, but how many children had mouths the same as that? The thought of not knowing Laurel split Thea in two. She fumbled into her pocket, wanting to look at the drawings of her daughter – to remember – but her notebook was gone. A sob built at the back of her throat. Jemima had tried to warn Thea against the pain of looking. She'd said it about the Archive, about the endless hours that Thea had spent scrolling, opening photographs, failing and reopening. It was a gentle steer, not judgement, and her words were laced with kindness. She'd phrase it as a question sometimes. After today, Thea knew she was asking the same for Laurel. *Thea. Sweet pea. Don't you think it's time to stop?*

She wrapped her arms around her body, wishing Jemima were there to hug her instead. Hope of finding Laurel had been holding her together. It had bound itself with her fear of what would happen if she didn't, and they'd drawn their wires through her, pulling her taut and yanking her upright. Without them, the grief was crippling. She had tried so hard to save her baby. To do right by her family. Somewhere in her heart Laurel would know that, wouldn't she? Thea hadn't abandoned her. She had done all she could.

In her lap Dom's screen vibrated, and Thea dragged the tears from her eyes with her fingertips and looked down, seeing another message appear from Dom's wife. *Dom, for fuck's sake, where are you?* A new wave of guilt hit. She pressed herself harder against the wall, bracing against the pain in her head, her legs and chest. If Dom hadn't come to at that instant, the gunman would have caught her. He would have been on her, right at her heels. She would never have escaped. Sprawled on the floor, Dom had looked directly at her, gifting her a precious few seconds. He'd done it without thinking, helping instinctively. Her lip trembled. He would have made a good father. She forced her fingers to move across the screen, one after the other, scrolling through Dom's contacts and finding who she wanted. Perhaps wherever Laurel was, someone like Dominic Nowell was with her. When Laurel was older, would whoever it was tell her where she'd come from? Not the truth, perhaps, but the version he knew of it. Thea hoped that if he did, he would say that her mother was dead.

You are loved, Thea said in her head. The screen flashed. She'd done it. She was calling.

She tried to summon her courage, and waited. She didn't want to do it, but she knew he owed him. Dom had saved her. Thea gripped the screen harder, her whole body trembling. Contessa Nowell answered and looked at her in horror. She was clutching the baby.

'I'm sorry,' said Thea. 'I'm so sorry. He's dead.'

25

The pain made Dom's eyes leap open. A hand clamped over his mouth, stifling any noise he might have made, and Garber's face loomed through the grey of his vision. He was staring down with panicked, pleading eyes.

'Shhhhhh!' he said. 'You're OK. For goodness' sake, be still.'

Dom tried to sit up, but the floor pitched, and his head thumped back onto the marble. At the entrance to the kitchen, Jemima was slumped in a motionless heap. She had her back to Dom, and there was a dent in her skull; a deep and rugged divot rimmed in bright white bone. Soft, exploded pinkness gummed her matted, bloodied hair. Horror overtook pain, and Dom tried to roll away from her – to stand and escape her – but Garber had straddled him, pinning him down. The professor was thirty years or more older than Dom, skinny and slight. On another day, Dom would have overpowered him with ease, but shock had winded him and his head was spinning, and though he struggled, he couldn't break free. There was a gush of cold liquid on his shoulder and a fresh blast of agony, and Dom rammed his knuckles into his mouth, biting down and crying into them. Garber waited for the worst of the wave to subside then peeled himself from Dom and slumped down. An empty vodka bottle hung in his hand.

'I've done what I can to clean the wound, but you're still bleeding,' he said. He wiped his face on the sleeve of his dressing gown and glanced at the bottle as though he regretted not saving some, then dragged Dom to a sitting position and propped him against the wall. 'We need to tie it off.'

Dom looked at his shoulder, at the tattered hole in his blood- and liquor-soaked shirt. Garber knelt at his side and tore the hole bigger.

'I'm going to be sick,' Dom muttered, seeing his gashed flesh beneath it.

'You're going to be fine,' replied Garber. He split Dom's shirt across his body, ripping free a section, balling the cotton and stuffing it inside the wound. Dom's vision blanched, and he bucked against the pressure, moaning as Garber held the makeshift plug in place and looped another thick ribbon of shirt around Dom's shoulder to secure it. He removed his dressing gown and snatched off his own t-shirt, manoeuvring it over Dom's head and navigating his arms into place before yanking the rope from the gown's waist and doubling it around Dom's wrist and neck to make a sling. He paused, skidding across the hallway on his knees, slipping through Dom's blood and teasing aside the curtain, peering through the thin glass panel beside the front door. 'You have to get away from here.'

Dom's mind swam. 'I can't move,' he said. His voice was more breath than words. 'I need a doctor.'

'No, you need to disappear. Find a doctor later if you must, but it isn't necessary. Once you've got your mind steady, you'll see you're alright. It's only pain. The bullet was a clean in-and-out, and the bleeding will stop soon enough. It missed everything that matters.'

Vomit surged in Dom's throat. 'How do you know?'

'You'd be dead if it hadn't. Now get up. It's time to leave.'

Garber pulled at Dom's uninjured arm, towing him to standing. The hallway spun, and Dom stumbled, hitting the wall. Garber gripped him by the elbow, holding him up and steering him towards the kitchen. Jemima watched with glassy eyes.

'Why didn't he kill me?' Dom asked, unable to pull his stare from her.

'He thinks he did,' said Garber. 'I told him the shot had landed, and he didn't look back. He was chasing your friend.'

Thea. 'Where is she?'

Garber shook his head. 'Gone. She might have escaped. I don't know.'

He pulled Dom into the kitchen and opened a cupboard, clattering to the back of it and seizing a medicine jar. He unscrewed the lid and shook three white pills into his palm.

'Here,' he said, stuffing them at Dom. 'These are for the pain. You need to hurry. Go.'

Dom collapsed against the countertop, staring at the tablets in his hand. His mind was thick and slow with fog. 'But you sent me the letter?'

'And I wish you'd bloody listened.' Across the room

Garber was fumbling at the bolts on the back door with his blood-slicked hands. He rammed the door open and looked at Dom expectantly. The cool morning air washed in. 'He's not going to be happy with either of us now.'

'He? Who's *he*?' said Dom.

'Carl Hamilton.'

The name pierced through Dom as painfully as the bullet had done. They'd been right. 'You work for Hamilton,' he said. It wasn't a question. He knew the answer.

Garber's face puckered. 'Not through choice, Dominic. Of course, not through choice.'

Dom's thoughts darkened. He stuffed the pills into his mouth and squeezed them down his throat, shoving himself up from the counter and lumbering towards Garber. 'But you chose to make a deal with him, didn't you? He spared your life and you told him how to invade people's minds. You chose to help him control hundreds of thousands of innocent Britons. You helped him kill them.'

Garber fired him a cauterising look. 'I *saved* lives. It's well known that FEB's use of chemical weapons decreased the longer they stayed in power. Who do you think deserves credit for that? I gave FEB ways to keep control without using violence.'

'Bullshit. You helped hold FEB together, helped prolong the suffering. How can you pretend otherwise?'

Garber jabbed a finger at him. 'I know better than you what I did, young man. Yes, I bartered my expertise for my continued existence. I'm not proud of what followed, and I could tell you now that I didn't know what I'd be asked to do or what it would lead to, and that my ignorance should somehow absolve my involvement, but the truth is that I didn't care what would happen to anyone else. I didn't consider it. All I knew was that I didn't want to die. Later – when my chances came – I did what I could to rein FEB in.'

Dom glared at him. 'But you still work for Hamilton. He's funding your research.'

'The past is a hard dog to shake off.'

Dom snorted, throwing his eyes around the gleaming kitchen. 'You don't look like you've tried.'

'Hamilton had me trapped long before he put me in this house. He killed me once when it was convenient, and he brought me back to life when he knew I might still be useful, but he wouldn't have had any trouble finishing me off for real if I stepped out of line. I've walked a wire for nearly twenty years, Dominic, my own instinct to self-preserve weighed against my desire to minimise the pain of others.'

'And now?'

'Now I'm old, and tired. FEB should be behind me. Behind us all. What Hamilton is doing with the children . . . He's starting on a new generation. I want no part of it. When the UN announced they'd captured Slade, Hamilton got scared. He knew that Slade wasn't tracked down by any journalist. He was outed. Nobody stays hidden for a decade without help. Whoever it was that had been protecting him stopped. It would be easy for the same to happen to Hamilton. He needs money to stay hidden; to pay off the people who are keeping him secret. But the way he's doing it? Its barbaric. He's rattled now, though. Not enough to stop – he's not the type for stopping –

but he's made a point of tightening his ship. The last few months, he's been directing so much more of his attention to his companies, keeping closer tabs on everyone who worked for them, whether they knew he was behind it or not. I thought I could strike whilst he was distracted. He even upped the checks on adoptive parents. You were flagged early, Dominic. They didn't like your FBI brother. Your file was sent right to his desk. He put eyes on you and your wife, and ghosts on your screens and watches to see what you were up to, just to be certain that you weren't fishing. He knew you'd been to that Box before you said a word to the orphanage. When you downloaded my paper, he had to act.'

Dom's head pounded as he struggled to comprehend what it was that Garber had said. The information was a flood, swamping him. Garber saw his confusion.

'That paper was all I could think to do,' he said. 'I couldn't risk going to the police or the press. They're too loud and too connected. They have their own agendas and are too easy to bribe. I wasn't sure that word of what I'd done wouldn't get back to Hamilton before it reached anywhere of use. I'm a coward, Dominic. I don't want to die today any more than I did back then. Writing my paper was the bravest thing I could manage. I tried to publish it under a false name at first, but the journals insisted on verifying me. I had to be myself. I hoped that Hamilton might not be paying attention to my work, and that I'd raise the flag with enough interested academics to cause a groundswell before he noticed. I hoped they'd pick it up and spread it further than his reach, quicker than his reach, so that someone who could do something might take note. I was still too weak to name him, though. Perhaps if I hadn't been, it might have worked. People would have listened. I blew my chance. At any rate, I underestimated Hamilton. He knew what I had done the moment I did it. Within a week he'd found a way to publish two dozen other papers in my name, on all sorts of madness, utterly discrediting me.'

The horrors of Garber's paper rushed over Dom anew, and Maya's beautiful face bobbed to the surface of his shock. 'So they're all stolen?' he said. He thought he might cry. 'The babies?'

Garber shook his head. 'Not all of them, no. Too many, though. Enough.'

'Is there a way to know which ones?'

'None. By the time the children are put up for adoption, their original identities have been obliterated. There are so many levels of deceit, so many pay-offs and falsifications that I doubt even the people making the changes could tell you which child was which.'

Dom plunged his head into his hand. 'But you said that Hamilton would kill you if you upset him. You wrote the paper last year. Why are you alive?'

'I made it complicated. If he'd have killed me – if I'd disappeared then – people would have been suspicious. It was better to humiliate me and leave me where I was. Who'd believe the senile professor? In less than a month, my reputation drowned beneath a sea of alien autopsy theories, hijacked planes and government-sponsored terrorism. With it, the truth about the adoptions perished too. UCL let me keep my office, but they took my classes and shrunk my budget to nil. I've spent the last nine months in purgatory. Until you.'

'Me?'

Garber stared at Dom like he should have known the answer. 'Yes, Dominic. You. You made this urgent. Hamilton's confidence was teetering, and you pushed.' He stepped from the door, back inside the kitchen so that they were standing face to face. His skin was almost as white as his beard. 'There's nothing more I can do – I expect I'm a dead man already – but you can keep pushing. Push harder, Dominic. Push the bastard right off.'

'But how?' Dom asked.

From the opposite end of the house there was a bang: the sound of the front door being thrown open. Garber's terror exploded out of him, and he snatched Dom's arm and yanked him forward.

'He'll have covered his tracks,' said Garber, forcing Dom outside. 'Start with Catherine Hilton-Webb.'

Dom clattered down the steep concrete step, landing on the decking. He hauled himself up and clambered back towards the house, trying to stop the door from slamming behind him.

'Wait. What about Catherine?' he said as he saw that Garber had plucked a butcher's knife from the block on the counter.

'Go!' Garber cried.

Dom froze, and their eyes met. For a heartbeat they hesitated, then Garber tore his eyes away and plunged the blade into his own scrawny thigh.

26

Sweat ran into Dom's eyes as he hurried down the street. The summer sun was creeping higher in the sky, his heart-rate was rocketing, and the pain in his head and shoulder surged with each step. People were staring at him, and his legs felt heavy and unsteady. He struggled against the urge to stop, collapse and fold in two. The image of Garber driving the kitchen knife into his thigh replayed in Dom's mind, blade after blade. He wanted to ring Tess and tell her to go to the embassy, but his watch was cracked, and it wouldn't restart. He forced himself to carry on, weaving through the growing number of morning pedestrians and willing himself towards somewhere he recognised. If he could find Kensington High Street – if he could only see the green of the gardens and get his bearings – he would know where to go. Returning to the Yeandle Hotel wasn't an option, no matter how much he wanted to see his wife and child. If Garber was right and Hamilton's people had been watching them, they would still be watching now. They might be doing more than watching, if the gunman had called his friends. The thought of leaving Tess and Maya exposed sent waves of terror though him, but Dom knew his decision had already been made. He glanced behind before turning the corner onto another tree-lined street. No one appeared to be following. The way to protect his family was to finish this, and he had the thinnest window of opportunity. He had run away once before, and where had it got him? For Tess and Maya – and for his parents, Thea and the other stolen children – he had to do what Garber said.

He swung right, spotting what looked like shops at the junction ahead. He quickened toward them, arriving with relief at a florist, a food bank and road he recognised. He traced the route from here in his memory, feeling Tess at his side as she had been before, half dragging and half guiding him. Ideas solidified in his mind, their shape, weight and colours intensifying as he made his way to the bright red archways of the Kensington Fire Station. He knocked and waited. Fire Officer M. Parks opened the door.

'Do you remember me?' Dom asked before she could speak. He saw at once that she did. Her eyes jumped from his face to his shoulder. Blood was seeping through Garber's t-shirt.

'Oh my god. What happened to your arm?'

'I need to talk to you.'

'You're bleeding.'

'Can I come inside?'

She threw a hesitant look down the street. 'Where's your wife?'

Dom's gut clenched. He couldn't bring himself to speculate. 'Are you alone?'

Parks tensed visibly, her hand gripping the door and

ready to close it. He realised his error and took a step back, raising his uninjured arm in the hope it would show that he wasn't threatening her. He dropped his voice to an urgent whisper.

'Sorry. I'm sorry. I didn't mean to scare you. Please. I need your help. The baby that we thought came from here, the one we wanted to adopt . . . We didn't make a mistake about her. Someone lied to us. We think she's stolen. We think there are more children like her. Hundreds. Maybe thousands.'

He tore through the details of Garber's report and Catherine's sob-story, the letter in their hotel room, Thea's missing newborn and finding Hamilton in the video, amazed at how the passing of a few days – a few hours – could lessen his shock at such atrocious facts.

Parks listened, rigid. 'You should be at the police station,' she said when he'd finished. 'Not here.'

A hot poker twisted into Dom's shoulder. 'I can't go to the police. I don't know if we can trust them.'

'How do you know you can trust me?'

He paused. The stack of rainbow-coloured blankets that he'd seen in his first visit to the fire station appeared in his mind's eye, and the way Parks had stroked their soft, knitted weave before shaking them out and replacing them with care. He stared at her. 'Gut.'

Parks didn't shift from the doorway. Doubt etched her face.

'Please,' said Dom. Dizziness rushed him, and he stumbled forward, leaning against the wall. 'I saw the love you gave those babies. It was written through every page of your records. You made so much effort, and you did it for the families they came from as much as the ones they were heading to. You know it matters that someone looks out for them. I don't want to take a child that isn't mine to take. I don't want anyone else to take one. I know you understand that. I won't ruin a family.' He stopped, feeling a thickness rise in his throat.

Parks winced, as though fighting better judgement. She eyed his shoulder. 'What do you need?'

'Can I use your computer?'

'That's it?'

'I hope so.'

She stared for a second longer then nodded and moved aside.

Dom let out a thick, shuddering breath. 'Thank you,' he said, stepping into the fire station. Parks shut the door, and he followed her to the desk. The fire engines that had been here at his last visit were missing, and their footsteps echoed in the empty hangar.

'Whatever you want to do, be quick,' said Parks, waking the first of the idling computers and logging in.

She pulled out a chair, and Dom sat down.

'We need to check your records against the official ones,' he said.

He called up the Ministry of Justice's homepage as he'd done at Jemima's house, skipping through the login and navigating sideways to the Ministry of Children. Out of the corner of his eye, he saw Parks shift, but she didn't comment.

'Do you have the file that you showed us?' he asked her. 'The one with the children's details?'

Parks turned on the second screen.

'How many records have you made for this fire station?' said Dom.

'One-fifty, maybe. Two hundred.'

'We need to know exactly. Can you count them, please?'

Parks sat too and pulled up her file, swiping through the pages and keeping count with lines on a scrap of paper. Dom delved deeper into the Ministry of Children's website, searching the menus for a clue that would lead him in the right direction. Garber guessed there were forty thousand children in the post-FEB adoption records. There must be a central database, Dom reasoned, a place where they all came together. He hit dead-ends at *International Adoptions* and *Parent Applications* before spotting *Adoptions Completed*. He tapped the link and was met with an empty search bar and a selection of options to refine the result. He keyed in *Kensington Fire Station* and clicked *OK*. The screen filled with hits.

'How many children?' he asked Parks.

She placed her pen on the desk. 'One hundred and eighty-three.'

Dom stared at the number in the corner of the screen. Two thousand, three hundred and sixty-five results. He selected *Location of Origin*. Re-tapped *OK*. The list shrank to four hundred and two.

Parks looked over his shoulder. 'They've not all come from here,' she said. 'There's no way. Pick one. We'll check it.'

He did as she asked, opening the top match.

'What's the record's date?'

'September 28th this year,' he said. '11.04 p.m. Boy. Lewis Roswell.'

Park swiped through her file. She shook her head. 'He's not here. Open another.'

'October 9th. 3.42 a.m. Girl. Constance Vine.'

Parks scanned again then sat back, the truth engulfing her as it had done Dom. Emotion trembled in her voice. 'And they did this to you?' she said.

Dom stared blankly at the screen. She meant his shoulder, but it was more than that. *This* was the adoptions, but it was everything that had been done and undone, excused and pardoned in the name of progress since he was thirteen years old. He nudged his chair away from the desk.

'Do you have a printer?'

Parks shook her head.

'Find one, please. Print a copy of your record, every page of it, and hide it in the safest place you can. And print the search summary from the ministry, the list of the children's names logged as found at this fire station. Hide that too. We need hard copies in case the files get wiped.'

He stood up, moving towards the exit. Parks stood too.

'Where are you going?'

'Do any other Boxes keep records like yours?'

'All of them,' she said. 'You don't mind a Box if you don't care.'

'You know how to get in touch with them?'

She nodded.

'Do it. Ask how many children they have on their records and check the numbers like we've done. Only speak to your friends. People you can trust. If the numbers don't match, tell them to copy their files and hide them too. Lie about why.'

He opened the door, shoving outside and squinting in the sunlight.

Parks burst after him. 'Wait! You can't leave. Let me look at your shoulder!'

Dom didn't answer. He left the station. Ran.

27

The truck that was parked outside BlueSkies Children's Sanctuary was almost full. Its trailer was open, its ramp was extended, and two men in Day-Glo jackets boasting a Renzo's Removals logo were manoeuvring a fridge-freezer into the back. Three more men were shifting a wooden cabinet the size of a grand piano through the doorway of the building. A fourth was standing and talking to Catherine, listening as she gave a terse instruction while pointing at the truck and then along the road. Dom hid behind an oak tree in the garden across the street, propping himself up on its broad trunk and trying to draw air deep into his lungs. His mind was fizzing. Catherine was leaving, fleeing in the brazen, orderly way that only the richest crooks could do. She and Hamilton were scared – but not *that* scared. It was like Garber had said.

Money. He should have thought of it sooner. How many times had he listened to Tim's stories of the most atrocious, wiliest criminals? Money was always what gave the game away. Dom and Tess had paid Catherine 18,400 credits for the privilege of having her arrange Maya's adoption. *It's not a donation if you have to pay it.* He'd said those words to Tess as a joke and not begrudged it for a second, but he hadn't stopped to think about it either. They were paying to secure their family's future. There wouldn't have been a price too high. He stared across the road, at Catherine and her discussion with the bored-looking removal man. She was wearing a purple scarf, the brightly coloured silk hanging in delicate pleats around her neck. Bracelets slid up and down her bare forearms as she gesticulated, and she tapped one toe of her pink, patent boots. *We don't waste our money on being flash,* she had told them. The smile she gave Dom was so forceful that he had blushed. In part, she'd told the truth. BlueSkies was plain, bordering on barren, though he'd been too blinded by the possibilities of Maya to clock the difference between the two. Not a credit had been spent on anything but essentials. The same frugality did not apply to Catherine Hilton-Webb.

He braced himself harder against the tree-trunk, rolling his shoulder in its damaged socket and clenching and flexing his fingers, trying to force the blood to pump into them and counteract his rising weakness, at least in his mind. When the realisation had first come to him, the idea that followed seemed simple. He hadn't thought it through. He smeared a thumb over his watch's shattered screen and pressed the button again, muttering an encouragement. The watch spat with lines and then fell black. It didn't matter, he supposed. Even if he had the option to contact Tim or Tess – if his watch had been working and he'd not known it was ghosted – he wouldn't have got in touch. Not yet. Tim would have agreed with Dom's logic but not his tactics. He'd try to call his bosses.

If the FBI picked it up, they'd want warrants. Subpoenas. Time. That couldn't happen. Hamilton was already covering his tracks. Dom couldn't risk the man finding a way to erase his connection before he worked out what it was. He needed a quick way in.

He peered from his hiding place, scanning the townhouse and racking his brain for what he should do. Catherine disappeared inside BlueSkies, and the removal men lifted the cabinet into the truck before pausing to chat to one another. Dom counted seven men on the pavement. The flash of a yellow Day-Glo jacket at an upstairs window meant there were more inside. The men on the street finished talking and followed after Catherine, leaving one to secure the truck's ramp. The shutter clattered as he hauled it down, then he climbed into the cab and fired the engine, shifting the truck a few feet backwards so that it was closer to the door. As he did, Dom saw a fluorescent jacket without an owner. It was slung over the railings by the BlueSkies sign. Without thinking, he darted from behind the oak and crossed the road, snatching the jacket up and throwing it over his shoulders, wincing as he ripped his arm from the sling Garber had made him and pulled it though. Tim would tell him this was madness, the most ridiculous long shot as well as being illegal. Dom's heart pounded. Tim was right. Dom didn't care.

He skipped up the steps and into BlueSkies Children's Sanctuary. What had been the nursery on the left of the hallway was empty, but he could hear voices in the back of the building, in the room beyond the staircase. From the floor above came the thud of furniture being shifted, followed by Catherine's muffled voice and a man's subservient grunt. Dom dipped his head and powered up the staircase towards the corridor where Catherine's office had been. When he'd first sat in that small, stuffy room with Tess and Maya, he'd felt so happy. By the time he'd retuned, everything had changed. On that second visit, Catherine had projected her screen onto the wall. Whilst waiting for her to retrieve their papers, Dom had sat and stared absently at the desktop. He'd seen the file labelled *BlueSkies Accounts*.

If Hamilton was in on this, accounts would be the way to prove it. Dom hastened his step, gripping the banister tightly with his good hand. Beneath the plastic jacket, he was sweating. What would he say if Catherine caught him? At the top of the stairs the corridor was deserted, but he could see that the door at the farthest end was open. Shadows moved, spilling into the hallway. Catherine's voice was clearer. He grabbed the handle of the office door beside him, praying. It opened – unlocked – and he almost fell into it. His chest heaved. The removal hadn't started in this room. It was exactly as it had been, with its hard plastic chairs, the oversized filing cabinet and Catherine's flower-patterned water bottle sitting by the window. The desk was strewn with papers. At one end was her handbag, toppled over and unzipped. Heart sprinting, he took her screen from its pocket. He tucked it into his jacket and bolted from the room.

28

Thea dragged herself up the Roundhouse's stairwell with one slow, heavy footstep at a time. It was the hour of the morning where many of the residents were starting their days properly, and the flow of people was heading in the opposite direction. Workers in grease-smeared factory overalls and faded care-home uniforms stared at Thea's bloodstained clothes, their half-eaten slices of toast pausing mid-journey to their mouths as they did a double-take. Mothers leaving the tower in search of open space to let their children run off the fizzling summer-holiday energy cast their eyes downwards and drew their little ones from her path. A few people may have asked Thea if she was OK – she saw their lips moving – but all she could hear was her own thudding heart. *Still alive*, it said. *Still alive. Still alive.* She didn't know how.

She reached the eighth floor and shoved the bar to release the fire door. The door swung shut behind her and she was swamped in hard fluorescent light, damp heat and air that was thick with the smell of burnt bacon. Her eyes roamed ahead, and her stomach sank. There were flowers on the floor outside her flat; pink and white lilies with their buds in drooping, unopened tears. She fumbled for her keys in her pocket, feeling for the one she needed and positioning it between her fingers in readiness. She couldn't deal with Springer. Not now.

At the farthest end of the corridor, a door clicked open. 'Thea?'

She pushed the key into her lock, not looking round. 'I'll talk to you later, Springer.'

'Did you get my messages?'

'I've been busy.'

'Where did you go?'

'I'm tired, Springer. Please.'

Springer ignored her, advancing. The bass of a stereo pumped from the floor below, followed by a shout to turn it down. Springer stopped beside Thea, his voice smaller and more anxious than before. 'Did you find her?'

Thea sighed. Her silence drew a line between them, as solid as a brick wall. She waited for the familiar feelings of rage to engulf her, for the words she needed to burst out and shut him down, but they didn't come. Springer's gaze skidded over the blood on her t-shirt, and his cheeks bloomed red. He shifted, twisting his mother's ring above his knuckle. He was sweating. For someone else – on another day – Thea might have felt pity. Instead, she felt exhausted. Numb.

'What do you want, Springer?'

He muttered the answer at his feet. 'I was worried.'

Thea stared at him. She wanted to go inside, to collapse into her parents' bed and curl up beneath the covers, to close her eyes and forget that any of this had ever happened. She wanted to be six years old again, picking sand from between her toes and beneath her fingernails, in a rickety Devon caravan, with her skin sun-pinked and salt-crusted, her hair wind-whipped and knotted, and to drift into dream to the sounds of her mother's laughter from the grass outside. She wanted to sleep and not ever wake up.

'I'm never going to find her, Springer. You know that, don't you?'

The disquiet on Springer's face deepened. 'I didn't think you'd be a bad mother, Thea. I swear it.'

She shook her head. 'You had no right to sign her away.'

'You weren't well. Not even conscious. What was I supposed to do? As soon as you were awake, you'd have been discharged. How would you have cared for her? You couldn't have gone back to the Oakwood – not right away – and you hardly had any credits.'

'I would have found them, Springer. I'd have worked something out.'

The mottled red in Springer's cheeks spread across his face and down his neck.

Thea felt a throb of pain along the split in her stomach scar. 'Did they pay you?' she asked. 'Is that it? Did you sell her?'

'What? No. I would never. They told me you'd get her back as soon as you were better.'

'And you believed them?'

Springer's mouth hung open. He rubbed his palm over his scalp, tipped back his head and blinked hard, as if trying not to cry. He looked pathetic. Yes, he'd believed them. Thea turned her back to him, nudging the flowers aside with her foot. Springer touched her wrist as she went to open the door. She shrugged him off. 'Go away, Springer.'

'I need to apologise.'

'Words can't fix this.'

'I know.'

He dug into his pocket and pulled out Thea's notebook, thrusting it at her. She froze. The thought of Springer seeing her drawings made her feel nauseous. She stared at the notebook, wanting to take it, but dread was worming its way through her gut. A slip of folded paper peeped from between the pages.

'You dropped this in the square last night,' said Springer. He was looking down and holding the notebook so the paper sat upright like a tiny white flag. 'I'm so sorry, Thea,' he muttered.

Thea felt her agitation rise. This apology was more than Laurel. Springer stank of fear. 'What's that?'

'Take it. Please.'

She reached out and plucked back her notebook, sliding the paper free, keeping her eyes on him until it was unfolded. Springer's handwriting. Her head pounded.

'His name is Samuel Cotton,' said Springer.

Thea stared at the address, not understanding.

'The officer.'

His words punched the breath out of her. She didn't need any more explanation. There was only one officer that Thea cared about, and Springer knew it. *Samuel Cotton*. The name ricocheted against the sides of her skull, crashing through memories, scattering them. She pressed her eyes closed, driving her thumbs into the sockets, seeing sparks. Cotton was the officer in charge of the Gritstone's kitchen for the rally. The officer who'd missed one measly chicken. The man who'd wrapped his fingers around her neck.

'How did you find him?'

Springer shook his head. 'I've known who he was for a long time. When Mum died, FEB sent me on ration runs sometimes. Turns out that Cotton was shipped around the country to manage the catering for all the FEB rallies. When there wasn't anything on, he was based at the barracks where they stored the grain. I saw him there a few times. Once, when I broke into the kitchens, I found his office. I was looking for something to eat, but there was a letter from before FEB. In a drawer, at the back. It was from a woman. His wife, I guess. She'd left him. The envelope was addressed to Samuel Cotton.'

Thea stared at him. 'Why didn't you tell me?'

Springer shrank back, his skin glowing berry. 'I don't know,' he said, not meeting her eye. 'I was scared of what you'd do, maybe. Thought you'd get yourself in trouble. Besides, it was clear that you would leave once you'd found him. I knew that when you didn't need the Archive, you'd get yourself as far away from the Gritstone as possible. I couldn't bear that, Thea. I couldn't bear living here without you. There are fewer and fewer people in the Roundhouse from our childhood, fewer and fewer who remember what happened here, and even fewer who know what it was like before.' He paused and swiped away a tear. 'What I was like before.'

Thea stared at the paper in her hand. She could feel the blood coursing through her body, an electrified current. Before.

Springer summoned a weak smile, but it wasn't

convincing. 'Your pictures are perfect, Thea,' he said. 'They're exactly as I remember him.'

'His address . . .' she asked. 'Is it current?'

Springer nodded. 'I got it last night. I was owed a favour at the police station.' He paused, his smile faltering. 'Do you hate me?'

'I don't hate you.'

'What are you going to do?' His voice was a whisper.

Thea pulled her key from the lock without turning it. She walked away, stuffing it back in her pocket. Springer called her name, but she didn't answer. She pushed into the stairwell. The fire door clanked shut.

29

Tess and Maya were the only lucid thoughts in Dom's mind. As he ran through the thronging London streets, his lips moved soundlessly, summoning the shapes of their names and bargaining with a god that he hadn't believed existed. He would give anything, everything, if only they were safe. Catherine hadn't seen him – he felt sure – but she, Hamilton and whoever else they worked with were already more than rattled. They'd shown they weren't afraid of taking action, however deadly. They were fleeing. Dom's heart pummelled, and he pumped his legs faster. They knew where his family was. They couldn't leave loose ends. He touched the inside pocket of his stolen Day-Glo jacket, feeling Catherine's screen against his sweat-drenched chest. Where would he look if Tess wasn't at the Yeandle Hotel? Guilt ripped through him. His wife would be apoplectic with worry. He hadn't even left a note. Was it better if he found that they weren't in the room? He tore into the hotel's lobby, hearing the concierge call his name. Dom didn't respond, and he saw the man reach for the telephone. Bypassing the lift, he went straight for the stairs, leaping double-step to the fourth floor and bursting into the corridor. Pain raged in his shoulder. He didn't have his room key. He hammered his fist against the door.

'Tess!'

He shouted louder, not caring who heard. The door flew open, and she stared at him, terrified. Her face was red and swollen, her nose streaming, her face wet with tears. She was pressing Maya to her body, cradling the child's head in her hand.

'Dom? Oh my god!' She turned to the room, and Dom saw his brother's haggard face projected on the wall. 'Tim! Tim, it's Dom. He's alive!'

She fell into him, howling the last words as he half pushed and half carried her into the room. He shut the door and bolted it behind them.

'I'm so sorry I left you,' he said, kissing her. He could feel how violently she was shaking, her body convulsing against his. She knocked his shoulder and he jerked back instinctively. Panic flared in her expression. She ripped back the jacket where it covered his shoulder, revealing the blood-soaked t-shirt beneath.

She cried out, recoiling.

'Jesus,' said Tim. 'What happened?'

'I'm OK,' Dom replied. He took hold of Tess, trying to pull her back into him. She squirmed away, searching his face for answers.

'You're not OK. You're bleeding.'

'It's not as bad as it looks.'

'It looks horrific,' said Tim. 'Where have you been? I told Tess to take Maya to the embassy. Thea said you were dead.'

Dom darted across the room, dropping on the bed and pulling Catherine's screen from his pocket. He jabbed the button to turn it on.

'What are you doing?' asked Tim.

'I need your help,' said Dom. 'Garber said that Catherine was the key to getting Hamilton.'

'You found Garber?' asked Tess.

'He was at an address near the children's home. Hamilton's people have him trapped. His report and the letter that he sent us were cries for help. He's on our side.' A chill ran down Dom's spine. *Was* on their side. Garber was most likely dead.

'Parks is collecting evidence of how many records have been falsified,' he said, ramming the thought from his mind. 'It's easily hundreds and probably many more, but we need to connect them to Hamilton.'

'Parks?'

'The woman from the Kensington Fire Station. Listen, I think Catherine is sending Hamilton money from the adoptions. Why else would he be doing this but for credits? We need to trace them.'

Tess was standing by the mirror, studying him. Maya blinked with her black-marble eyes. 'Whose screen is that, Dom?' Tess asked. 'It's not yours.'

'It's Catherine's. I think the evidence we need is on here, Tess. I saw a file when we were at her office for the custody agreement. Accounts. I want to look at it.'

'You stole Catherine's screen? She'll be after us.'

'She's already after us.'

The screen fired up, and a grid of fifteen silver dots appeared. Dom tilted the glass towards the window, letting the light catch the smears from where Catherine's fingertips aligned with her security pattern. He traced them from top to bottom, left to right, as he knew was most common. The desktop loaded, and he felt a flicker of relief. The simplest hacks were often the ones that worked. He accessed her settings quickly, disabling her geo-locator and hoping she'd not yet realised that her screen was missing. He turned to Tess.

'The link to Hamilton will be here,' he said. 'I know it will. We paid Catherine nearly 20,000 credits for Maya. We didn't even think about it. She told us that BlueSkies had completed more than two thousand adoptions. If every couple paid the same amount, that's 40 million credits they've been given over what . . . ten years? We saw for ourselves that money wasn't spent on the orphanage, and the actual legal costs – the ones that go to the government – are a pittance by comparison. So where's the money? I'm only talking about BlueSkies, too. Thea's daughter disappeared from a different home, and we know from our adoption research that there are dozens and dozens of orphanages in the UK. How many more are run by Hamilton? How many hundreds of millions of credits flow his way?'

'I don't like where you're going with this, Dom,' said Tim. 'Nothing you find on that screen will be admissable in court. You know that, don't you? Not like this. You have to hand it over to the FBI.'

'This won't end up in court if we wait. Catherine's closing the orphanage. Running. We haven't got time.'

'You could go to jail,' said Tess.

'We'd all go to jail,' said Tim.

'Fine.' Dom stared at them. 'This isn't only about Maya. We can't let Hamilton disappear for another fifteen years. Perhaps forever.'

Tess closed her eyes and pressed her face into Maya's neck. The child gave a gurgle of delight, bobbing her head and smiling. Tim rocked back in his chair, exhaling deeply.

'I can't trace it through the banks, Dom,' he said, relenting. 'That's too much. It'll flag on the system. Someone will notice.'

'I know,' said Dom. He found the file that he'd seen before, labelled *BlueSkies Accounts,* and opened it. An accounting app that he didn't recognise loaded, but it looked intuitive enough. He whipped through the navigation options presented to him: *Invoices, Statements, Remittances* . . . 'I'm not asking you to hack anything. Just tell me what to look for.'

'You better be right about this.'

'I'm right.'

Tim let out another long, hard sigh. 'OK,' he said. 'Find the payment records. We need to see what's outgoing.'

Dom found *Payments* in the menu, and the app opened into a spreadsheet, its lines shaded alternately in washed-out peach and grey.

'How far does it go back?' Tim asked.

Dom scrolled. 'Six years, looks like.'

'And where's the money going? People or corporations?'

Dom scanned the list. 'Corps, mostly. Or the Ministry of Children.'

'Let's discount the Ministry for now. The corps payments – are they large or small?'

'Mixed.'

'Alright. So what type of corporations might an orphanage reasonably need? Food and catering. Consumables. Kids' clothing. A staffing agency, perhaps. Furniture occasionally. Do you recognise any names? Are they categorised somehow?'

Dom frowned as he searched down the list. Tess lowered herself onto the bed beside him, looking too. The spreadsheet gave so little away. How were they meant to know who sold what without checking every vendor's name online? *Mosdbys.* Was that the supermarket delivery chain? It was the largest regular appearance, with a twice-weekly payment of several thousand credits each time. He tapped on an entry, and an invoice popped up showing a long inventory of groceries. Seemed legitimate. He closed it down and continued scrolling. Nothing stood out.

Tess touched his wrist. 'Dom, look,' she said, pointing to the bottom of the screen. 'That payment was the biggest last month by a landslide. All the other entries have checked the box marked *Vendor*, but that one didn't. There's just an invoice number.'

Dom stared at the company name that was listed beside the payment for 55,200 credits. *Saxons LLC.* He'd never heard of it. He tapped on the invoice, and it opened.

'There's no detail,' he said. 'Payment for "Professional Services Rendered". What does that mean?'

'It means you've found a red flag,' Tim replied. 'When an invoice is as vague as that, it's usually deliberate. They're counting on no one looking too closely. Well done, Tess. See if there's anything similar.'

They scrolled further, backing through the months and

picking out the entries where the *Vendor* box remained unchecked and the payments were larger than the rest. 110,400 credits in June. 36,800 credits in April. 55,200 credits in March. The pattern continued. They were split between Saxon LLC and another company that Dom didn't recognise, Athelstan LLC, and all for Professional Services Rendered. He opened a new window on Catherine's screen, typing each company name into the Internet search engine in turn. Nothing obvious came back to explain who they were or what they did. He returned to the names. Saxon and Athelstan. Had he heard them before?

'Can you look them up on your system, Tim? There's nothing illegal in that, is there?'

Tim nodded and typed. The clack of his fingers hitting the keys filled the air.

'You see anything?'

He squinted, reading. 'We're in luck,' he said. 'They're both US-based companies. They have different registered agents but . . . *wow*.' His eyes widened. 'Dom, they've got the same registered address and were incorporated on the same day. June 5th. I'd bet my last credit they're shells.'

Tess was still staring at Catherine's screen. 'Look at the values,' she said, reaching over and tapping open another bare-bones invoice from Athelstan LLC. 'We gave Catherine 18,400 credits. This is for 73,600. That's exactly four times our payment. The other payments are multiples too. She's creaming it straight off.'

Dom looked. Tess was right. He scrolled to July, three weeks previously, when they'd made their own payment. 55,200 had been transferred to Saxon LLC; precisely three times what they'd paid Catherine, the day *after* they'd paid it to her. Three donations. Catherine had been waiting for their money to land before she side-streamed it. 'Is this enough to act, Tim? Can we get her arrested?'

Tim shook his head. 'You're not getting an arrest yet, but it's certainly enough to order an investigation. Uncovering fraud is like treasure hunting, but I'd say you've got a solid first clue and second clue.'

'But how do we link it to Hamilton?' asked Tess.

'By following the payments once they've left BlueSkies. We'd need to see what Saxon and Athelstan did with them next. Most likely they'd send the credits onwards to another company, not a person, but the more we know, the more likely a connection will make itself known. What was the name Hamilton was using at Grateley Profiles?'

'Thomas Fox.'

'Right. Fox. So perhaps we'd be able to find a reference to him or a company he's done work for somewhere down the chain. It would take a slip-up, though. He's too smart to leave his name floating around, even if it is an alias.'

In the dark of Dom's mind a light flared. 'Oh god, Tim. The museum.'

Tim and Tess stared at him.

'The night we slept at the British Museum with Mum and Dad, we'd been to see the Saxon exhibit, hadn't we? The Anglo-Saxons. The founders of modern Britain. Athelstan was a Saxon king. He was the first king of unified England. He enforced the first full code of law. Don't you remember Mum telling us? At Grateley.' Tim looked at him blankly. 'It created the British state, the first framework of national politics. It laid the way for the first

– 254 –

parliament. The companies, Tim. They're a set. Saxon, Athelstan and Grateley.'

'You're kidding,' said Tess. 'You remember that?'

'Tim,' said Dom. 'Look up Grateley Profiles.'

Tim typed. 'What am I searching for?'

'It might not be a shell, but Hamilton's more than a board member. He's in charge. He's named his companies for what they signify to him. No corner of Britain untouched by his power. Complete control.' He paused and looked at Tim, expectant. 'Have you found it? What's the address? The incorporation date?'

He shifted to the edge of the bed. He knew the answer. He'd found the link.

Tim frowned at his computer. 'They're not the same, Dom.'

'Are you sure?'

'They're all from Colorado, but that's as far as it goes.'

'That's something, isn't it?' said Dom. Pressure was spiking in his head. A wave of tiredness and emotion was rising up and threatening to crash.

'I'm sorry, Dom,' said Tim. 'There are hundreds of thousands of companies registered in Colorado. It's not a connection. You're clutching at straws. This isn't how fraud works. You're not just going to stumble across an affiliation to Hamilton. It takes months to work the leads in cases like this and find something we can use as evidence, if it's even possible. It's time to let me pull in my team, OK? I won't tell my boss you stole the screen. I'll get the case opened properly, then I'll guide them in the right direction. Find what we've discovered today, again. OK? You've found enough already to trigger a search for him if we take it to the right people, and even if we don't find the link to the adoptions, they'll get him for FEB.'

Dom shook his head. The disappointment was a bludgeon. FEB wasn't enough. It wasn't everything. He wanted justice for Maya. And for poor Jemima. And Thea. He went back to Catherine's screen, typing *Grateley Profiles* into the accounting app. There had to be something that showed they knew each other. He hit search, knowing nothing would come up, but hoping all the same.

Tess's hand closed over his, stopping him. 'Let Tim do his job, honey,' she said gently.

'We'll miss our chance, Tess,' Dom whispered.

'We don't have a choice.'

Tess peeled Maya from her shoulder and passed her to Dom. The child turned her dark eyes on him, gurgling out a smile as he drew her into him and kissed her soft hand. He breathed her in, feeling the tears back up at the rim of his eyes. From the desk, the telephone bleated.

Tess went rigid. Tim stared from the projection.

'Dom,' he said. 'It's time to go.'

30

There was a litter-strewn garden out front, a rectangle of land no bigger than a double bed, filled with waist-high, sun-baked weeds and grass gone to seed. Thea stood by the gate where it clung to its hinges and stared at the door of the ground-floor flat. Green-black moisture trickled down the wall beside it, collecting in a rotten slick on the step. Where the diamond of glass at eye-height was broken, someone had pinned up a scrap of wood or cardboard so it wouldn't fall through. The curtains were drawn, despite it being lunchtime. No sound came from inside. Her stare slipped sideways along the block, then upwards. The buildings in this part of the city were squat and crammed down every backstreet without any room to breathe, but the smells and sounds and feel of them were exactly like the Gritstone. There were flashes of colour amidst the rows of windows – plants on ledges, washing hung, children's playthings – that broke the pattern of boarded glass and blacked-out rooms. Thea could hear music, loud and frantic, and the echo of teenagers swearing and smashing bottles from the underpass. A shudder ripped through her. In all her years of imagining this moment, she hadn't pictured it would happen in a place like this.

She glanced down the street, dipping her hand into her pocket and fingering the smooth wooden handle of the knife she'd stolen from Garber's kitchen. She waited for the German Shepherd to drag its owner around the corner, the dog choking itself on its leash as it did so, then she slipped up the path. The flat was on the corner of the building, and she darted sideways into the narrow alley that ran beside it. A cat leapt from its perch atop a dustbin, mewing and rubbing itself against her ankles, and she nudged it away and cupped her hand to the window, peering in. A kitchen sat beyond the glass, dark and still. The window was open a crack; she dug in her fingertips and pulled at the frame as carefully and quietly as she could. A rush of fat, black flies escaped, along with the stink of decomposing bins, and she heaved herself in, holding her breath and easing past the teetering stacks of dishes on the countertop. A light was on in the room across the hall, and she picked her way across the tacky linoleum towards it, feeling sweat prickle on her skin. The light brightened, strobing through colours. Her heart thumped harder. In the centre of a room as cluttered and rancid as the kitchen, someone was sitting and watching a projection. The crest of a head peeked above an armchair. Wisps of grey hair were lit from behind.

Thea's hand crept to the knife in her pocket. As she stepped forward again, there was a clatter at her feet.

'Edie?'

A face appeared at the side of the armchair. Thea froze, glancing down and cursing inwardly at the crusted cereal bowl that was overturned on the floor. The man looked at her, concerned, and then at the spaces to the left and the right. He was groping for his cane.

'Edie? Is that you?'

In the dim light, Thea saw his useless, clouded eyes jump over her, unseeing. She held her breath, taking in his features. Age had thinned him, darkened his skin and tugged it looser, but the man she saw was unmistakably the same.

Did your parents take the chicken, child?

We'll find out.

We'll find you.

Don't make this worse.

Her body convulsing.

The terror.

Yes.

The chair creaked, and Samuel Cotton dragged himself up. He was moving towards her, advancing in slow motion, and suddenly she was eight again, in the square outside the Roundhouse and frightened beyond measure. Like the last time she'd seen him, she couldn't think. Her mind was screaming. He was wearing a vest, too big for his thin frame and stained with food and sweat. On his wrist was a faded *epa* tattoo. He said the name again, and a new rush of fear hit her. Edie? His daughter? Someone on their way to see him. Thea's eyes fired to the window, to the ways in which she could escape, but her legs wouldn't move. Cotton lumbered into her, wrapping her up and pulling her against him. He buried his filthy, stubbled face into her hair.

'Edie. Oh, Edie. I'm so glad you came home.'

Thea couldn't breathe, couldn't move. The touch of

him was like rope around her body. He stank of urine and decay.

Cotton drew back, gripping her shoulders and looking blindly at her face. 'You're not happy, love? Not happy to see me?'

The projection flickered, making Thea feel drunk. It was the verdict, she realised. Cotton had been playing the trial. Billy Slade was in the dock, and Judge Lyons was taking her seat on the bench. A barrage of flashbulbs flared as the world's media clambered for a photograph of the moment Lyons spoke the words they all knew she'd say.

Thea gasped as Cotton's fingers pressed harder into her. There was a photograph on the wall beside the projection. It was Cotton as a young man, beaming on the steps of a pretty grey-stone church, with a flower in the buttonhole of his navy suit. The woman beside him was wearing white and laughing, throwing her head back and reaching for flakes of confetti in the air. The frame was engraved. *Edie and Samuel. 9 July. Congratulations!* Thea's thoughts sprinted. Not his daughter. Not just *someone*. Edie was Cotton's wife. Her eyes darted around the room. Edie watched from other photographs, dozens of them, in frames of all sizes. In one she was sitting beside a swimming pool, wearing sunglasses and combing her wet hair. In another she sipped a glass of wine in a garden. She posed with a Labrador on a jetty above the sea. In not a single image had she aged a day beyond the wedding. Beside Cotton, and in the fetid room, she looked so fresh and out of place. Thea settled on a picture above the mantle. The young woman was glancing over her shoulder, staring down the camera's lens without smiling, as if she had known she was going to flee. Springer had said that Cotton's wife had left him. When had she done it – before or after? Had she known what Cotton would become?

Thea flinched, and Cotton released her, looking embarrassed.

'Where have you been, love?' he said quietly. Thea could hear his desperation. 'What are you doing back?'

She licked her lips, the taste of bile strong in her mouth. What was she doing here? She had come because she could, and because she'd always said she would. It had been a reflex action, a limb striking out. She had always expected, too, that Cotton wouldn't recognise her. She had been prepared to remind him of what happened – had looked forward to it, even. She wanted to recount the day to him, to witness the moment of dawning, to see the fear as his memories clicked into place. She hadn't expected he'd have half lost his mind.

Cotton whimpered at her silence and thumped back into his armchair, hanging on his cane and seeming ready to cry. As he landed, he clunked the table at his side. Thea's stomach lurched when she spotted what was there. The FEB party logo glowed like a beacon. She touched it with one finger, as though she thought it might scold. It was on the cover of a magazine – a printed one like she hadn't seen for years and years. *The Free and Equal Review*. The date was from before the election. The headline read *Cast Your Vote for a Free and Equal Future* and beneath the words, the FEB Five waved at a crowd from an open-topped bus. She slid the magazine aside and saw another, and another, and then a poster she remembered from somewhere in her subconscious. *Unite and Rise. Salters before Spoonies*. There was an image of a cage being unlocked and a boy emerging from inside. The time and location of a rally. Another. *Don't Be Spoon-fed. Embrace the Liberation.* A toddler crying as a woman wearing a crown stuffed coins into his mouth.

Thea sped through the pile. There were pamphlets from door-drops, FEB party posters, newspaper cuttings, leaflets advertising events, newsletters. She stopped, the past ploughing into her. She recognised the next cutting without a second's hesitation. There was a photograph at the top, and the light was the same: the sun slatted between the towers in the morning – Boscastle, Shackleton, Lipson, Roundhouse – and tumbling down the overpass's steep steps. The square was dressed exactly like in her memory, too, with blue and white bunting to distract from the graffiti, and the angle was such that you couldn't see the A-frames. Thea didn't need to see the crowd's faces to know that they were her neighbours. Her eyes skimmed the words. The rally had gone ahead the following day, as if nothing had happened. The news channels reported more fervent support for FEB than ever, and the Gritstone was simply *thrilled* to be visited by their Dear Leaders. No reference was ever made to Thea's parents, nor to Thea.

She stared at the cutting, horrified. At the bottom of the report, beneath the grand, panned-out Gritstone vista, was another, smaller photograph: a group of nervous, hand-picked residents, trying not to look famished as they tucked into their feast.

'Why would you keep this?' she whispered.

Cotton slipped back in his chair, his breath rasping. He looked at the table like she did, his stare holding the paper for a long time, drinking it in as if he could see and was remembering too. He turned his face to Thea like the answer was obvious.

'I kept them for you, Edie,' he said. 'At first I wanted to prove that you were wrong. I wanted to show you that FEB had made things better. They'd made *me* better. I had a good job. People respected me. I was someone, love. Someone! Later, I kept them to say sorry. You were right.'

Lightheaded, Thea grabbed the chair. This stack of dog-eared magazines and papers was Cotton's record of the events that he'd catered. It was a record of the things he was culpable for. The projection strobed again with flashing cameras, the volume seeming to grow louder, and Judge Lyons hushed the courtroom as she prepared to read her verdict. The hall was packed but fell utterly silent. Slade stood in the dock, his hands on his hips. Everyone in Britain knew that Lyons would find him guilty. He would spend the rest of his life in jail. As the judge spoke, the crowd's physical reaction was invisible, but Thea felt the charge shoot through the air. There wasn't celebration, nor relief, nor anger. Nothing about any of this could cause the slightest happiness. There wasn't the space left for any feeling but sadness, and a tiredness that went right down to her core.

'I didn't want to argue with you, Edie,' whispered Cotton. His eyes were pointed in the direction of the projection, too. 'I didn't want you to leave, that's all. I thought it would be OK. I didn't know. But I'm glad you left, love. I'm glad you got out.'

Lyons finished speaking, and the courtroom setting was replaced with a newsroom and two sombre-looking anchors. Thea swallowed down her revulsion and shoved aside the cutting on the table. She wanted to see her parents' faces – her own face – and to cast herself back to the time before the rally happened, when she'd still had a different choice she could have made. She snatched up a new magazine – *Meet Your Leaders!* – and threw open the cover. There was a biography of Billy Slade, then one for James Easton, then Eric Simmons. She flicked through them, rage bubbling. *Vision and ingenuity! Men of the people!* She turned the page again. The corner had been folded, presumably by Cotton. Her nausea redoubled. She had seen the same image on her bedroom wall yesterday, projected from her watch as she searched online for Carl Hamilton. In it, Hamilton was young, fit and happy on his wedding day, absorbed in the joy of a moment not dissimilar from the one which captured Cotton and Edie in the photo on the wall. He was standing with his bride at a pedestal decorated with white roses, and their hands were clasped over a long, thin knife. The crown of laurel leaves was tucked on the woman's head. The couple were beaming. *Family First for Hamilton,* boasted the caption. Thea pressed her hand to the barely-healed gash along her stomach. To her daughter's absence. Dom's limp body flashed before her vision. Cotton had circled the cake in a neon-yellow marker, drawn a smiling face and written *MINE!!!*

'You baked Carl Hamilton's wedding cake,' said Thea, breathless. Her disbelief was as much at the culmination of the past week as the fact before her.

Cotton's lips parted as if he was about to laugh, but no sound came. His smile fell away. 'It wasn't a patch on the one I baked for our big day.'

She shook her head.

'Edie?'

'I've got to go,' Thea muttered.

She turned to leave, but Cotton snatched her wrist, stopping her dead despite his featherweight touch. The veins stood in bulging blue ridges along the back of his hand. She gagged, her mind overflowing with Hamilton and Dom and Laurel and her parents, and she couldn't bear the feel of him, the way he'd held her that day long ago.

'We all have our shame for the parts we played,' said Cotton. He stared right into her eyes, and his voice was crisp and steady. 'We all said *yes* when we should have said *no*.'

The projection blared. Edie watched from her photographs.

'Do you understand, girl?' said Cotton.

Thea's tears were falling.

Of course she understood. It was all she'd thought about since she first went to the Archives. She looked at the table – at the image of Hamilton having fun on his wedding day, his wife with her beautiful laurel-leaf headdress – then back to Cotton. She dug her hand in her pocket and drew out the knife.

31

Tess and Dom stood with Maya at the centre point of Westminster Bridge. The breeze from the river was cool and gentle. The Houses of Parliament were ahead of them, rose-gold and glowing resplendent beneath the bright midday sun. Tim had said that he'd get them a car to the US embassy – tried his hardest to push it – but Dom had insisted they would make their own way. If this all went wrong and they never proved the link between Catherine and Hamilton – if Hamilton somehow made certain that Dom would never be safe in London – he needed to walk through the city of his childhood one last time. He didn't want to be chased out again. He dipped his trembling hand into his pocket for his pills. Even before he and Tess had outed the truth about Maya, returning to Britain had felt so unexpectedly complex. Deep wounds that he'd thought were healed had rent apart. He swallowed a tablet then stroked Maya's soft head. She was sleeping, strapped to Tess's body; she sighed and her eyelids fluttered at his touch. Getting Maya was meant to heal him, but they still weren't parents. Could they ever be now, after this? Tim had told the embassy all that they'd discovered about the adoptions. Would they take her from them? His chest ached at the thought of having to hand her over. He had let himself fall so completely into possibility, into loving this child. To give her away would break his heart.

He wrapped his arms around his girls, pulling them into him.

'I'm sorry, Dom,' Tess whispered.

'Me too.'

He exhaled a long, hard breath into her hair, knowing how many things they were both sorry for. Maya was never the one who would fix him. He was wrong to put that on her. The fix had needed to come from within. He looked down at the River Thames, calm, bright and rippling, and the breeze caught the tears as they slid down his cheeks. He wiped them away with his palm, feeling guilty. He had spent the last nineteen years underwater. It had held him deep, its pressure keeping him contained and compressing him, slowing his movements – his ambitions – without him knowing. The world above was muted. It had taken the London tides to reveal him, to let him break the surface and gasp for air.

'I'm glad I came back,' he said into Tess's hair, and he meant it. Nothing had gone like he'd planned or wanted. He would spend the rest of his life fighting to find Hamilton if he needed to, but at least he now knew that he was brave enough to fully face what happened. If nothing else, he was proud that he'd tried.

He kissed the top of Tess's head then felt a familiar vibrating sensation pulse against his wrist. His vision slid to his watch. It had resurrected. The gears of his mind ground into motion, piecing words together though the egg-shelled glass.

Connect to screen?

He peeled back from his wife and looked around, instinctively.

'What is it?'

'My screen,' he said, glancing left and right, along the bridge. He stepped into the road, skipping through the cars and onto the top of the concrete barrier that separated the lanes. He scanned the faces of the people on the pavements.

'Dom?'

'It's Thea,' he said. 'I saw her grab my bag when she ran from Garber's house. She kept it, Tess. She's here.'

Fear whipped across Tess's expression. 'You can't know that. What if it's not her? It could be Hamilton's men.'

Dom jabbed at his watch, bringing up the map and seeing the blue line wind its way to Trafalgar Square.

'She was well ahead of them, Tess,' he said, jumping from the barrier, returning to the pavement and striding north. He grabbed Tess's hand, pulling her with him. 'We need to find her. She has to know about Catherine. It might help her find her daughter.'

They hurried past Big Ben, Tess holding Maya's head steady in her hand as they turned along Parliament Street. It melted into Whitehall, the grand old buildings towering over them, just as they had done in Dom's childhood, suspended in time. He quickened his pace. The crowds were visible in Trafalgar Square before they reached it, overflowing into the side streets and blocking the traffic. They heard the loudspeakers before they saw the big screen too, sounds crystallising from indecipherable, rumbling bass into clear words as they made their approach.

'What's happening?' Tess asked.

'It's the verdict,' said Dom, remembering as he said it.

They nudged into the mass of people, following the directions on Dom's watch and heading to the monument. Judge Lyons was on the screen in front of the National Gallery, giving an interview outside the Old Bailey courthouse. The square was transfixed by her, watching quietly and eerily still. He held Tess tighter and slowed to a walk, weaving towards Nelson's Column. At its base, he stopped. He looked from the map to the hordes, and then he saw her. She was perched between the paws of a bronze lion, her knees pulled to her chest and her head buried into them so he couldn't see her face. There was blood on her bright white trainers. His bag was at her side.

'Thea?'

Dom shouted, and Thea startled. She looked up, her eyes skittering through the crowd without recognition. He shoved forward, raising his hand at her and shouting again. Tess followed, and Thea's face crumpled when she found them. She slid from the plinth, her legs appearing to buckle beneath her weight. She was clutching his rolled-up screen to her chest.

'Listen, Thea,' said Dom, helping her from the floor. He held her up, dipping his head to catch her harried face. She looked as grey as ash, and confused. 'Catherine – the woman who ran the BlueSkies agency – she's been stealing money from the adoptions. The US government is going to investigate. My brother's helping – he works for the FBI – but we know we've got her nailed. There's work to do, but she'll be arrested. Sent to trial, most likely. The evidence is there. She's been forging records, too. It's only a matter of time before the authorities prove the children in her care weren't orphans. I know it, Thea. Perhaps she can tell you what happened to Laurel? Once they've got her in custody, she might cooperate. Give you the information you need to cut a deal.'

Thea's lips puckered like she was going to cry. 'Laurel's gone,' she said, and she squirmed away from him.

'You don't know that.'

She didn't answer.

Dom shook his head at her. 'Didn't you hear me, Thea? You can still find Laurel.'

She flinched as though he'd hit her. 'It's not going to happen, Dom. You heard how many children Garber said had been adopted. Laurel isn't Laurel any more. She could be anywhere in the world. And who am I? I'd need a thousand lifetimes to search.'

Dom felt his desperation rising. 'Thea. Please. You can't give up.' He grabbed Thea and pulled her closer. 'We'll help.'

Thea let out a moan of pure pain. She snatched herself free of him and slumped to the bottom of the plinth, dropping Dom's bag and his screen. As she did, the screen unrolled, and a slip of paper slid from the centre of the coil. Shell-shocked, Dom stared down before dropping beside her.

'Where did you get this?' he asked, picking the paper up. He felt dizzy.

Thea shrugged and smeared her nose on the back of her hand. 'I found the man who murdered my parents. After all the years of looking, there he was. Right there. I went to his flat. He was half dead, and blind, and completely bloody raving, but I felt like a kid again. I was useless and terrified. I wanted to scream, but I couldn't say anything. I saw the picture on his table.'

'And you took it?'

'He had his own archive in that room, Dom. That's what it felt like. He lived in it, filthy deep. He'd kept photographs and posters and magazines from everything he'd ever done in the name of FEB. It was disgusting. But I'd seen this picture before. After we'd found Grateley Profiles, I was searching online for Carl Hamilton, and when I saw it again . . . I don't know. I panicked. I'd thought the man I was looking for would be a giant. I thought he'd be rich and fat and happy, but he wasn't. He was just as scared and miserable as me. Jemima was always on at me to look to the future. I didn't think I could do it, but you managed, didn't you? Hamilton killed your mum and dad like Cotton killed mine, but you didn't do what I did. You got out, and you got married and you're happy, mostly, aren't you? I want that. I want to be happy, too. I went there to kill him, Dom, but I couldn't do it. Look, they're laurel leaves in the woman's headdress. Can you see them? Plain as day. If I killed Cotton and they caught me, how would I find Laurel? How could I track her down from jail? How could I be with her? Tell her I loved her? Say sorry? The knife was there, in my hand, and he wouldn't have fought me. It would have been easy. But when I looked at all he'd held on to – what he'd done and what he'd lost and how weak it left him – I didn't want to do it any more. I'd be letting him ruin my life all over again. I swear he knew who I was. He remembered. I saw it. I understand what Mima meant, now. I want to walk forwards, like she did. Like you've done. I cut the picture from the magazine because Laurel needed me to do it. To tell me to look ahead.'

Dom's head swam. He clung to the photograph. 'I'm not walking, Thea. I'm dragging myself. I've spent two decades limping.'

'That's still moving.'

She sniffed and pulled her knees to her chest. Dom stared at Hamilton, reeling. He was younger than Dom had ever seen him: fresh-faced, clean-shaven, smartly dressed and beaming at a cake that was four tiers of bright white icing. In Dom's head the flood of relief was overwhelming. Thea had found the link. Hamilton couldn't escape this. It tied him completely. On the big screen, Judge Lyons was winding up her interview. Somewhere in the crowd, people started clapping. The sound spread like a drumbeat, until Trafalgar Square was trembling. Dom's heart thrashed. He closed his eyes, and an image of his parents lit behind his eyelids. Tess bent to the ground and looked at the picture.

'Oh, Dom,' she whispered, wrapping herself around him.

It was Hamilton and his young bride, Catherine Hilton-Webb.

ONE YEAR LATER

44-86B, Queen's Bench Division
The Royal Courts of Justice
Strand
London
WC2A 2LL

Dear Mr and Mrs Nowell,

At this point in the proceedings, I would like to take the time to write and express my sincerest gratitude for the role you have played in bringing Carl Hamilton to trial. The information and evidence you were able to provide the prosecution, at great personal risk to yourselves and your family, was invaluable not only in locating him after more than a decade of evasion, but also in building the foundations of their secondary case. Your bravery and determination have ensured that not only are we able to call him to account for his crimes during the years of Free and Equal Britain, but that when the trial concludes next year he will once again stand in the dock against the charge of child trafficking, alongside Catherine Hilton-Webb, Levi Garber and their accomplices. Whilst I am aware that some quarters of the media view this second trial as unnecessary, since Hamilton will invariably be sentenced many times to Life, I believe – as I know you do too – that it is only by acknowledging FEB's full, heinous and continuing legacy, that we can begin to truly heal a damaged nation. Following the example you have set, we must continue to be bold in our conviction not to view the task of achieving what is just as being too complicated or overwhelming, nor to be tempted to excuse crimes committed by or against certain persons in favour of prosecuting those easier to prove or deemed more 'worthwhile'. The moral authority we can claim by charging Carl Hamilton and his associates despite their incarceration sends a message more important than ever: democracy and justice are not open to hierarchy. Freedom and equality will only prevail when they represent all.

As a personal aside, I feel privileged beyond measure that you sought to trust me with your discoveries at a time when they were most sensitive and fragile, and when you must have been most scared. I am thankful for the lengths you went to in ensuring your evidence reached me without compromise, and I will continue to ensure that your names are kept from the media, as you've requested.

I have written to Ms Baxter to thank her also, and to assure her that the search for her daughter Laurel continues to be the highest priority of Operation Reunite. I cannot begin to imagine how conflicted your emotions must be following Maya's return to her birth family, and I wish you the greatest of luck and happiness with your new adoption journey in the US.

Yours sincerely,
The Honourable Ms Justice Mabel Lyons DBE

ACKNOWLEDGEMENTS

I am lucky to have extremely supportive people around me, and I am particularly grateful to Rowan Jones, Lucy Hoile and Sophie Yates for their friendship, encouragement and feedback on drafts. Similar gratitude goes to my parents, Carol and Keith Abbott, to Annette and Andrew Cruickshanks, and to Lesley Davis. Thanks also to Nic Dunlop, Virak Tep and Robert Dinsdale for their early input and the support of the Society of Authors. Thanks to Nyree Ambarchian for the pep talks and shameless bias.

For having faith and bringing this book to readers, thanks go to Edward Crossan and the Polygon team, and to Justin Nash at the Kate Nash Agency.

My biggest thanks are reserved for my family. Thanks to Fluffy, for being my constant – if slightly intense – literary companion. Thanks to Scott, as always, for enduring the madness, gently pushing (sometimes shoving), and making space. Thanks to Miles, for the inexhaustible kindness and energy. Thanks to Tate, for being the motivation when I needed it most, and for trusting without reservation when I promised. And for the hugs. Forever the hugs. This one is absolutely for you.